"A doyen of humorous Regency-era romance writing."*

**Raves for
Barbara Metzger's Romances**

"Metzger's gift for re-creating the flavor and ambience of the period shines here, and the antics of her dirty-dish villains, near villains, and starry-eyed lovers are certain to entertain."   —*Publishers Weekly* (starred review)

"An extraordinary book that commands the reader's attention and lingers in the mind long after the last page is turned."   —*Booklist* (starred review)

"Funny and touching—what a joy!"   —Edith Layton

"Lively, funny, and true to the Regency period ... a fresh twist on a classic plot."   —*Library Journal*

"A vivid backdrop for a fast-paced, sometimes funny, always rich romance of rare quality."   —*BookPage*

"Barbara Metzger is a true artist with a palette of words."   —Romance Reviews Today

"Witty, spicy dialogue, and intelligent characters."   —*Romantic Times*

"The complexities of both story and character contribute much to its richness. . . . [It is] exciting when the layers are peeled back and savored."   —*Affaire de Coeur*

"Remarkable. . . . An original, laugh-out-loud, and charmingly romantic read."   —Historical Romance Writers

"A true tour de force. . . . Only an author with Metzger's deft skill could successfully mix a Regency tale of death, ruined reputations, and scandal with humor for a fine and ultimately satisfying broth."   —The Best Reviews

Also by Barbara Metzger

The Bargain Bride

Barbara Metzger

A SIGNET ECLIPSE BOOK

SIGNET ECLIPSE
Published by New American Library, a division of
Penguin Group (USA) Inc., 375 Hudson Street,
New York, New York 10014, USA
Penguin Group (Canada), 90 Eglinton Avenue East, Suite 700, Toronto,
Ontario M4P 2Y3, Canada (a division of Pearson Penguin Canada Inc.)
Penguin Books Ltd., 80 Strand, London WC2R 0RL, England
Penguin Ireland, 25 St. Stephen's Green, Dublin 2,
Ireland (a division of Penguin Books Ltd.)
Penguin Group (Australia), 250 Camberwell Road, Camberwell, Victoria 3124,
Australia (a division of Pearson Australia Group Pty. Ltd.)
Penguin Books India Pvt. Ltd., 11 Community Centre, Panchsheel Park,
New Delhi - 110 017, India
Penguin Group (NZ), 67 Apollo Drive, Rosedale, North Shore 0632,
New Zealand (a division of Pearson New Zealand Ltd.)
Penguin Books (South Africa) (Pty.) Ltd., 24 Sturdee Avenue,
Rosebank, Johannesburg 2196, South Africa

Penguin Books Ltd., Registered Offices:
80 Strand, London WC2R 0RL, England

First published by Signet Eclipse, an imprint of New American Library,
a division of Penguin Group (USA) Inc.

First Printing, November 2009
10 9 8 7 6 5 4 3 2 1

In memory of Edith Layton—
a great writer, a better friend

Chapter One

Lord and Lady X were wed in a match arranged by their parents. They have been blissfully ecstatic ever since the wedding . . . an entire month ago.

—By Arrangement, a chronicle of arranged marriages, by G. E. Felber

Three years was a long engagement. Thirteen years was ludicrous. It was an insult, an error of judgment, an affront to good manners and good sense, but, damn, it was thirteen years of freedom.

And it was over now, blast it to hell.

West regretted the loss of his liberty almost as much as he regretted the supposed slight to Miss Goldwaite, but he would not take the blame for the entire decade's debacle.

He had not chosen the bride.

He had not chosen all the delays. The bride was too young; then she was in mourning. Soon after, West joined the army, where he wished he was now. He resigned his commission when his father and brother died, after which he spent years trying to restore the family's fortunes. He'd thought that if he could repay the settlements, he could rescind the agreement between his father and Mr. Gaspar Goldwaite.

Hah! The banker was as tenacious as a bulldog, and twice as ugly. West shuddered to think what the daughter looked like now. At thirteen, she had been sunburned, scrawny, and had scraped knees. She had been pale, still scrawny, with swollen eyes at sixteen, at her mother's funeral. He had not seen her since.

He had not chosen to see her today.

Likely she was a skinny, sour-faced spinster at twenty-six, he thought, with her father's spectacles, if not his sparse hair. She'd be purse-lipped and prunish, saints preserve him, countrified and coarse. Just look where she and her grandfather lived, he considered as he read yet another signpost to Little Falls. Lud, he lived in London. What could he have in common with a common-born rustic female? Not that he was a snob, but he was a titled gentleman of university education, worldly-wise, politically minded, and socially accepted. Zeus, what had his late father been thinking?

The previous viscount, God rest his gambling soul, had been thinking that he had nothing but leaking roofs, debts, and spare sons. Gaspar Goldwaite, on the other hand, had everything except entrée to the polite world for his only daughter, Persephone. It was a match made in heaven . . . thirteen years ago.

West, Kendall Westmoreland, was well aware that he had to marry. With his father's passing, and then his elder brother's, he was Viscount Westfield. He had never expected or coveted the succession, but he had stepped into his father's shoes vowing to be a better holder of the venerable title. He was thirty-two years of age, and the sense of duty weighed heavily on his shoulders. He liked his bachelor existence, but he knew he owed his patrimony more than leaving the estates and obligations to his younger brother, Nicholas, a scapegrace pleasure-seeker with pockets perennially as empty as his head.

West sighed as he passed through Little Falls—which was little more than a church, an everything store, and a smithy—on his way to Littleton Cottage. He'd rather be facing French cannon fire.

He had to marry, and it seemed he might have to marry Miss Persephone Goldwaite. The banker had made it abundantly clear that his choice was a proposal or pistols at dawn.

Shoot at a balding banker with bad eyesight? Impossible. Almost as impossible as wedding the man's daughter. Damn. West knew he should have settled the whole matter earlier, repaid his debts and convinced the female to cry off years ago. He'd always thought—when he thought about the engagement at all—that Miss Persephone Goldwaite would have found another poor chap to marry. Hell, she was an heiress. There were scores of men with titles and debts eager to make such a match, even if they had to compromise the girl or kidnap her. Instead his betrothed was rich and unwed at the age of six and twenty. The woman must be as ugly as her father.

West almost turned his horse back the way he had come, but he was no coward. He might refuse a ridiculous challenge, but he could not ignore his own conscience. Honor, not a dawn meeting, had him up early this morning, and desperation drove him forward, seeking out his fiancée before her financier father was out of bed at the inn six miles south. He could have driven with Goldwaite to this village in the middle of nowhere later this afternoon and listened to his prospective father-in-law plan the wedding and his forthcoming children's lives. West chose to ride ahead, alone, early, on a hired horse from the inn's stable.

At least he got to make one decision for himself.

*   *   *

Penny scrubbed as hard as she could as she tried to get rid of the stains and smells of paint on her skin. Or else she was trying to rub away the stench of her father's message. They were arriving this afternoon. *He* was coming, the cad who had ruined her life. Penny reached over the side of the copper bathtub for another can of hot water. No amount of soap and suds was going to wash away that stain, but heaven take it if she wouldn't try.

While she rubbed her skin raw, Penny tried to regain her equilibrium. She was not going to let that man affect her one bit, never again. And, she told herself, dunking her head under the water, sending soap bubbles flying across the room, he had not actually ruined her life. She would not give the toad that much credit. She liked the life she had, running her grandfather's country house, supervising the staff, managing the nearby orphanage and school, helping the vicar care for the aged and infirm in the parish. She led a worthy, rewarding life. Not like some London rake who cared for nothing but his own pleasure.

No, her life was fulfilling. It simply was not the life she had imagined before he entered it, then left without a second glance. Granted, he was not responsible for his father's debts, the war, her mother's death, or her father's remarriage, but nearly everything else in her life could be laid at his door. Why should her new stepmother keep Penny on in London's marriage mart when she was already promised? Why pay for new gowns and more Seasons when the new Mrs. Goldwaite had two young daughters of her own—less well favored, considerably less well dowered—to raise? Why have another mistress at Goldwaite House—one used to running the household and adored by the servants—when Penny's maternal grandfather in the country had no one to look after him? So Penny had been sent to Yorkshire to wait for her fiancé to come.

He had not.

He had not rescued her from the wicked stepmother. He had not saved her from banishment to a hidden castle. He had not slaughtered any dragons for her. Kendall Westmoreland, now Lord Westfield, was no fairy-tale hero. He was no hero at all. What he'd killed was her childish dreams; that was all. The first time she had seen him, when their fathers met to sign contracts, he'd been kind. The second, at her mother's death, he'd been comforting. He was the handsomest, noblest young man in the entire kingdom, a prince from her storybooks, a god from the myths she read, a creature of magic and wisdom and beauty and sweetness and strength.

She was a child, and a fool. He was a weakling. And cruel.

He should have escorted her the year of her comeout, before her father remarried, when Mr. Goldwaite hired a widowed baroness to chaperone Penny, but he was with the army on the Peninsula. He should have visited her before he went off to war. She would have followed the drum gladly if he asked her. He should have come to see her when he reached his majority, rescinding those contracts and ending the betrothal while Penny could have found another man to marry. She had been certain he would come four years ago when he succeeded to his father's title and sold out of the army. No one would have expected a viscount to wed a banker's daughter. She was suitable enough for a second son, but not the heir. He had not come to York even then, nor sent for her to come to London. He stayed in Town enjoying himself, likely using the engagement to keep himself safe from matchmaking mamas, if he mentioned it at all.

Penny would have stopped scanning the London newspapers when she started seeing her fiancé's name in the society columns instead of the war dispatches, except she had to read the papers to her grandfather. According to the *on-dits* columns, his lordship's current inamorata was a Lady MG, dubbed the Colorful Widow, whatever that meant. Penny assumed she was buxom, beautiful, and wealthy, to boot. Not that she cared, of course. Westfield obviously did not care about her or her feelings. He never once came, or wrote, or sent a message. Never.

Now he was arriving this afternoon. Likely because her father had been made a knight, probably for paying Prinny's debts, the same way he had paid the previous viscount's. Perhaps her father's new title made Penny a more acceptable bride for his lordship's puffed-up pride.

She tossed the washcloth across the room with enough force to knock over a bottle of perfume. No, by heaven, he'd come to ask her to cry off, finally, because he had to start his nursery. Women who wanted to be mother to his sons must be lined up in London, waiting six deep.

Good. Let one of those silly twits have him and his care-for-naught manners. Let her worry when he rode off to war, and let her weep when she read about actresses and opera dancers. Let her spend thirteen years waiting for love.

No, Viscount Westfield had not ruined Penny's life. He'd broken her heart. Now she would not marry him if he were the last man on earth. He was here only because everyone knew a gentleman did not break an engagement. He simply made his betrothed so miserable that she was eager to end the arrangement. Cry off? She would shout it from the rooftop this very afternoon, if she had any skin left.

A boy ran around the side of the building to lead West's horse away, but no one answered when he let the brass door knocker tap on the door twice. No one answered, which would never have happened in a properly run gentleman's residence in London. Even more telling of the difference between city life and country dwelling, the unlocked door creaked open when he rapped again.

"Halloo?" When no one answered his call, West stepped through the entry and found himself in even more unfamiliar territory. Bright splashes of color assaulted his sensibilities from every inch of the narrow hallway, from paintings—no, he amended, smears—of every size and shape, that were hung ceiling to floor. The Academy of Art was known to fill their walls, but with art, not these ... these ... Words failed West. The closest description he could give was the works on display might have been painted by a cow with a brush tied to its tail. Great daubs of color flew across the canvases with no rhyme nor reason that West could see.

He shook his head. Here he'd been worried that his promised bride was no beauty. He should have been concerned that she was cockle-headed, and color-blind to boot. How could anyone live in a place like this? He thought of the quiet refinement at Westfield Manor, the few cherished heirloom masterpieces he'd been able to reclaim. Then he thought of Miss Goldwaite being chatelaine there. "Great gods."

"Magnifique, non?"

West turned, and shook his head again. Maybe he was the one with attics to let. A large man stood there, carrying a ribbon-wrapped spear. The man's size did not intimidate West, although his own six feet were overshadowed by the other's height, nor did the spear seem threatening. What had him nonplussed was the fellow's attire, or lack of it. He was wearing a feathered headdress, a beaded leather breechclout, and war paint, lots of war paint. Now he pointed the spear at one of the paintings and answered for West. "A masterpiece, *oui*."

"*Oui . . . ,*" West sputtered, eyeing the spear's sharp point.

The Indian raised a thick red-striped eyebrow. "We are early?"

"We . . . that is, I, have come to call on Miss Persephone Goldwaite. Please tell me I have the wrong address."

The Indian bowed with all the pomp and punctilio of a London upper servant. "This is the home of Monsieur Cornelius Littleton and his granddaughter."

West's spirits, already low, plummeted to his feet, where at least he wore boots, unlike the barefoot butler. "Please tell them that Viscount Westfield has called." He reached into his pocket for a calling card. At least he had pockets, unlike the red-skinned retainer.

The Indian took the card and bowed again. "Monsieur may wait in the library." His expression said it might be a long wait.

Before the man turned to lead him farther into the house, West asked, "Are you a French-Canadian Indian, then?"

The butler straightened to his considerable height. "I am sitting."

The viscount smiled. "Odd—I've never heard of that tribe."

West could swear he heard a muttered French imprecation that had more to do with his own parentage than the Indian's. "*Je suis* Marcel. Monsieur Littleton is an *artiste* of great note."

West took one last look at the paintings on the wall before following Marcel. That great note must be a sour one, indeed. Then he realized that the back side of a beefy man in a breechclout was even less attractive than the paintings. To exacerbate the matter, Marcel flounced down the corridor to the library. There was no other word for it. The model-cum-majordomo swung his hips and jiggled a jig right down the hall.

Good grief, this was no bucolic bride's abode. This was Bedlam!

Chapter Two

Lord and Lady G. lived happily ever after, after their arranged wedding. He lived in London; she lived in Leeds.

—By Arrangement, *a chronicle of arranged marriages, by G. E. Felber*

The view from the library was a lot better than the one from behind Marcel's behind. The windows overlooked a terraced garden, with an orchard in the distance. Inside, the decor was far more pleasing than the hall's. Here, at least the few paintings carefully placed against the dark wood paneling were truly works of art, skill, and composition. West particularly admired a landscape that hung over the table where Marcel had directed him to liquid refreshments. The artist had captured a storm in the woods so well that West could almost see the branches of the trees moving. The painting was signed *C. Littleton*, so the man actually did have some degree of talent. He had excellent taste in brandy, too. West poured himself another measure. Lord knew he needed it.

With the library door left partially open, he could hear shouts and footsteps, curses, and slamming doors.

From the feminine tones of some of the imprecations, he gathered he would need a bit more fortification.

He made a more thorough survey of his surroundings while he waited and sipped his brandy—or brandies. For the first time since coming on this benighted journey, he was pleased with what he saw. A man could be comfortable here. The walls were high, with bookshelves to the ceiling, the windows letting in light to read in the inviting leather armchairs. A wide cherrywood desk was placed in a corner, with what appeared to be the estate ledgers neatly arranged on the shelves behind it. As he examined the other walls of books, West noticed classic literature, plays, and philosophy mixed in with the latest volumes of poetry, fiction, and scientific speculation. One glass-fronted cabinet held a few valuable editions that any collector would prize. The volumes appeared well read and carefully handled, not merely arranged for show, so the household was not entirely filled with barbarians. Here was a gentleman's library, West decided with relief, not a madman's. And the brandy was excellent. He eyed the crystal decanter with longing, but set his glass down. He needed all his wits about him if he was to leave Yorkshire alive and a bachelor.

Eventually Marcel returned. This time he was dressed in proper butlerish attire, from spotless white gloves to dark tailcoat to powdered wig, all of which made the war paint on his face look even more bizarre. He made a formal bow at the door, then announced his master in tones sonorous enough for a bishop. "Monsieur Cornelius Littleton, my lord." He stepped aside, then led a slender old man into the room by his arm.

West stepped forward, bowed, and put his hand out. It was Marcel who placed Littleton's hand in West's for a shake, before guiding the impeccably dressed gentleman—except for a streak of crimson in his white hair—to one of the leather chairs. That explained the splashed paintings in the hall, West supposed.

Marcel started to place a blanket over Littleton's knees, but the old man patted the butler's hand and said, "Do not fuss, *mon ami.*" That explained Marcel, West supposed.

The smell of turpentine and linseed oil replaced the comfortable aroma of the old books and brandy as Littleton sat back against the cushions after Marcel left to fetch refreshments. West hoped his host couldn't see him take out his handkerchief to rub at a spot of yellow ochre on his thumb.

Littleton appeared to be waiting for West to begin the conversation, but the viscount's mission was with Miss Goldwaite, not her grandfather, which left idle chitchat, the weather and such. "A lovely day, sir."

"I have not been out."

A comment on the local scenery was obviously impolite, as was praise for the paintings in the library. The artist could not produce such again. Neither could West compliment the books when Mr. Littleton had not read those latest novels on the shelves. He settled on, "Excellent brandy."

"Helped yourself, did you?"

Now West felt like a thief, besides a tongue-tied trespasser. "Marcel directed me. May I pour you a glass?" He got up and refilled his own.

"What, in the morning? Some of us have better things to do than addle our insides and benumb our brains."

"Uh, quite."

"And some of us do not need courage from a bottle."

West pushed aside his glass untouched. He resumed his seat, noting that Littleton's head followed his movements. The awkward silence fell again, as thick as the smell of paint. For all his thirty-two years and experi-

ence as an officer, West felt as if he'd been called before the headmaster in school, waiting to find out which
of his many infractions had been discovered this time.
There was no doubt he was already judged guilty.

He would not be accused of ill manners. "Your home
is lovely, sir. And I appreciate your kindness in seeing
me so unexpectedly and interrupting your, ah, work."

"It is love, of course."

For the painting? West prayed they were not discussing Marcel. "I can tell you are devoted to your art."

Littleton waved his hand around, narrowly missing
the decanter West had unknowingly moved. "I paint for
love, yes, but for the money also now."

People paid for the monstrosities in the hall? West
made a noncommittal sound of assent.

Littleton cleared his throat. "I am speaking of my
granddaughter. I love her."

"I, ah, see." West was as in the dark as the old man.

"I care only for her happiness."

Ah, he was being lectured, or warned. "Quite. I am
sure we all wish Miss Goldwaite the best life has to
offer."

"Some of us more than others. Some of us even consider what it is that would make her happy. I don't suppose my son-in-law is hiding in the drapery?" Littleton
peered into the corners of the room. "Marcel did not
mention Greedy Gaspar."

"No, Mr., ah, Sir Gaspar was still asleep at the inn
when I rode out this morning. He made a late night of it
last evening."

"Most likely with the help of the barmaid."

Actually it was the innkeeper's wife, but West chose
not to report on his prospective father-in-law. Goldwaite's affairs were his own business, the same as Mr.
Littleton's . . . and Marcel's. "He will be arriving later."

"Hmm. Best that way, I suppose. You and Penny can get the thing settled between you without his interference."

"That was what I thought."

Littleton leaned forward to stare at West, making him wonder just how much the artist could see. Finally the old man nodded and said, "So you are not as foolish as your father."

"I hope not."

A slight smile flitted across Littleton's face, replaced by a fierce scowl that would have matched Marcel's war paint. "If you hurt her, you'll be sorry."

"That is not my intent, sir, I swear."

"It better not be. I might not be handy with my sword anymore, but Marcel can use a carving knife to good purpose, and his fists when he needs to. Or I can paint your portrait with warts and fangs and horns and get it hung in a London gallery and printed on broadsheets. You wouldn't like being a laughingstock, would you?"

"No, sir."

"Don't think I cannot do it. I have great influence in the art world."

"Yes, sir."

"Good. Then I can get back to my work while the light is still good."

What did the light matter? West wondered, but the old man brushed his help aside and made his own way out of the room. West sat back to wait some more.

Marcel brought in a tray with a plate of biscuits and a pot of coffee. West noticed two cups on the tray, but no one came to join him. Since breakfast had been hours ago, West decided to eat without waiting for his hostess. He supposed such insubstantial fare was enough for the frail old man or his scrawny spinster granddaughter, while he would have preferred eggs and steak and ale, but beggars could not be choosers.

When the last crumb was gone, West stared out the window, walked around the library, picked up a book, then put it down and wandered back to the hall to look at Littleton's current works. He might not be any connoisseur, but dash it if he could imagine anyone buying the garish, sloppy pieces. He could not even tell whether they were landscapes or portraits.

Just then he heard a loud noise from the end of the corridor, as if poor Mr. Littleton was falling down the stairs. West rushed through the hall to help, but no one was tumbling to the bottom. Slight Mr. Littleton would not have made that much noise, either. Instead, a woman was clomping down step by furious step in heavy wood-soled boots that were half unlaced. So was her gown, which gaped at the neck. Her hair was wet, with half of it crammed under a beribboned lace cap and half trailing down her shoulders. Her gown was green, her ribbons were yellow and purple, her eyes were blue, and her face was as red as a cooked lobster's. Jupiter, the female had been dressed by the blind artist!

She paused when she saw him, ceasing her teeth-jarring descent. She straightened her shoulders and started to step down as gracefully as one could in unfastened boots.

Ah, West thought, here comes the bride.

When she reached the bottom, he bowed. Miss Goldwaite bobbed her head in the merest expression of civility and manners. West held his hand out to assist her. She pretended to be as blind as her grandfather, stepping past him back down the corridor.

West took a deep breath—at least she smelled of rose water, not turpentine—and said, "Miss Goldwaite, I sincerely apologize for arriving so early."

She spun on her awkward heels to face him, coming nearly to his chin. Her own jutted out. "Early? Early? Why, you, sir, are late. Thirteen years late, to be exact!"

It seemed that Miss Goldwaite had used up her politeness by bobbing her head, nor did she believe in sparring with gloves on.

West bowed, acknowledging his sins. "I apologize for that also, although I do not believe you wished to wed at the age of thirteen."

"I do not wish to wed now, either."

Which was the best news he'd heard in ages. "I think we should discuss this further, perhaps over a cup of coffee." Or another brandy.

Instead of stopping at the library, the woman marched on toward the front entry. "There is nothing to discuss." She opened the door and nodded in the direction of outside. "Good day."

West did not take the unsubtle hint. "I am afraid things are not that easy. Your father—"

Her face lost the red flush so suddenly West was afraid she was going to faint. He took a step closer, but she squared her shoulders and said, "I will deal with him when he gets here. I am no longer a child. And I will be no man's chattel, no matter how you men write your foolish laws."

"If I might say that I regret what has happened—"

"You might have said it any time these past years. You have not been a child for ages, either."

"No, and I should have come, or written. I know. But you were too young to discuss such matters, and then I was in the army."

"You resigned your commission four years ago."

"Yes, but I spent—"

"You spent your money on fast horses and loose women. Gambling and wenching and drinking. Do you think we do not get the London gazettes here in the north? Do you think I cannot read, sirrah?"

Not if she was the one who maintained that fine library. He was not going to discuss wine, women, or wasting money. "No, I spent my funds trying to restore Westfield Manor by establishing a farm for horse breeding and training."

"So you have thrown away the fortune my father paid, and that is why you are here today? I suppose your plans failed when you frittered the money away, the same as your father did. Do you think my father will pay more to see the deed done while I can still provide grandchildren? Well, you are wrong. My father is as clutch-fisted as they come. How do you think he became so wealthy? He won't pay you more. And my money— yes, I have funds of my own, now that I have reached my majority—is tied into trusts so firmly that you will never get your hands on a shilling of it to support you or your high-strung racers."

Now West was growing angry, that she thought he would take money from his wife, that he was here to wrest more gold from Goldwaite, that his stud farm had failed. He was making a tidy profit selling his horses to the army, not gambling on them to win races. "You mistake my intent. I spent my time trying to recoup the loan—"

"That was my dowry, not a loan."

He nodded, not arguing semantics. A dowry was not paid until a ceremony took place. A loan was a loan. "I wished to repay the sum to cancel the contract our fathers entered into."

"Fine. If you do not have enough funds, I will add to that. It will be a worthwhile expenditure."

The entire time they had been speaking, or shouting, Miss Goldwaite had been edging West closer to the door, almost pushing him out.

West hated to leave her so pale and rigid with rage. "Your father still wants us to wed."

"If he wants your title in the family so badly, then he can marry you off to one of my stepmother's daughters."

West had seen the stepdaughters. Oh, Lord. "You are certain?"

"Certain? Lord Westfield, I would jump off Little Falls before I married you. No, I would jump off Big Falls before I joined my future to yours. The past thirteen years have been more than enough."

She was certain, all right. "Then thank you." He meant for speaking with him, for the biscuits and coffee, for letting him escape so easily.

"Thank you?" she yelled. "Thank you? For offering to kill myself? For not wanting to marry you?" Now her face grew red again and her blue eyes narrowed to slits. "You insufferable, self-important, swellheaded swine!" Then she hauled her arm back and slammed her fist into his jaw.

West staggered back, half falling out the door, which slammed behind him.

Well, at least she wasn't scrawny anymore.

Chapter Three

*The farmer needed a mule, not another daughter.
The blacksmith needed a wife to cook and clean
and tend his children and his vegetable garden.
They traded. The daughter considered all three of
them jackasses: her father, her new husband, and
the mule.*

—By Arrangement, *a chronicle of
arranged marriages, by G. E. Felber*

Penny leaned back against the door. She'd fall down
without its wooden support, for there was not a
muscle in her body not gone limp. She was gasping for
breath, her cap was listing over one eyebrow, and one
of her shoes had flown across the hall with the force of
her blow, but she'd done it. She'd tossed out the rubbish.
She'd told him how she felt, and then she'd tossed him.
She did it, Penny Goldwaite, the disposable daughter,
the forgotten fiancée, the woman without a choice.

Well, she'd chosen now, she thought with pride. And
she'd chosen before Westfield, which was even more satisfying. Whether the fortune-hunting scum was here to
claim her or jilt her made no difference. She'd struck the
first blow.

Then it hit her: She'd struck the first blow. She had actually hit a man. Her own betrothed. She'd never raised her hand to a creature larger than an insect, and now she'd punched a peer. How uncivilized, how unladylike, how good it felt, except for her stinging knuckles. The dastard's skull was so thick she might have broken her hand!

She checked. Her fingers moved, even if she could not yet. She was whole and she was free! Penny kicked off her other shoe, tossed her cap onto the floor, and filled her lungs with clean, fresh air only slightly tainted with the scent of brandy, horse, her own rose water, Grandpapa's paints, and . . . ? Penny wrinkled her nose. And some spicy scent that was manly and exotic and exciting. No, she was merely basking in her victory, not inhaling the devil's own cologne.

She was free, and free to forget all about the slug, his smell and his smile. So what if he was tall and broad-shouldered and even more handsome than she recalled? So what if his dark hair curled onto his forehead in boyish innocence, and his brown eyes gleamed with gold flecks? His smile when he first saw her, despite her appearance, still held remembered sweetness, but his voice was deeper and richer. Mellow tones did not make his words—or him—one bit more trustworthy. Penny had no idea if anything he said was true or sincere, and she refused to ponder over it. Perhaps he had tried to raise the funds to end the betrothal honorably before coming to speak to her, as he had said. Perhaps his horse-raising enterprise was successful. Or perhaps he was here to steal Grandpapa's silverware. No matter, she had now seen the last of Kendall Westmoreland, Viscount West-field, former fiancé.

Then she heard a rap on the door behind her and felt it vibrate through her skin.

She yanked the door open. "Yes?"

His hand was raised to knock again. "My hat and gloves and riding crop. I left them in the library."

"Oh." Sure enough, his hands were bare except for a signet ring on one, a gold band set with a dark garnet on the little finger of the other. There was nothing for it but to let the maggot back in, despite the fact that she had no shoes on and her hair was curling down her shoulders in ringlets. She could tell Westfield was trying to hide a smile when he noticed her further dishabille, so she turned her back and silently led the way to the book room. There was nothing more to be said.

He thought otherwise. As they walked, he asked, "Who taught you to make a fist like that?"

She looked around, surprised at his question. Oh dear, he was rubbing his jaw, where a fist-sized red mark stood out against his healthy complexion. It might even turn black and blue, so he would wear her brand for a sennight. Served him right. "You did. When we first met, and our fathers were closeted in the office so long."

"I thought I remembered that. You said some boys in the neighborhood were teasing you, pulling your hair. I don't blame them." He almost reached out to touch those golden curls himself, now that they were drying in tumbled waves down her back. She glared and he rubbed his chin again instead, pretending that was his intention all along.

Penny put more distance between them. "You said I ought to know how to defend myself."

"Did they ever bother you again?"

"No, but not because of the fist I clenched in front of their faces. I told them I was an engaged lady now, promised to a real lord's son. I said you would come break their noses if they insulted me."

"At least I was good for something."

Her silence spoke volumes.

When they reached the library, West retrieved his belongings. While he put on one of his gloves, he asked, "Is it you who filled these shelves with treasures?"

She smiled for the first time since receiving her father's message, pleased with the compliment to her beloved books. "I added to an already extensive collection, yes. The books have been my friends and companions." She quickly held up a hand. "Not that I am complaining or trying to win your sympathy or make you feel guilty. My life in the country is rich, with running my grandfather's household and helping the less fortunate in the community. Nor am I a mere bluestocking do-gooder. The neighborhood has an active social life with assemblies every month and frequent dinners and dance parties among the local gentry."

"And none of the local beaux caught your fancy? None of your dance partners or dinner companions measured up?"

How could they, compared with him? She picked up a book from the desk and flattened its pages open, as if she were going to read it as soon as he left, which could not be soon enough.

When she did not answer, he gestured toward the high shelves. "I suppose you are far better-read than your possible suitors."

"You sound surprised. Did you think I was an unlettered, ignorant country lumpkin? I had governesses and tutors, and a year at Miss Meadow's Select Academy."

"I did not know what to think, honestly."

"Or you did not think."

He spread his fingers, smoothing the soft leather down each finger, then smiled at her. "I believe we have settled that issue comprehensively. I acted wrongly, perhaps for honorable reasons, although that is not sufficient excuse. I can only apologize again. I truly am sorry, Miss Goldwaite, for any ill I caused you."

Men did not apologize easily, Penny knew, especially proud men used to having their own way. She could do no less than accept his apology, which did not mean she had to forgive him. "And I apologize for having struck you," she said graciously, which did not mean she meant it.

Before putting on his other glove, Westfield asked, "Have you never done anything else you regretted?"

Yes, she'd let him back in, him and his heart-stopping smile. "I did not say I regretted punching you, only that I was sorry. There is a difference."

"And in my own defense, let me say that I never knowingly caused you harm. I did not know your circumstances. I should have made it my business to find out how you were situated; I see that now. I can only plead youth and the war, and abysmal ignorance. Our fathers made the arrangement, so I suppose I was waiting for them to finalize the wedding plans. After my father died and I never heard from yours, I simply assumed you had found a gentleman of your choice to wed. A wealthy man, one your father would approve. I was going to return your funds as soon as I was able, and all would be well."

Perhaps someone else had hit him earlier, Penny thought, and scrambled his brains. "How could I encourage another man's attentions when I was already promised to you? I was honor-bound by our betrothal from seeking another beau."

"There is that again." He studied his other glove before putting it on, the fact that he had not felt constrained by the contract a palpable presence between them. His mistresses and society misses might have been in the room, except none of them were interested in books. She had come a hairsbreadth away from impugning his own honor, but West could not fault her for that. He cleared his throat and tried to sound cheerful. "Well, you are no longer bound. Have you a gentleman in mind?"

Now she laughed, but without humor. "Eligible bachelors are not thick on the ground in the country. Little Falls is not Almack's, you know, and I am no longer a blushing debutante. No one here considers me an heiress, either, only an eccentric old maid, which is just as well, for I would not wish to be wed for my money. Besides, Father wants a title. Rich men with peerages seldom look to bankers' daughters."

"But your father is a knight now. And you are an attractive, intelligent woman. Surely in London—"

"I am not in London. I meet my father and his family in the Lake Country for a summer holiday. Grandpapa and I travel to Bath in the winter."

"Bath is better," he said, relieved. "Lots of chaps go for the waters, some with their ailing relations, of course, but some of my officer friends stop in Bath to recover from various injuries. Or you might try convincing your family to go to Brighton for the summer. A younger crowd vacations there."

Penny had never thought past this day. "Perhaps," she said.

The viscount must have heard the doubt in her voice, for he smiled again and said, "You are free, little butterfly. Go spread your wings."

"As you will? Blithely celebrate your release from bondage?"

Now he did reach out to lift a bright curl. "Not so blithely. Perhaps I will feel a bit of regret."

The practiced rake might be saying that to make her feel better, Penny knew. It did.

He did not release her curl, just stared into her eyes. "Perhaps I will feel more than a little regret that I never got to know you. But now we are both free to make our own choices, find our own paths. That is better, isn't it?"

"Much better," she answered too readily to be polite. His nearness was disturbing. "That is, we shall both benefit from the end of this unfortunate experience."

"Shall we seal the end of our betrothal with a kiss?"

A kiss? Gracious, he really was a rake. She was well out of the engagement. "I do not believe that is at all proper."

"No, I suppose not." He lightly touched his lips to hers anyway. "Farewell, my onetime bride-to-be. Be happy with your independence."

Penny would be happy if her legs could hold her up. She really ought to hit him again, she thought. Or kiss him again so she'd know how a practiced womanizer did it—for future reference, of course.

He was smiling, the devil, knowing his effect. His confidence gave her the strength to smile back and say, "Yes, now I can go find my own Prince Charming to wed."

"Like hell you can," came a loud voice from the open doorway. "You are marrying Lord Lustful, for good or for ill, and not a moment too soon, it seems. And you, sir, unhand my daughter. The wedding ain't taken place yet."

"Father?"

"Sir Gaspar?"

Penny's father stepped into the library. "Who were you expecting, King George? Although I had to be as mad as the king to let Westfield ride ahead. But I suppose no harm's done, an engaged couple and all."

"You are mistaken, Sir Gaspar," West told him. "We were saying good-bye. There will be no wedding."

"Like hell there won't." He looked around for a place

to put his hat. "Havey-cavey household altogether. I always said so. I sent a note to expect me and what do I get? No butler, no footman, no chaperone for my daughter."

"I am too old for a chaperone, Father."

"Not by the looks of you." He peered over his spectacles at her bare feet, unfastened gown, and disordered hair. "Your mother would be ashamed."

"It is not what you think," Penny insisted.

"Miss Goldwaite is totally innocent," West said.

"When the gal's cheeks are rubbed red from your beard and she looks like she's been dragged through a bush backward? Deuced hard to think anything but you were anticipating the wedding vows."

"There will be no wedding, Father."

Sir Gaspar finally set his hat on the desk. "Are you telling me you behave like a wanton with any stranger who walks through the door?"

"Of course not."

West was growing irritated at the older man's stubbornness. "You insult your daughter, sir."

"Hmph. I wasn't the one pawing at my betrothed."

"I wasn't—"

"I'm not his—"

"I need a drink. Does the old man still keep that fine brandy?"

West brought him a glass and the decanter, much less full than it was when he arrived. Sir Gaspar sank into one of the leather armchairs and took a deep swallow of the brandy. "I needed that, just getting through the hall."

The man most likely needed it after a night with the innkeeper's wife, but West said, "The paintings are somewhat of a shock, aren't they?"

"That and finding my daughter dressed like a Covent Garden convenient." He shook his head. "Thought she'd cause a dustup, but I can see you handled the gal right. I guess you were smart to come a-wooing on your own. Not surprising, a fellow with your reputation with the ladies."

West almost snarled, "I did not come a-wooing and I did not handle your daughter."

Sir Gaspar snorted.

"Well, not in that way. We have agreed we do not suit, so there will be no wedding."

"Hah. You, miss, go make yourself presentable while Westfield and I settle a few details."

Penny crossed her arms over her chest. "I am not leaving. It is my life you are discussing."

"Well, I ain't talking while some buck ogles my daughter's ankles. And assets."

More red color flooded Penny's face, and she was glad her arms were making certain her gown stayed almost modest. There was nothing she could do about her bare feet or her hair. "Fine, I shall go." She glared at both of them. "But you are not to talk about me or my future until I return." To make sure they did not have the opportunity, she told her father, "Speaking of propriety, you ought to pay your respects to Grandpapa, if you are going to drink his wine."

"Suppose the old loon is off painting, or whatever he calls it nowadays."

"He calls it art."

Sir Gaspar snorted again. He grimaced, but got to his feet.

When they were both gone, West eyed the decanter. Then he eyed the door.

Chapter Four

After their arranged match, Lady Y. presented her husband with five tokens of her affection. Three were dark-haired like him; two were redheads like the affectionate footman.

—By Arrangement, *a chronicle of arranged marriages, by G. E. Felber*

West did not take either of the coward's ways out. His pride would not let him run, for one thing, and lending his sober support to Miss Goldwaite was the least he could do under the circumstances, for another. Besides, Sir Gaspar returned quickly, mopping his brow, muttering about immorality, and finished off the brandy.

West was curious to see how the two strong-willed Goldwaites were going to deal with each other. Miss Goldwaite could not very well plant her father a facer, but she seemed as adamant as the banker. West's jaw still ached, and his self-esteem still suffered from her sharp words, proving the female could defend herself, but the knight appeared deaf, dumb, and blind to anyone else's opinions.

As curious as he was to see the outcome—and to ensure that outcome did not involve leg shackles—West was even more curious to see what Miss Goldwaite would look like in what her father considered proper female attire, if she owned any such apparel.

He was not disappointed. Miss Goldwaite looked every inch the lady now, with her hair neatly braided into a coronet atop her head, like a golden crown. Well, he had to admit he was disappointed in that. He'd looked forward to seeing her glorious blond curls rioting around her face and shoulders again. Now only a few ringlets were permitted to caress her cheeks.

She wore a gown made of costly watered silk, perfectly fitted if not in the latest London style. The lower waist than he was used to became her, showing off a willowy figure. The lower neckline than the green sack she'd had on earlier became her more, showing off a well-formed bosom for such a slender female. He quickly raised his glance.

The shimmering blues of the gown made her eyes appear luminous, especially reflecting from the chain of round-cut sapphires at her neck, any one of which could have purchased another mare or two for his breeding stock. Her hair was the sun, her eyes were the sky, and her lips were rosy dawn. Her complexion had lost that hectic choleric color—which her father's red cheeks now bore—and instead had the clarity and glow of fresh cream. Altogether, she reminded him of a clear country morning, except for the expression on her face.

If she was not careful—or if no one made her laugh—Miss Goldwaite could end up looking like the bulldog banker who fathered her, with her mouth permanently turned down and scowl lines etched between her eyebrows. If not for that, and the fists she kept clenched at her sides, his former fiancée would be a diamond of the first water. For now she was merely stunning, unless his opinion was formed by surprise at the transformation a careful toilette made.

No, West told himself, the woman was attractive in herself, and intriguing for the emotions that she did not try to hide. The usual well-bred London miss kept her expression bland, afraid to cause wrinkles, and afraid to show any kind of passion lest she be considered loose, flighty, or difficult. Miss Goldwaite was difficult, all right, but her father—or any other red-blooded man—could not fault her appearance. She even wore satin slippers on her feet.

West went toward her, to lead her to the chair opposite her father's, whispering, "Don't let him intimidate you. I will be right behind you." He took up a position at her back, his hand resting on the leather cushion an inch from her shoulder.

Before Sir Gaspar could start the rant he was nearly choking on, a footman wheeled in a cart and Miss Goldwaite was busy pouring out tea and filling plates. As soon as the servant left, while her father's mouth was full of the cook's best strawberry tart, Miss Goldwaite began. "Father, no matter what you say, I shall not marry Lord Westfield. We have decided together that we do not suit."

West had to smother a laugh at that. Was that what they decided, when she bashed him? Still, he admired her tactics: attack while the enemy was distracted.

Sir Gaspar choked on a bite of pastry, then gulped at his tea. He looked at Westfield, ignoring his daughter. "That so? What about what *we* decided?"

"We had not come to any conclusion. You threatened to challenge me to a duel; I agreed to come meet with Miss Goldwaite."

Penny set her cup down. "A duel, Father? At your age? With your poor eyesight?"

Sir Gaspar huffed. "Nothing wrong with my age, and I've got my spectacles, haven't I? And I wasn't going to let him pick swords, no matter if it was his choice. A duel's how gentlemen settle differences, don't you know. Otherwise I could hire a ruffian to beat him up in an alley."

West ignored that last. "There will be no duel. There was never going to be one. I would not shoot at a man old enough to be my father. Nor shall I be coerced into a marriage I never agreed to. I told you I was ready to repay the money you gave to my father. With interest."

"Of course I'd collect the interest if I was going to accept your bribe. But I told you, I will not take your blunt. A deal is a deal."

"I made no deal."

Sir Gaspar set aside his plate and cup altogether. "You paid your father's gambling debts, didn't you, even if you never held the losing cards? You weren't the one who took my girl's dower money and spent it on fast women and too-slow horses, but you paid those chits."

"My father's debts were a matter of honor."

"And his promises are worth less? In my world, a man's handshake is as binding as an IOU, a gentleman's agreement, same as play and pay. Hmph. Seems to me you pick and choose what you call honor."

"One is only money. One is trading your children."

"Only money, eh? I guess I can see why you were mucking out stables yourself. Well, no matter. If you won't respect your father's integrity and his intentions, maybe you will respect the law. If you won't duel, I'll sue you for breach of promise. See if I don't. And drag you and your family name through the courts. Asides taking every shilling you have. I can afford the finest barristers in the land. You cannot." Satisfied he had made his point, Sir Gaspar reached for another strawberry tart.

West could imagine his horse farm sold, his lands mortgaged, his younger brother forced into some trade to pay the cost. He was horrified.

So was Penny. "You cannot do that, Father. The scandal would reach as far as France, much less Little Falls. Everyone would wonder what was wrong with me that Lord Westfield had to fight the betrothal. Besides, that is blackmail."

Her father brushed crumbs off his waistcoat. "No, that is justice. Obeying the law. What do you call reneging on a contract? I call it a crime."

Perhaps West should accept the man's challenge after all, he thought, and choose sabers. Instead he said, "I call your behavior barbaric. Your daughter does not want to marry me."

"Of course she does." Goldwaite turned to Penny at her gasp. "You ain't stupid, girl. You'll never find a more pleasing partner."

"Pleasing to you."

"And half the women in London. Just ask Lady Greenlea."

West growled at private matters being mentioned in polite company, much less in front of a young lady, especially his betrothed. He should simply run the banker through and be done with it.

Penny gasped again while West was thinking of murder. So that was his current, colorful flirt, and the color was green. Definitely green. "You would have me marry a womanizer I loathe?"

"Bosh. You were kissing him, weren't you? Asides, I'd have you wed a real man who can give you sons."

Before West could stop her, or say anything in his own defense, Miss Goldwaite leaped to her feet. "I am not a broodmare for his stables, Father, nor for yours. I will not do it, I say. Since I am of age, there is no one who will marry me against my will, so you are wasting your threats."

Sir Gaspar steepled his fingers over his stomach, unconcerned. "Very well, missy, where will you live if you do not wed Westfield?"

"Why, here, of course. Grandpapa would never throw me out."

"No, but I doubt Littleton can afford to keep you, or the roof over your heads. For sure I will not pay an allowance to some chit who defies me."

"Grandpapa would take care of me."

"He mightn't be able to, when he has no income."

"Nonsense. He makes ample money on his paintings. I keep his books, and he is very well-to-pass."

"Hah! Who do you think buys those wretched things he calls paintings? The fool wouldn't take money to keep you, but a Goldwaite pays his own way. So I have an arrangement with that art dealer in London where you send the canvases. I have a whole warehouse full of the scribbles and splotches."

"You buy them? Oh no, Grandpapa would be heartbroken if he knew. He is so proud that he can still support all of us."

Sir Gaspar merely smiled. "He doesn't have to find out."

Now it was West's turn to claim that was extortion of the worst kind.

Penny was not willing to concede. "I have funds of my own. I can pay Grandpapa's bills."

"Of course you have money. It's invested with my own bank, ain't it? I know to a farthing how much you have and how long you could support your grandfather, his, ah, butler, and the rest of the household. Not very long, I figure—not without my help. That brandy doesn't come cheap, nor do his fancy paints."

"How could you be so cruel?" Penny cried, sitting back down, as if she felt comfort in West's nearness.

"Cruel? How cruel is it to want my only offspring settled and secure? That's what every father wants, ain't it? Just think, girl, what will happen to you when the old man passes on? Not even Littleton can live forever. You cannot want to come home to London, not as some old maid who's been jilted."

"I can find a cottage somewhere and live an independent life."

"A dried-up old stick with no family of your own? Is that what you want? You'd be prey to every charlatan and fortune hunter, and plagued by scandal besides, a woman living alone. I know the way of the world, even if you do not. What kind of father would I be if I did not protect you from withering away like that?"

Penny looked stricken, and West wished he could comfort her, but he half agreed with her father. A woman like Miss Goldwaite should have a lovely home, fine gowns, servants at her beck and call, tousle-haired children at her feet. She should not take in stray cats in a shack.

"Why now, Father?" she asked. "Why are you doing this now?"

For the first time, Sir Gaspar looked embarrassed. "None of us is getting any younger. I want to see my grandchildren. And I want the best for you, no matter what you think."

"But now? Why did you not settle this years ago, or when Westfield came into the title?"

"I didn't want any son-in-law I had to support, coming to me for loans to repair that old pile of his."

She looked up at West as if to say "I told you so."

Her father was going on. "He's solvent now and can support a wife in decent style, especially with the wedding gift I intend to give. In fact, I'll sweeten the deal and pay to refurbish his London town house for you. The place looks too shabby for a viscountess."

West might have argued that point, but he knew the older man was right. He had not spent money on Westmoreland House, not when the estates needed so many repairs. He and his brother lived spartanly in one wing of the mansion.

Penny did not care about the state of Westfield's house, which she hoped never to see. "And if Lord Westfield were not able to keep me in jewels and furs, would you leave me here?"

"Well, he is, so that's not to the point. I didn't like sending you off, you know. But with a new wife, I did not have much choice. Couldn't have two women in the household, now, could I?" he asked, turning toward West.

When West did not answer, he added, "Besides, there was Nigel."

"Who the deuce is Nigel?" West wanted to know.

"M'wife's son, Nigel Entwhistle."

"The ivory turner?"

Penny looked at both of them. "An ivory turner?"

"A cheat, a Captain Sharp," West explained, while her father claimed nothing had ever been proved.

"But neither is Entwhistle welcome in the more discriminating gentlemen's clubs. He is your stepson?"

"To my regret. I sent him off to India to make his fortune. He lost a parcel of mine, instead. He came back with the fevers—and the idea that he ought to wed Penny. No blood relation, don't you know."

Penny almost shouted, "What?"

So did West. That bounder with West's fiancée? That is, Miss Goldwaite was not his betrothed any longer, but he still felt protective of the woman.

Sir Gaspar shook his head. "The jackanapes thought to keep my blunt in his family. Counting the days until I shuffled off, I suppose. I wouldn't put it past him to compromise my gal, so I had to get you out of London. His mother wouldn't hear a word against him, of course. You can't say I didn't have your best interests at heart, poppet, protecting you from that. Westfield is a far better choice."

"I am safe here. I still want to know why you will not let me stay where I am happy, if you say you care for me."

"I told you, I want grandsons. Besides, it's not right, you living in this harum-scarum household. A blind painter, his Frenchy friend . . ."

"What's wrong with Marcel? He takes good care of Grandpapa."

Now the banker blushed. "He's in the backroom studio, half naked except for some feathers. That ain't right. You need the company of females."

"You were the one who dismissed Lady Bainbridge after my come-out."

"She insulted your stepmother."

"She told her the Egyptian style looked ridiculous in our London house and that her daughters were spoiled brats."

Now Sir Gaspar took off his spectacles to polish them with his handkerchief, not meeting either West's eyes or Penny's. "Yes, well, that's, um, another reason I need you wed to his lordship and back in London."

"You want me to redecorate your town house?"

"I want you to take the girls in hand."

Penny saw her stepsisters twice a year, once when they met in Bath in the winter, once at summer when she traveled to the Lake Country. Lady Bainbridge had been correct: They were horrible children. They were horrible young women now.

Her father was still polishing his glasses. "They're both of marrying age, you see, and ready for their come-outs. Constance doesn't have the same connections a viscountess would, not even with my knighthood."

"You want me ... to marry this man, this person who ignored my existence for thirteen years ... so that I can bring out your wife's daughters? That is how much you care about my happiness?"

Sir Gaspar looked up. "Here, now, I planned your wedding before I ever met Constance. I always wanted you to be a lady like your mother, and I am not ashamed of that. I saw you were brought up for the position, didn't I, with all those books and schooling and some snooty baroness to haul you to the Queen's Drawing Room for a formal presentation?"

"Yes, you did that, Father."

"And your father agreed, Westfield. My gal was good enough for him, and she is good enough for you."

"It was never that she is not good e—," West began.

Sir Gaspar did not give him the chance to continue. "I have the special license in my pocket, and the innkeeper's wife says she can bake a cake big enough for the whole village for tomorrow, right after church. I already sent a message to the vicar."

"Tomorrow?" Penny asked with a groan. "You have waited thirteen years, and now tomorrow?"

Her father nodded. "I don't want to have those females around the rest of my life."

And that, Penny and West both supposed, was as good a reason as Sir Gaspar needed to force them to wed. Tomorrow.

Chapter Five

In an arranged match, George, Prince of Wales, was
wed to Caroline of Brunswick. Need I say more?

—By Arrangement, a chronicle of
arranged marriages, by G. E. Felber

"What are we going to do?" Penny cried once her father left to make the rest of the arrangements.

West was pacing. "What do you think we are going to do? We are going to get married tomorrow morning, it appears."

"But . . . but I do not even like you."

He rubbed his jaw. "That much is obvious. At least I am not a totally rotten fellow. Not like Nigel."

"You do not like me, either."

"I just met you! And you struck me."

"Will you forget about that incident already! I apologized, and now we have more important things to discuss."

"More important than wedding a violent woman?"

"Botheration, I am not usually so ill-tempered. But if you liked me, you would have been here years ago."

"Deuce take it, I could repeat your own words and advise you to forget about that episode already. I also apologized. And unlike your vehement antagonism, I had nothing against you. I was simply not ready for marriage."

"But now you are?"

He was tugging at his neckcloth while he paced, destroying the careful arrangement of folds in the snowy linen, as if he could feel the noose of matrimony growing tighter by the second. "According to your father, I am ready. I just never expected it to be so soon."

"Soon? After thirteen—no, I shall not mention the wait again."

"I would not wager on that," West muttered, just loudly enough for Penny to hear.

She glared at him, or at his back, since he was pacing away from her. "I do not suppose I could convince you to return to London, could I? Or go shooting in Scotland? Best of all, jaunting off to Jamaica? Perhaps there is another war for you to fight."

He'd thought of it, but was offended that she did, too. "What, leave my bride at the altar? Now, that would be shabby indeed. I would look no-account, and you would be disgraced. No, my honor demands I make an appearance. You could always cry off, though. Brides do it all the time, I understand. There might be a dustup here in Little Falls, but that will blow over with the next rainstorm. No one in London knows the wedding is to take place tomorrow, so no one will notice when it does not. Our reputations will survive."

Her voice was low and sorrowful. "You heard my father and his threats."

He had. "Surely we can come up with another solution. Let me think."

She watched him pace, back and forth, back and forth, like a caged animal. He did not want to marry her any more than she wanted to marry him, the toad. She had good reasons, thirteen of them. His reasons were that he was, simply, a cad of no character. "Well?"

"All I have been able to devise is offering you a home at one of my estates, so you are not dependent on either your father or grandfather. But your reputation would be in tatters, and I cannot think you would enjoy being ostracized in a new neighborhood."

"Everyone would think I was your mistress." Just like Lady Greenlea.

"Exactly. And no, before you get up in the boughs again, I am not suggesting anything improper, just a refuge. I suppose I could ask one of my aunts to take you in, but what kind of life would that be for you, especially after you are used to managing your own household?"

"And I should not wish to abandon Grandpapa. How would he get on? Besides, what if my father cut him off out of spite, or told him about the paintings?"

He paced some more, while she wrung her handkerchief as if it were her father's neck—or the viscount's.

West turned. "I have it! You could claim to be ill. We could paint spots on your cheeks, or dose you with laudanum or feed you something rancid. No, not that, I suppose. But you get the idea."

Penny thought a moment. "Anything short of my death would only postpone the inevitable."

"And your father would likely drag you to the church anyway, even if he had to prop you up at the altar. Hmm."

"There is no hope for it," she conceded. "You have to leave. Bother your honor. I would rather be disgraced than be forced into a lifetime of misery."

"Well, I am not going to play the villain, no matter what you think of me. For that matter, many a female would be happy to wear my ring. Damn it, I do not have a ring."

"I have my mother's," she answered without thinking,

then caught herself. "No, no. The ring is not the problem. You are."

"Thank you. I do not know when I have been more insulted, at least not since you hit—since I arrived."

"I am sorry, but I do not want to be your wife. Furthermore, you do not want to be my husband."

"I never said that." Not in so many words, anyway. "But if we must wed, perhaps we can learn to rub along. Maybe marriage between us will not be as bad as you fear."

She made a rude noise.

He ignored it. "If, as you say, the deed is inevitable, we can try to make the most of it. I find you attractive, and that is a start. Your hair, your form. Your expressive face." West thought he could watch emotions color her cheeks for days, and spend at least a week learning the surprises of her slender figure. A week in bed with no clothes on.

She waved her hand, and her handkerchief, in dismissal. "Faugh. Looks have nothing to do with building a marriage."

"If that is what you think, you know less about men than a mongoose. Your hair—" He could not wait to see it loose and curling again, free for his fingers to slide through the silky tresses, preferably against his pillow. "That is, your care for your grandfather. I admire your loyalty, your intelligence, your spirit in fighting for what you want." Her sun-kissed hair. "And your good deeds for the neighbors. You did say you are involved in charitable enterprises?"

She went back to twisting her handkerchief between her hands. The silence went on.

"Um, did I mention your spirit? I appreciate that you have not flown into a tantrum, swooned, or dissolved in tears at a crisis."

"No, I would not do any of those things," she said

with a sniff, quickly using her mangled handkerchief to blot at her eyes.

He looked at her with suspicion. "Good, for men hate a woman's tears. They make us feel helpless."

"You are helpless, if you have no other plan to offer."

"Other than making the best of things? I see no alternative. But can you not think of one thing about me to admire?"

After too long a pause for his self-esteem, Penny said, "You are handsome, I suppose some would say."

That was a start, even though she had claimed looks did not matter. "Yes?"

"And you like horses."

"Good grief, ma'am, I am searching for crumbs here. Very well, since you will not credit me with the quality of a clam, let me say that I am honorable. I was an officer and deemed brave. I do not cheat at cards; I rarely drink to excess or gamble more than I can afford to lose. I am an excellent shot and handy with my fists."

"All excellent qualities in a husband," she mumbled to herself.

"I am not a fortune hunter. You cannot accuse me of plotting and planning to get my hands on your dowry or whatever moneys you possess, for I never knew you had any."

"That is true," she said grudgingly.

"I have never struck a woman." He ruined that by adding "yet."

"And . . . and I do not snore."

Her head jerked up. "We would share a bedroom?"

Saints preserve him from maidenly modesty and a virgin's vapors! And his own heated thoughts of her naked, beneath him. He hurried on, erasing the image. Discussions of the marriage bed could wait until after the marriage, thank the gods. "Not if you do not wish, except occasionally, of course, for the sake of children. You will have your own room, and you can decorate it any way you wish. In fact, you will have all of Westmoreland to redecorate. Although I would ask you to ignore your stepmother's preference for the Egyptian motif."

"What, no mummies in the morning room?" She smiled at last. "It would serve you right if I did."

Her smile entranced him. "Quite. Um, I am sure I have more to offer a woman than a crumbling pile to furnish. There is my title, of course, the country property, and a hunting box. Our first son will be an honorable, and he'll have lots of horses to ride."

None of his assets seemed to impress her, so he stood by her chair and reached for her hand. "I am sorry I cannot be your Prince Charming after all, but think on it, my dear. You have no better way to protect yourself and your grandfather than by marriage, and I have no other way of satisfying my honor. Then there is duty, a daughter's to her family, a viscount's to his heritage, a son's to his father's memory. My father did give his word on the betrothal, and I am bound not to betray him."

"I understand," Penny said. "But I need time to think about all this. I wish to speak to Grandpapa and reflect on my choices, limited though they are. This decision is for a lifetime, after all. I should have more than a few minutes to decide."

The decision was made when she was thirteen, but West held his tongue. Let the poor girl think she was in control of her destiny. He raised her hand to his lips, then said, "Very well, I shall return later this afternoon for your answer."

That was not late enough for Penny. "Why do you not come to dinner? With my father, I suppose. We can speak afterward, and perhaps if Cook's food is good and Grandpapa's wine is flowing, Father will listen to reason."

Maybe they could get him so drunk he could be put on a ship for the antipodes, West thought on a moment's optimism. But, no, Goldwaite would only come back. And no wine that West knew of turned solid marble into something malleable.

"Later, my dear."

"Grandpapa, I need to speak to you," Penny said after Westfield left. Her grandfather and Marcel were just finishing the day's work in the studio, so she helped clean up, as usual. She did not reveal her father's threats or the truth about the painting sales, but she did not need to explain about his insistence on the wedding.

"I heard all about it, poppet. But Grasping Gaspar told me to stay out of it. He is set on getting that title for you. And in a way he is right. Fathers have always made matches for their children, being older and wiser and with a larger view of life. Why, I never met your grandmother until a month before our wedding, and I came to love her with all my soul. Your mother caught young Gaspar's eye, but it was his father who approached me about an alliance. Daughters especially were expected to wed where their fathers decreed. Only recently have love matches become fashionable."

"Then you think it is my duty to obey Father's wishes?"

"I do not know what is in your heart, or in the viscount's, so I cannot advise you, even if I wished to go against your father's whims. You are always welcome here, but Gaspar is right. I will not live forever, and then you will have given up your chances of a life of your own."

"But I could be miserable in that life!" she said with a wail. "Doesn't that matter?"

"Of course, but you might also be happy. I have never heard ill spoken of him, and he has made good on his father's debts, which shows he is a man of honor."

"And he is *très beau*," Marcel put in. "Those shoulders, those muscles, such a distinguished air. Not an ounce of fat, I'd wager, and, oh, the legs of a horseman. Marry him, *chérie*, before someone else does."

"Yes, yes, he is good-looking, Marcel, but it is his character that matters."

Mr. Littleton stepped back from the work in progress and squinted his eyes as if that might bring the colors and shapes into focus. "Well, I could not comment on the gentleman's appearance, but he seemed pleasant to me."

"Is that enough? He has a mistress. A string of them, I suppose."

The old man shook his head, whether at the painting or her question Penny could not tell.

"Forget the past and look ahead, poppet. I always wished you to find a forever romance, but here? Tending your old granfer? You will make a good mother, and I would not have you miss that chance. And who knows? Perhaps you will find that your viscount is not the reprobate you have pictured. I have known so much love in my days: my sainted mother, my darling wife, your blessed mother, and Marcel, even my dog. Then I was fortunate to have you for these last years. All the loves of my life were different, yet all are to be cherished, in memory and in what time I have left."

"Do not talk like that, Grandpapa."

"What I am trying to say is that there is no easy answer, no one definition of love. Yet however and wherever you find it, in whatever shape or form, your life will be richer for it. If you cannot find a grand passion, at least you can make a comfortable marriage. The union will be what you make of it, my dear."

"But I have no time to get to know him, to see if even friendship is possible."

Littleton shrugged. "If you are going to do it, best do it quickly, like having a rotten tooth pulled. Sooner it's done, sooner you will feel better."

Penny had to laugh. "I doubt his lordship's pride will appreciate being compared to a rotten tooth."

"Better that than a boil on your behind."

Chapter Six

After their arranged marriage, Lord DH had his clubs; his wife had her committees; they had three children. All expectations were met. They were content.

—By Arrangement, *a chronicle of arranged marriages, by G. E. Felber*

Cook was furious she had to plan a dinner with so little time. She was even angrier that she might have to plan a wedding breakfast for the very next morning.

"What do you mean, 'might'? Either you are getting married or you aren't. Cooking a roast is like being with child. It's either yes or no. You don't cook it, you don't eat it."

Penny did not feel like discussing beef, babies, or Cook's problems. She had enough of her own. "We can have the neighbors over either way, so yes, plan on a meal after church tomorrow."

Then Cook was outraged that she was not getting to make the wedding cake. If there was a wedding, of course. By the time Penny had calmed the woman, planned the menus, picked flowers for the centerpiece, and helped

Marcel polish the silver, she was more frazzled than before, with no answers.

Then the vicar called. The Reverend Mr. Smithers was a gentleman in his midyears who wore the weight of his position around his waist. He was not pleased with the tidings of the day, either.

"I came as soon as I could after reading Sir Gaspar's note," he told Penny, after settling his bulk into a damask chair in the parlor, a cup of tea balanced on his meaty thigh. "His request to hold a marriage ceremony tomorrow during church came as a great surprise."

"Not as much as it was to me. That is, I had not planned on it quite yet."

He frowned, possibly because the few offerings on the nearby platter were so sparse, Cook being far too busy to make more tarts and tea cakes. "I did not so much as have a hint that you and this Lord Westfield had a long-standing agreement."

Penny thought he looked affronted not to know every detail of his parishioners' lives.

"It never seemed important. I never supposed an actual wedding would come to pass."

"I must say, I am disappointed."

So was Penny. She had thought, for an instant, of asking Mr. Smithers's advice, of telling him her doubts and fears, her broken dreams and impossible hopes, looking for his wiser counsel. Now he seemed too disgruntled over the supposed insult to his authority. She did not speak of her own disappointment.

"Yes," he was going on, scowling at the last biscuit, "very disappointed. I had hopes. . . ."

"Hopes?"

"You are an excellent addition to our little congregation, Miss Goldwaite, modest and helpful. Just what is wanted in a vicar's wife."

"Wife?"

"Why not, with my own wife gone to her reward these six years? I am not too ancient to wish a companion to share my days, and my nights, heh-heh." He dabbed at his mouth with his napkin, hiding his impious pleasure in the thought. Then he frowned, remembering both his position and Miss Goldwaite's imminent marriage. He waved the napkin in the air. "Ah, that way Little Falls could have the benefit of your kindness forever, and I would have a helpmate again."

The day was certainly full of surprises. Penny would not be shocked to find an elephant in Grandpapa's garden at this rate. Two suitors in one day, when they had been as rare as pachyderms in pantaloons. "You . . . you never spoke of it, sir. That is, I had no idea."

"Of course not. That would have been improper, giving rise to expectations before I had made up my mind. I felt that in time—"

"Time? I am six and twenty, Mr. Smithers. Time is fleeting." Her mind was fleeting, too, hither and yon. If she had married the vicar when she reached her majority, she would have been safe from the viscount and her father's finagling. Of age, she would not have needed anyone's permission.

She must have spoken the last words aloud, for Mr. Smithers tut-tutted. "Oh, I would never have taken a bride without her father's blessings. There is the matter of a dowry, you know. And the dignity of my calling. Why, the bishop would have been appalled to think I had wed another man's betrothed. That might have been grounds for an annulment, although I am no legal scholar. There would have been a scandal, certainly, which would have put an end to my hopes for advancement in the church."

Penny did not know the vicar had any hopes. Unless he had hoped to use her money to further his career.

He was not finished. "And of course there is the duty owed a daughter to her father. Why, I could never encourage a female to disobey the authority God gave to her guardian, who, after all, must have his own daughter's best interests at heart. Sir Gaspar was quite correct in making an advantageous match for his dear child, despite my own sorrow at his choice. A viscount, after all. Quite a feather in your cap, my dear, although one never knows about Londoners and their wicked ways."

Penny knew all too much for her own comfort.

The vicar had finished the last biscuit, but not his musings on his loss of a warm woman and a warm-pocketed father-in-law. "Then again, I am not certain the bishop would have approved of your connections."

"My connections? My father is a knight, a wealthy, respectable man of business who advises the Crown on occasion."

"Ah, but your grandfather is a . . . an artist. Not even a portraitist, which might be more acceptable, but a dauber of colors. Not at all the thing, my dear."

"Grandpapa's paintings sell," she said in clipped tones, disregarding the fact that they all sold to one unwilling buyer. "And there is nothing disgraceful about his profession in general or his artwork in particular." She stood, signaling an end to the conversation.

Good manners forced the vicar to stand also. "Ah well, one man's loss is another man's gain, as they say. I should have spoken sooner."

Then she might have been already wed . . . and dead of the tedium. Penny had punched one man today. What was another, even if he was a man of the cloth? Instead, she decided to deflate the pompous windbag another way. "I thank you for the kind offer you might have made. But you must not lament your own dillydallying. I would have refused your honorable proposal, Mr. Smithers."

"What? What's that? Oh, the previous engagement. Of course."

"No, sir, Lord Westfield was not on my mind, as I was not on his. I would have refused you because we would not suit. But do come for dinner tonight. You and my father have much in common."

Marcel kept pouring, the vicar kept preaching, and Penny's father, the devil take him, kept proposing toasts to his daughter, the peeress. Mr. and Mrs. Carne, Penny's friends who ran the local school, kept raising their glasses with him, until the schoolmaster almost fell off his chair and his wife started giggling. Grandpapa sat morosely at the head of the table, feeding scraps of Cook's finest meal to his fat pug under the table.

Penny could not eat a bite. She had not been able to speak to her father over sherry before the dinner, and he would not listen to her pleas now, not while he was celebrating.

"Just think, my grandson will be a viscount," he repeated every time Marcel filled his cup. Instead of being more amenable to reason, Penny's father appeared to be growing as hard of hearing as her grandfather was blind. Could drink do that to a man? Maybe it would make Penny forget that tomorrow was her wedding day unless she found a miracle. She drank down another glass of wine. And got a blinding headache.

Surely this was the worst meal of her life. Of course the wedding breakfast was bound to be worse, with her having to act the happy bride for her pride's sake, knowing she had been bartered away to an unwilling groom. Everyone knew Westfield would never have chosen Sir Gaspar's daughter, Mr. Littleton's grandchild, an on-the-shelf spinster with little else to recommend her besides her father's money and her books.

Why, look at him now, she thought, although she'd hardly looked elsewhere than at where he sat across the wooden table from her. The man was as handsome as sin, and committing it already, right in front of her! His smile flashed as brightly as the garnet on his finger. The dastard was actually flirting with Mrs. Carne, Penny's own friend, setting her to blushes and eyelash flutterings. And Mrs. Carne was forty if she was a day.

The last thing Penny wanted was a husband with a roving eye. Her father had always kept mistresses. Her mother knew, and now his second wife, Constance, must. The servants always did, and they always gossiped. Penny could not bear the shame, the insult, the disloyalty. She could not bear a man who prided himself on his honor, then lied and cheated to the one he owed the most fealty. Then again, she disliked her husband-to-be. Perhaps his straying would be a blessing. Let him take his smiles and seductions to his Green widow, she thought over another glass of wine. See if she cared.

Finally the last course was served and Penny led Mrs. Carne out of the dining room so the men could smoke and drink and gossip. With any luck, and a bottle of Grandpapa's best port, her father would be more open to Westfield's last efforts to change his mind.

The viscount shook his head when the gentlemen joined the ladies. The schoolmaster was staggering and the vicar was humming a hymn—no, that was a ditty from the tavern. Grandpapa fell asleep as soon as he sat in a chair, and the pug was so full it could barely waddle to the fireside. Her father was red-faced and grinning, happier with the coming nuptials than ever. Why not? He had the innkeeper's wife's company instead of his sour wife's for one more day. He was getting rid of his stepdaughters, and his grandsons would be lordlings.

Lord Westfield was as sober as a judge, one who was about to condemn the prisoner, Penny, to a lifetime sentence.

He stayed behind when the others left. He had ridden again, rather than sharing the coach with Sir Gaspar. The banker raised an eyebrow, but with only one night to go before the wedding, he winked and went on his way. He'd have a grandson that much sooner, and still legal.

"I tried," West told her. "I swear I tried, but your father is determined. He would see us both ruined, and your grandfather, too, if he does not get his way in this. All the while he smiles and says it is for our own good."

"Then there is no hope?"

"Barring earthquakes, floods, or a sudden plague of frogs, it seems not." He poured himself a glass of brandy and brought another one to Penny.

And then he did an amazing thing, or Penny's brain was more addled than she thought. He set his glass down, dropped to one knee, took her hand, and asked her to marry him!

She blinked to clear her aching head. "What did you say?"

"I said, 'Will you marry me, Miss Goldwaite?' I promise to be the best husband I know how, which is not much, but I am a quick learner, and I am certain you will teach me what else I need to know."

"With my fists?"

"With your smile, which is far more potent. I swear I will try to make you happy. I have already promised your grandfather."

"Penny."

"What?"

"You should not propose to someone as formal as Miss Goldwaite. I am Penny to nearly everyone."

"Very well, and you may call me Westfield, or Kendall, although my friends call me West."

"West," she said, in two syllables.

He set her wineglass farther away. "Penny, will you make me the happiest of men?"

"Will I?" she asked, that line between her eyebrows sharp. "Will I make you happy, that is?"

"I hope so, and believe that with respect and trust and affection, we may both be content. If you feel that is impossible, I shall try to smooth things over with your father. I will not let anyone force you."

She shook her head and pulled her hand away. "I do not understand why you are so resigned to this marriage. You are not inebriated, are you?"

He stood, facing her. "I told you I seldom drink to excess."

"I thought you would be raging and raving against my father and yours, and fate. And me."

"First, none of this was your doing. Secondly, I always knew I would have to marry someday, especially since coming into the title. That is the job of the second son, to step into his brother's shoes and bring forth future viscounts who are trained for the job as my brother was. I am still learning."

"But you could have wed a London belle, a toast. A political hostess, a duke's daughter." A wealthy widow, she thought, but did not say it. "Anyone better suited to the way you live."

"I could have wed a Spanish senorita or an Austrian princess, too. But you were the one chosen for me. And I am happy enough with my bargain. What of you?"

She had to look up at him, at his intense dark-eyed stare. That was too disconcerting, so she stared at his feet. His large feet, to her dismay, as Penny recalled Mrs.

Carne's naughty comment. "I have been thinking, when I had the chance."

"I could tell you were, instead of eating."

"You noticed?" Penny had thought he was too busy charming her friend.

"Of course I did. I do not want my bride fainting in church tomorrow. People would think it was me, not hunger. I, for one, think better on a full stomach. Empty belly, my old sergeant used to say, empty head. But tell me, what was the result of your musings?"

"That I cannot displease my father. But I cannot give my hand and all my life to yet another man, not without a few terms of my own."

West started pacing again. "Terms? As in terms of surrender?"

She raised her chin. A Goldwaite did not surrender. "Terms of negotiation, rather."

"The details were all spelled out in the original contract. I assure you, your settlements are generous, as are your widow's benefits. You shall never be in need. And I told you, I would not take my wife's life savings. Your money stays yours, to invest or to spend or to give to our daughters, God willing. I can support you and my sons, especially since I will not have to give back the dowry money. I will let your father pay for repairs to the London house to assuage his guilt, but my estates are showing profit and the horse farm is successful."

"What if the war ends and no one buys cavalry mounts?"

"I breed and train strong horses, not racers. There is always a call for good hunters and hacks. We shall not be poor."

She brushed that aside. "I leave fiscal matters to my father. I am speaking of far more important matters. Like faithfulness." Lady Greenlea's unspoken name hung in the air between them like one of the pug's emissions. "I could not bear knowing my husband preferred another woman, or women, so that I became a laughingstock, or a creature to be pitied. If you cannot be faithful, I demand discretion."

"A wife deserves nothing less, but I always meant to honor my wedding vows, when I got around to making them."

"Excellent. Next, I wish us not to con—" She could not say it. "Not to become, that is, not to make—"

He helped. "You do not wish for intimacy with a stranger?"

She was relieved. "That is it."

"That makes faithfulness a bit harder, but I can understand your reluctance to consummate the union until we get to know each other better."

"Thank you."

"Very well, we shall stymie your father's plans for an instant grandson, without his knowing it. But I must warn you that I cannot be patient—or celibate—forever. Is there anything else? Although anything might be easier than staying out of my own wife's bed."

Penny could feel the blush heating her cheeks and rushed on: "Grandpapa comes to London with us. He will enjoy being in Town, seeing all his old friends."

West shrugged, still thinking of how soon he could convince Penny to renegotiate that bedroom clause. Giving up his freedom was one thing. Giving up sex was another. "If he wishes."

"And Marcel."

"I, ah, already have a butler at Westmoreland House."

"Marcel can act as Grandpapa's valet and assistant. No one will question a blind man having a personal aide."

"They will if he parades around the house half naked."

That bright color flooded her cheeks again. "He will not."

"Then, done. It will be your house also, to organize the staff. What else?"

"I do not want a husband making rules and demands. I am used to making decisions for myself."

"As am I. I respect your intelligence, my pet, and I would not think of ordering you about. As long as you stay away from my horses," he added with a laugh.

"And you won't wish to select my clothes and arrange my schedules and choose my friends?"

"Good grief, I am no jailer, or governess, and you are an adult. I assume you will conduct yourself as befits a viscountess, that is all."

"And you will not hate me?"

"Is that one of your terms? Why should I hate you? I will be proud to call you my wife."

"And you will not mind that I do not like you?"

He smiled again. "I am a likable chap. Everyone says so. I will grow on you; depend on it. In fact, that is one of the terms I propose. Fair is fair, right?"

"Of course."

"Very well, I propose that you try to make something of this arrangement neither of us asked for."

"That is what Grandpapa and Marcel said I should do."

"They are both eccentric, but wise. And as for your not liking me, you hated me when I did not marry you, so you cannot hate me now, when I will. That is not fair."

"Grandpapa always said that life is not fair, but the alternative is less appealing."

"So you will try? We have a bargain?"

She took a deep breath. "We have a wedding tomorrow, yes. Heaven help us."

Chapter Seven

Miss L. ran off before meeting the man her father had arranged for her to marry. When her carriage overturned in a snowstorm, she fell in love at first sight with the handsome hero who rescued her ... the very same man her father had arranged for her to marry.

—By Arrangement, *a chronicle of arranged marriages, by G. E. Felber*

"Too bad Constance and the girls could not be here," Penny's father said as they waited in the back of St. Cecilia's Chapel. "The gals would be tickled pink to be bridesmaids."

At least Penny had been spared that horror.

This was not the wedding she would have chosen. Not that she was haughty enough to demand St. George's, but Penny had always imagined her marriage taking place in some majestic church amid elegant guests, not in the dark and drafty country chapel that someone had tried to make festive with flowers and ribbons, while sheepherders and farmers and their wives gawked at the suddenness of the ceremony. The children from the orphanage had been scrubbed and seated in the back, where they squirmed and whispered, almost as loath to be here as Penny.

The special license her father held meant she could wed anywhere, at any time of day, but Sir Gaspar would not hear of the smallest delay, not when victory was at hand. His victory, her hand.

For that matter, her father was not the man Penny would have chosen to give her away. She did love her father, but he was not giving her; he had sold her. She'd rather her grandfather took the last steps of a single woman with her, as he'd been with her these years of her exile from London. Grandpapa was acting as best man for the viscount, however. Marcel had offered to be her attendant, but he was joking, she hoped. It was Mrs. Carne who stood next to the vicar as Penny's witness, although the schoolmaster's wife had eyes only for the groom.

This was not the gown Penny would have chosen for the momentous day. She had her mother's bridal ensemble set aside in the attics, but there was no time to alter the white satin dress for her thinner figure. And the white lace overlay had yellowed with age. She would have dyed it with tea leaves, to a color more becoming her pale complexion, had there been time. When she complained, her father had offered to pay for her new London wardrobe as her trousseau. Meanwhile, she wore her favorite pale pink merino gown, with rosebuds in her hair and a single strand of pearls at her throat. The gown had the advantage of long sleeves and high neck, necessary in the unheated chapel. Penny shivered anyway.

The church, the gown, the wedding party—all meant nothing. Kendall Westmoreland, Viscount Westfield, was simply not the man she would have chosen to marry.

The tall, dark, and handsome gentleman waiting for the vicar to finish his Sunday reading before going on to the wedding ceremony was a stranger. In his London finery, to say nothing of his proud stance, his air of authority, Lord Westfield was as out of place here as Grandpapa's pug would have been. Little Falls might never have been visited by a real live viscount before, for all she knew. Like Mrs. Carne, no one was even looking at the bride, only at the splendid groom.

He spotted her in the back and smiled.

Oh no, she would never have chosen to wed such a man. Attractive, charming, titled, educated, he was a fairy-tale prince without the happy ending. Westfield would break her heart, over and over again, if she let him. She would have high rank and a fine address and, thanks to her father, a fancy wardrobe—she would get him to buy a new carriage, too, before the day was over—but she would not have what every woman wanted: a loving marriage to a good man. Westfield was neither loving nor good. Why, as soon as he had his heir, the rogue was liable to forget about Penny's existence for another thirteen years.

And he brought out the worst in her, all the bitter resentment, all the anger. That could not be a good sign of things to come. In less than two days she had committed violence and blasphemy and lies. Even now she wanted to strangle the vicar with his own clerical collar. Furthermore, she had resorted to blackmailing her own father.

Penny had agreed to the wedding, but at a price. There had never been a choice—everyone knew that—but her father had bargained to avoid another scene. Now he was not just financing the refurbishing expenses for the London town house and the trousseau, but he was going to keep paying Penny's allowance, and Lady Bainbridge's salary as her companion. He could not expect Penny to bring out his stepdaughters on her own, could he, while she was a stranger to the *ton* herself?

Her father would have acquiesced to anything— except Marcel in a gown tossing orange blossoms and rose petals—when Penny started crying. Maybe he was assuaging his own guilt with his gold, but Penny was not going to turn down his conscience money. She had pride, but she had some recompense coming, too, she decided, with interest. She was her father's daughter, after all.

West had proved right: Tears worked better than screams and shouts. Penny had not even had to threaten to disrupt the ceremony with cries of how she was being coerced, of how Sir Gaspar was an unnatural parent, or how he'd bedded the innkeeper's wife. No, a few tears— honest ones, too—and he had agreed to her demands. She had to remember that for the future.

Mr. Smithers was turning pages in his prayer book, ready to begin this addition to his Sunday service. Penny's future was now, waiting at the altar, smiling at her. West had been decent about the whole mess, she supposed, kinder than she might have expected or de- served, after her rant. Hadn't he given her the pearls at her throat, saying they were the best he could find in Upper Falls? There were heirlooms aplenty in the fam- ily vault in London, but he wanted her to have some- thing new, all her own, as a wedding present. Hadn't he sent the bouquet she carried and the roses for her hair? Probably he was the one who thought of decorating the chapel and bringing the children from the orphanage, knowing how much they meant to her.

He'd also been reasonable about her conditions, without adding impossible demands of his own. Later, he had agreed that they could stay on in Little Falls for a few days, rather than traveling back to London right after the wedding party, as her father was going to do. Penny needed time to pack, to settle her accounts, and to help her grandfather with the move. The house had to be closed, instructions left for caretakers and gardeners. She had to find willing hands to take over her responsibilities at the orphanage.

She thought—she hoped—that West would go on ahead without her. He could busy himself with sending the marriage notices to the newspapers and readying his own home for additional guests. Instead he said that her father would see to the notices, gladly, and notify West's staff at Westmoreland House. He would not let them make any changes until she approved them, anyway. Besides, they would stir the scandal broth worse by not appearing together in Town. He also volunteered to help her with her chores, the rotter.

The scoundrel was trying to make her like him. Charming a female must be second nature to a rake like him. Why, every goosegirl and dairymaid on the hard pews sighed when he flashed those dimples, and he had never given them anything. Yet.

Penny clutched her bouquet more firmly, and her father's arm with her other hand, to keep it from trembling. Now she knew how a convict felt on that last, slow walk to the gibbet.

West could not keep a grin from his face. Zeus, his bride was a beauty. She carried herself with such grace and dignity, one would think she was a duchess or a princess. For once in his life, he'd rolled the dice and come out a winner. Who would have thought it? And why did he wait so long?

"Thank you, Father," he whispered, looking up to where he supposed his dead sire resided, then added, "You, too," in case anyone else on high was listening.

Miss Persephone Goldwaite was not merely a fortune with a pretty face and figure. She was a delightful creature with a sound mind and strong opinions of her own.

She would never bore him, unlike the milk-and-water misses of proper society who never had two thoughts to rub together. They certainly never gave voice to temper or showed their emotions with every touch of pink across their skin. They never, ever disagreed with a gentleman. Hah!

According to her friend Mrs. Carne, the vicar, and the servants, Miss Goldwaite had progressive ideas, and never minded putting her own money or hand to furthering a good cause. Heaven knew there were good causes aplenty at his seat in Westfield. As soon as they had fired off Goldwaite's stepdaughters, they could go to the country and see what needed to be done.

When he'd come into the title, the fields and farms were in such poor state it was a wonder any tenants stayed on at all. His conscience forced him to reduce their rents, his gambling father and wastrel brother having made no improvements in years except to their own standards of living. At first, West's primary concern had been with the horses, to have some income to invest back into the land. The estate was finally showing a profit, but he still had no time or money to see about schools and hospitals. Now he'd have a partner who, it appeared, excelled at bettering conditions for those less fortunate. She had already bettered his by agreeing to the marriage.

So he would have a lovely, interesting, helpful bride ... who hated him. Well, a man needed a challenge. He smiled again, to see his pearls at her throat, his flowers in her hair. His. Soon he would be able to take the pins out of that golden crown and spread it down her shoulders, feel the curls twine around his fingers, smell the rose water. He'd get to touch her skin, her full breasts, make her nipples harden, make her turn rosy, this time with lovemaking. His.

He wondered how long it would take. Tonight could not be soon enough.

He took her hand when she reached his side, and could feel hers tremble. Or shiver with the cold, damn it. Even through their gloves he could tell that her hands were cold. He rubbed his thumb over her knuckles, but she frowned across at him. Maybe her hands were not the only things cold about his bride. He prayed fate could not be that fickle, putting an icy heart in an inviting body.

He turned forward and tried to listen to the vicar natter on about the married state, a wife's duties, a husband's responsibilities. Great gods, there had to be more than onerous obligations or no one would get married. He knew a brief moment's panic to think he was taking on those burdens, forever. Then he knew a deeper panic when it seemed he might not be taking a wife today after all.

"Do you?" he whispered to Penny when silence followed the vicar's repeated question.

"Do I what?" she answered, as if in a trance. Panic was as pervasive in the tiny chapel as the cold. She hadn't been listening to anything but her own heart's galloping beat, wondering whether it would stop altogether, and whether that might not be a blessing. If the viscount had not been holding her hand, she would have collapsed for sure. Was he supporting her or dragging her closer to the abyss?

"Devil take it," West swore, earning him a frown from Mr. Smithers and a reminder where he was. "Hell," he swore again, "if we weren't in a church, I wouldn't care what she replied."

The vicar cleared his throat. "Miss Goldwaite?"

West squeezed her hand, too hard to ignore. "Yes?"

"Do you take this man, et cetera?"

"Oh."

"Do not turn craven on me now, my girl," West urged, while he could hear mutterings behind him, and a growl from Sir Gaspar. " 'Oh' is not the proper response. Do you want to marry me or not?"

"I . . . I think I do. That is, I do." He squeezed her hand again, this time in gratitude, she thought, so she spoke up louder. "Yes, I do."

She did.

West raised his eye heavenward again for another prayer of thanks and apology for his harsh words. A breeze blew through the chapel, as if the entire congregation had exhaled the breaths they'd been holding.

She did.

Then he got to kiss the bride. Not that anyone told him he ought, but he did anyway. The kiss was not a hasty formal finalizing of the vows, either, but a real kiss, a deep kiss, a kiss as if no one were watching. A seal on their union, a promise of the union of their bodies as well as their fortunes and fates.

Her lips were cold until he warmed them with his. And then his bride—no, his wife—kissed him back.

She did!

Lady Westfield was not cold at all. West smiled. Her cheeks were aflame, and her breaths were coming in gasps, and her eyes were still closed.

The vicar cleared his throat.

Penny opened her eyes, blinked away the dazed expression, and muttered for her new husband's ears only, "I still do not like you."

The sound of West's laughter warmed the whole chapel.

Chapter Eight

To avoid an arranged match, Lord J. wed an actress. She promised to love, honor, and obey. She was acting.

> —By Arrangement, *a chronicle of arranged marriages, by G. E. Felber*

Now, that was unfair. No man should kiss like that. Or laugh like that. Penny felt hot and cold, weak-kneed and paralyzed, humiliated, humbled, and—heavens, the man could kiss! How could she have reached the advanced age of six and twenty without knowing that a kiss could make a woman's stomach do somersaults, her heart skip a beat, and her mind skitter off? Well, the answer to that was simple: Penny did not know because her promised husband had never shown her. He'd waited all those years and then he chose today, in the chapel, to demonstrate what she'd been missing. He'd had almost two decades of practice to perfect his skills, practice on other women.

He was despicable. And he had dimples. What was a woman—nay, a wife—with newly discovered wanton tendencies to do? She would not fall in love with him, Penny swore. She absolutely would not.

Proud that she had survived the kiss, and the wedding ceremony, Penny imagined the rest of the day would be easier. It was not. She had to sign the register, and sign the papers her father's solicitor had drawn up, making her feel like a purchased pig. Then came the congratulations and well wishes of people she had known the past years. Some were angry they had not known about her betrothal to an aristocrat, as if she had misled them about being one of their own class. Some were disappointed she'd be leaving, and leaving the charities to them to manage. Some were genuinely happy for her, and some—every unwed woman and half the married ones—were jealous. During it all, Penny had to smile and coo and pretend to be thrilled with her good fortune. Her pride demanded no less.

They left the chapel in a hired coach, festooned with ribbons and flowers, leading a merry procession back to her grandfather's house. Everyone in the surrounding villages was invited, it seemed, from Baron Whitstanley to the butcher's boy. Trestle tables were arranged on the terrace, filled with a roast, a ham, the wedding cake, and kegs of ale. Champagne was served to the family and closest friends in the parlor. Two fiddlers were set up in the cleared carriage house for dancing. Songs and laughter spread throughout the gardens as people moved from one area to the next, delighted with the unexpected treat.

Everyone insisted the newlyweds lead off the first dance.

West was an excellent dancer, of course. Penny expected no less. What did surprise her was that the viscount was not half as high in the instep as she feared, dancing with Cook and the village seamstress as well as the baroness. He even applauded the Sunday school children when the vicar led them in a hymn of celebration;

then he handed them each a coin, winning the hearts of the locals, if not his wife.

After an hour or so Penny was used to being called Lady Westfield, instead of looking around for some dowager to curtsy to. After another hour, she was sick of hearing her new husband's praises sung by every man who shook his hand and talked about horses or asked about his regiment. She was thoroughly tired of watching the women ooh and ogle. For heaven's sake, hadn't they ever met a god come down from Olympus? She sighed. No, no one had, not around here. Not around anywhere, Penny feared.

He was just a man, she told the awestruck admirers, lying through her teeth.

The party went on until dark, with more toasts, more food, more noise and laughter. Penny was trying to appear so merry, so gay, she thought her face had frozen in a false smile. Her toes ached from the blacksmith's dance and her throat burned from trying to speak over the music. Her favorite gown was stained with someone's wine, her hair was falling out of its careful topknot, and beads of perspiration dripped down her back. She had not slept last night, and had not been able to eat since yesterday. Her grandfather looked pale and weary, and the magistrate was looking at Marcel with hostility. Her father was looking at the baroness, the blacksmith's wife, and the barrister's daughter. And this was supposed to be the happiest day of Penny's life?

What made it worse, Penny decided, was Westfield. There he was, as poised and polished as he had been this morning, a few tousled curls the only sign that he had stood up for the last country reel. His neckcloth was still starched and spotless, and his smile never wavered. He was eating and drinking and dancing and flirting. The worm was enjoying himself!

If he could, she could.

Penny threw herself back into the party, dragging her father into the carriage house for a waltz. He huffed and puffed, but beamed with pride.

"My daughter, Viscountess Westfield."

At least no one would call her Penny Gold or the Golden Penny anymore. Now she was more than the banker's daughter.

"And you are happy, aren't you? I can see you are. I knew I did the right thing for you, my girl."

Happy? Penny thought she might cry, but it was too late for tears. She had another glass of champagne.

The guests finally started to leave when the sun started to go down. Many had distances to travel; most had work and chores early in the morning; some were already passed out from the revelries. Carriages and carts were organized to get everyone home, parcels of food and wedding cake sent with them.

Sir Gaspar was the last to leave. Penny's father would spend one more night at the inn, then head out for London the next day without stopping at Littleton's.

"Wouldn't want to disturb the newlyweds, eh?"

Penny accidentally spilled her wine down his shirt-front when she kissed him good-bye.

Marcel led Grandpapa into the house and up to his room for the night. The servants began to clear away the rest of the mess until Penny told them to leave it all for tomorrow. They had worked hard enough to deserve the night to themselves.

"What about supper?" Cook asked.

Penny knew the woman had been up all night, too, preparing the feast. "I could not eat another thing," she said. "You go on to bed. If my lord is hungry later, I can fix him a cold platter."

Cook winked. "If he's hungry later, it won't be for leftover ham."

West laughed back, not in the least offended. He put his arm around a blushing Penny and guided her to the edge of the terrace, to watch the sunset.

"Beautiful," he said, "all the colors."

"I have always loved dusk in the country."

"I meant your face, your hair."

She blushed all the pinker, and he smiled, but turned to watch the sky. "I thought that went well," he said after a moment.

Penny looked at the trampled garden, the broken glasses, the dirty dishes, and the crumbled wedding cake. "Lovely."

"The best wedding I have ever had," the viscount said, placing a gentle kiss on her forehead.

She leaped back. Oh, no, he was not going to play off his charms on her. They had an agreement. "I am filthy and exhausted, my lord."

"West."

"West," she said. She decided she had to be obliging about something lest he think she was going back on her word to try for peace between them. Peace and twenty feet was what he was getting between them. She feigned a yawn. "Why, I am so tired I might fall asleep right here on the terrace. And I need to check on Grandpapa."

"He is fine. I looked in on him. Marcel left him with a toddy, his journal, and a magnifying lens."

Penny headed back into the house. "Thank you. I will, ah, leave you to smoke, then. You do smoke, do you not?"

"No, I am glad to say. Filthy habit."

"Yes, well, you must be tired, too."

"I am used to London hours. The *ton* rarely begin their evening's entertainments until far past sundown. They often party until dawn. I am not tired at all."

Penny could see his wide, white-toothed grin, like a jungle cat's, ready to pounce. There would be no pouncing tonight, by all that was holy. She yawned again. "I am used to country hours," she lied. "You know, up with daybreak, in bed by dark."

"That is all right, too."

Penny worried what he meant by his smiling comment. He could not mean to join her, could he? "I am barely awake now, so I shall bid you good night."

West bowed. "Good night, wife."

He made no effort to detain her or kiss her again, so Penny made her escape. She flew up the stairs, raced into her bedroom, and slammed the door behind her. She tore off her clothes—the gown was ruined anyway—and wished she had asked one of the servants for a hot bath before dismissing them for the night. But they had worked harder than she, so she made do with a pitcher of lukewarm water and a washcloth. She pulled the pins out of her hair, tugged on the night rail laid out on her bed, and threw herself backward onto the mattress. Great heavens, she was married.

Her body was exhausted, but her mind was wide-awake, racing in circles like a hound after two foxes. She was married, after so many years of thinking such a thing would never come to pass. Her dreams had changed; her plans for her life were not the same. Yet she was indisputably, irretrievably married. She felt no different, but a stranger was in the house: her husband. And he would be there, or she would be at his home, until death did them part. Maybe if she put a pillow over her head . . . ?

She did not have the energy to raise her head, much less a pillow. So she did not move when she heard a knock on her door. Perhaps one of the maids was bringing more hot water. She lay flat, but called out, "Yes?"

West opened the door and stood in the entrance, a bottle of champagne in one hand, two glasses in the other. His neckcloth was gone; so were his coat and waistcoat.

Penny screeched and jumped up, off the bed. "What are you doing here?"

"It is our wedding night, my pet."

"But we agreed not to . . ."

He smiled. "We agreed to delay the consummation until we got to know each other better. I thought this was a good time to start."

She shook her head. "It is not. I have a headache." She rubbed her temples as evidence.

"Impossible. We have not even been wed for a whole day."

She looked puzzled.

"I apologize." And she did have that pucker between her brows. "Perhaps I might soothe your pain with a massage, or a cool cloth on your forehead." He looked for a place to set the glasses and the bottle.

Touch her? He wanted to touch her? "Thank you, but I believe I merely require a good night's sleep. Uninterrupted sleep."

"I see." What West saw by the candlelight was his exquisite wife in a sheer white gown that caressed her soft curves when she moved, and turned transparent when she stood in front of the fireplace. What he saw was a cloud of fair hair around her head like a halo, and shadows below that could tempt a saint. If she was all the colors of dawn when he first saw her—lud, was it only yesterday?—she was moonlight tonight, her skin so pale, her hair a yellow nimbus, her body an unexplored mystery, her eyes as bright as stars.

What he saw was a long, lonely night. He made one last attempt. "But it is our wedding day."

Penny raised her chin and narrowed her eyes. "I know what you are after, what all the ribald jokes were about. But we agreed. You have waited thirteen years for the wedding—you can wait another while for the bedding."

"That was not my only intention." He was honest enough to admit his lust. How could he not, when her eyes dropped to his bulging breeches? He held the champagne bottle lower. "But I am not here solely to make love to my beautiful bride, but to make friends with her. How can we become accustomed to each other if we do not speak?"

"We shall have decades for that. I see no need to begin tonight."

"But—" The door shut in his face. His Penny might look like an invitation with her sheer gown and flowing curls and bare feet, but she was still shutting him out. West felt as if she'd punched him again, he was so disappointed.

Penny blew out the candles and went back to bed. This time she got under the covers and pulled the sheet over her head, trying to hide the image of West in his shirtsleeves and smiles, bent on seduction. Gracious, that memory would keep her awake another night, drat the man.

He knocked on the door again.

She muttered a French word Marcel had taught her, but got up. She crossed the room by the light of the fireplace embers and pulled open the door, knowing what she would find on the other side, his loutish lordship. "What now?"

West smiled. Penny looked like an angry kitten, her fur all ruffled, ready to hiss. "I am sorry to disturb you again, my lady wife, but I need to know, where am I to sleep if not with my lovely bride?"

"Oh." Penny hoped the darkness shielded her blushes, for once. "Marcel was supposed to show you to your room."

West raised the champagne bottle. "Marcel is a romantic. He handed me this before going to bed."

She sniffed. "Your things are across the hall. We have given you George's room. Good night."

She started to shut the door again, but he called out, "Wait! Who is George?"

"Do not worry," she said. "He is friendly."

Chapter Nine

*At the orders of their parents, Mr. and Mrs. Z. said
"I do." Those were the last civil words the couple
spoke to each other for the next forty years.*

—By Arrangement, *a chronicle of
arranged marriages, by G. E. Felber*

She expected West to bed down with one of her grandfather's friends? Bloody hell, if the woman thought
that, she was missing a few spokes to her wheel. And her
understanding of men was sadly warped by her uncon-
ventional upbringing.

West decided he'd sleep on the couch in the parlor
instead, or in one of the stuffed chairs in the library. He
had no idea if there would be a fire in either room, so he
decided to fetch a blanket and a pillow.

No one was in the room she had indicated, as far as
he could see. A warm fire glowed, and an oil lamp was
left burning on the bedside next to a book. The sheets on
the large canopied bed were turned down, with West's
own robe spread across the foot. His bags were neatly
stored beside the wardrobe, and his brushes and shaving
supplies were on the washstand. He saw no one else's
clothes or possessions. George must have moved to an-

other room. And the wide bed did look inviting. The past few days and the wedding had been a strain, and the next few did not look to be any easier, as he dealt with his skittish, sexy bride. He needed his rest, not a sore back from a makeshift cot.

West started to undress. He was used to doing for himself after years with the army, then the years of scrimping and saving when he returned to England. He did have a valet in London now that his social obligations and hence his wardrobe were so extensive, but he'd left the man behind, rather than have any more gossip about the proposed betrothal and possible wedding. He'd shared Sir Gaspar's man on the road north and he supposed Marcel or a footman could iron his neckcloths on the way south.

He folded his clothes in a military-neat pile, then washed, climbed beneath the sheets, and picked up the book left beside the bed.

Love Lasts Forever, he read, and grimaced. Well, a book of poetry was certain to put him to sleep. Then he read the inscription: *To Cornelius Littleton, in honor of his sixty-fifth birthday, with love from his devoted granddaughter.* It was signed by Persephone Goldwaite, and dated from when West's bride would have been eighteen. Motherless, sent away from the only home she knew, her place usurped by her father's new wife, his Penny had written a book of poems for the grandfather who had taken her in and shown her affection.

The vellum pages were small, neatly lettered, and bound with string. The pasteboard covers were encased in brown velvet, with the title and a few delicate flowers painted on the front.

Only Marcel could have left this for West by his bedside, and only at Mr. Littleton's orders. The downy old bird must have known the path of this marriage was a rough one. He was trying to smooth the way by letting West get to know the girl his wife once was.

No one would believe West was reading amateur, amatory verses on his wedding night, but he turned to the first poem. Some young women were mothers at eighteen. Some were still girls. In his experience, most were emotional, sentimental, and immersed in high drama, so he was not surprised to read about love and loss, unrequited affection, heroes who went off to war, and callous fools who deserved to die long, lonely deaths. West learned a great deal, as the old man must have intended.

He learned his Penny was a dreadful poet.

He also learned she had loved him once, idealistically, worshipfully, foolishly, before he betrayed her by neglect.

And he learned that first, young love did *not* last forever.

His was a rocky road indeed.

West finished the last poem, a paean to the artist who had painted a new world of bucolic pleasures for his granddaughter, and turned down the lamp. He had much to think about.

Despite his troubled thoughts and the early hour, West was sound asleep in minutes without a dream or a nightmare in his mind until something landed on his chest. He instantly rolled over, smothering whatever assailant was attacking him. If he'd had his pistol under his pillow, the dastard would be dead before answering a single question. If he had his sword—

Something whined. He raised himself up to his elbows, and got his face licked.

"George?"

In the last faint glow from the fire, West could see Littleton's fat old pug panting and trembling from being rolled on. "This is your room?" West was panting and trembling, too, from the shock of the assault.

In answer, the fat old dog shook himself and moved to the other pillow on the bed. He circled thrice, then lay down, his curled tail inches from West's nose. The viscount answered his own question: "This is your room." But this was not the view West had imagined on the pillow next to his, not on his wedding night.

He tried to get back to sleep, but the dog snored. That explained why the creature was not sharing its master's bedchamber.

West turned over; George growled at him. West nudged George farther away; George showed his teeth. "She said you were friendly."

And she'd said it was George's room, so West was the interloper and the pug was defending his territory. West sighed and thought about the chair in the library, but the bed was comfortable here, the blankets warm. He'd have to get dressed, find his slippers, relight the candles, and make his way down the stairs without disturbing the rest of the household. That felt like too much effort, so he tried to fall back asleep again, thinking about the young girl's poems instead of the old man's pet. Then he tried to recall Penny's rosewater scent instead of the pug's bad breath, her willowy shape instead of the four-footed barrel beside him in bed. It was no good. He could not sleep through the dog's gasping *whuffle*s.

He remembered sharing a tent with an Irish officer once, one who could alert the French to their position just with his loud, rasping, openmouthed breathing. West tried what had worked on McMann. He rolled the pug over.

But the pug was not a burly Irishman. West pushed too hard and the pug fell right off the high bed. It wheezed a few times, and then was quiet. Too quiet. West lay still, waiting for the snore that never came. Instead of letting him slip into slumber, the silence put his every sense on guard, kept every muscle rigid, as he waited for the heavy breathing.

West scrambled to the other side of the bed, tangling in the sheets, and leaned over. He could see the pug on its side, not stirring. "George? I say, old man, I did not mean to shove so hard. George?"

He touched the dog's flank gingerly, not willing to lose a finger to gain a night's sleep. George did not move.

Holy hunting hounds, George was dead! First West had broken his bride's heart, then he'd wed her against her will, and now he'd killed her grandfather's pet. He doubted that was a harbinger of a happy marriage. He untangled himself from the covers while he considered his options.

He could ignore the dog altogether, pretending surprise in the morning when a servant came in to relight the fire. Not only was that devious and underhanded, but how could he sleep with a dead dog next to his bed? Shutting George in the wardrobe was no solution, and no one would believe George put himself there, or that he jumped out the window, for that matter. West thought about carrying the corpse elsewhere, for someone else to find. That was cowardly, and someone might see him, besides. He leaned over and nudged the dog again. Oh, hell.

Someone had to tell the old man. What if the news killed him, too? West ran his fingers through his hair in despair. What to do?

There was nothing for it, he decided, but to ask Penny what she thought best. He'd ask Marcel, but he had no idea where the servant slept. Yes, he'd ask Penny. The woman had an opinion about everything, and she loved her grandfather. He jumped out of bed and hurried toward the door. Then he came back and put on his robe. The sight of his nudity might give his virgin bride an apoplexy. Just think, he could wipe out the entire household in one night.

He scratched softly on the door across the hall. Penny did not answer, so he pushed the door open and crept in like a sneak thief—or a dog murderer. The room was dark, the fire out. Damn. He waited a minute for his eyes to adjust, but he need not have waited. He was guided to the bed by his bride's snores. Damn again. Her snore was not as loud as the dog's had been. In fact, it was almost a sweet little ruffle of breath. He could live with that, he supposed, if she ever let him near enough after this night's work. For a craven moment he thought of moving George into her room while she slept so soundly, then mentally chided himself for the unworthy idea. Wasn't there something in those wedding vows about love, honor, and protect? If there wasn't, there should be. A gentleman's code of honor insisted he defend the weaker sex from harm, anyway. And a decent man did not deposit dead things under his wife's bed.

"Penny?" he called softly when he was near enough to make out her pale hair.

She did not miss a snore, so he shook her shoulder.

"Yeoow!" she screamed, thrashing her arms, kicking her legs, fighting like a wildcat, or like a woman being attacked in her bedchamber in the middle of the night. One of her fists caught his nose before he could catch her arm.

"It's Westfield, by George," he yelled, feeling to see if his nose was broken or bleeding. Did someone say they were the weaker sex? "Well, bygone George."

She sat up, furious. "What are you doing in my bedchamber? What kind of monster assaults a woman in the dark?"

"I have never assaulted a female in the dark or otherwise, and I take offense that you might think I would. Dash it, I merely tried to awaken you. Next time I will throw water at you. From a distance." He rubbed at his sore nose again.

"Water? Is the house on fire?" She started to bolt out of bed. "Grandpapa!"

He put a hand on her shoulder, cautiously. "No, the house is fine. So is your grandfather. It's George the pug. He, ah, fell off the bed and now he is not moving. I do not know what to do."

Penny rubbed at her eyes. She got out of bed and reached for her robe, giving him a brief, tantalizing glimpse of soft curves left uncovered by the clinging nightgown. West tried to dampen his wayward thoughts. He'd murdered the mongrel and now he was leering at his maiden bride? Devil take it, he used to be a man of principle, with a straight nose. Marriage was having a decidedly ill effect on him.

And his wife was bossy, besides having a streak of meanness.

"Light a candle," she ordered, "and stop trying to see through my clothes."

She took the candle from him and stomped across the hall. She went to the far side of the bed when West pointed, and knelt down. "He has only fainted."

"Dogs faint?"

"This one does." She propped the dog on its feet and blew in its nose.

"Should I find a vinaigrette?"

"This works. Unless you want to breathe into George's mouth?"

He stepped back. "No, you are doing admirably."

George took a deep breath, staggered a bit, then licked Penny's cheek. She lifted him back onto the bed, where he promptly circled again and curled up . . . on West's pillow this time.

"Thank you," West said, so relieved he reached out to pat the dog. "But you might have warned me."

Penny was still watching the pug. "He does not go off frequently. It must have been the excitement of the day."

Or being knocked to flinders by a trespasser in his bed. West lit the oil lamp and put another log on the fire. "I do not think he should stay here."

"Why not? Now you know what to do."

"Yes, I need to find another room. I do not suppose I can share yours for the rest of the night?"

Penny looked at him, in his brocade robe, bare feet, bare chest, a loose sash keeping him decent, a sultry smile on his lips. A sensible woman did not invite the devil into her chamber. "George will be fine," she said.

"He snores."

"Most of his breed does."

Since she was showing no pity, West said, "You snore, too."

"I do not!"

"I just heard you with my own ears. But do not fret. I find it attractive."

"I could not care less what you find attractive." But she did care, because she turned seven shades of scarlet when her stomach let out a loud rumble.

"You are hungry! It's no wonder, for you hardly eat anything at all. You are not one of those foolish women starving themselves to be stylish, are you?"

"Do not be absurd. I have been too busy, is all. I suppose I could have a piece of wedding cake now that I am awake."

West ignored the reproach in her voice as he led the way down to the kitchen and raided the pantry. He filled plates with the cold ham and cake, while she heated water for tea and set places at the worn wooden table in the center of the room.

They were too busy eating to argue, for once.

West liked the companionship. He'd eaten many a solitary midnight meal, but this was far more pleasant. Mistresses demanded dining in style and conversation, while the young women of the polite world giggled and simpered their way through supper, under their duennas' watchful eyes. Penny simply ate, and enjoyed the meal.

She reached for a second slice of wedding cake. "I suppose I no longer have to put a piece under my pillow."

He eyed the icing. "Good grief, why would you want to do that?"

"Young girls do, you know. That's why we sent so many pieces along with the guests, carefully wrapped, of course. If you lay your head on the pillow, atop the cake, you are supposed to dream of your future husband."

"Did you?"

"Put cake under my pillow? A few times."

"But did you dream of me?"

"I dreamed of cake and woke up hungry." But she smiled. And she did not shy away when he used his finger to wipe a dab of icing from the corner of her mouth. That was progress.

When they were done, she was yawning again, this time for real. Her eyes were heavy, her movements less graceful. West held the candle on the way up the stairs. She made no resistance when he set the candle down outside her door, raised her hand to his mouth, and kissed her fingers. That was more progress. So he turned her hand over and kissed the palm, and the wrist, and— progress ended with the door in his face again.

"Well, George, it's just the two of us. And only one of us gets the bed."

Chapter Ten

Lord and Lady M. were promised at birth. They wed at eighteen, and died within days of each other, decades later. They were best friends and lovers from the cradle to the grave.

—By Arrangement, *a chronicle of arranged marriages, by G. E. Felber*

If Penny Goldwaite, now Lady Westfield, had been with Wellington's army, the war would have ended years sooner. She had her whole household fed, organized, and in action by nine in the morning.

Except for the viscount, who slept until ten. Someone had come at dawn to retrieve George for his morning constitutional, so West had a few hours of uninterrupted sleep. He worried that his wife had less, since she already had her lists in hand when he entered the dining room.

She did not appear as tired as he felt, with her hair held back with a yellow ribbon that matched the color of her gown. The day was overcast and damp, but Penny looked like sunshine. She had the usual pucker between her eyes, however, which deepened when she saw him, also as usual. Whatever ground he'd gained last night, West knew, had been lost with her remembering that he was a profligate London beau, sleeping half the day. The prickly female was determined to remember that, but not the dog, the late-night meal, or her own appeal, which had kept him awake. He wondered how long she was going to blame him for everything from the bad weather outdoors to the price of corn. Forever, he thought with a sigh, pouring himself a cup of coffee.

"I do not suppose you dreamed of me last night," he said, hoping for a smile, something to brighten the gloomy day besides the color of her gown.

"Why should I dream of you, with no wedding cake under my pillow? Besides, that is for unmarried girls. I already know who my husband is."

He thought she might have muttered, "Unfortunately."

"Ah, but there is no rule saying a woman cannot dream of her wedded spouse, is there?"

She ignored his flirtatious tone. "Did you dream of me?"

If waking up in a state of half arousal counted, yes. "In fact, I did. And wished you were beside me instead of George."

If he could not get a smile, he could get a blush. He laughed at how his bride was so mature and efficient, and yet so like a schoolgirl. He liked the combination much better than he would have enjoyed a silly young wife with more hair than wit who was wise only in the ways of the world. Penny must hate her telltale coloring, he thought as she hid her face behind her pages of notes. She would lose that touch of innocence soon, he knew, when she faced flattery and flirtation as a steady diet in London. Now, that idea did not please him, anyone else bringing an embarrassed flush to his Penny's cheeks. Or flirting with his wife. Lud, married a day, by law if not biblically, and he was jealous already. He swallowed a mouthful of coffee without thinking and burned his tongue.

Penny ignored his cry of pain, and his later attempts at polite conversation. Yes, the day was gloomy; no, she did not think she would be ready to set out before the end of the week.

He had left London, his appointments, his investments, his duties at Parliament, within a day of her father's visit to his town house. He could not see why she needed so much time.

"Yes, but you had no one but yourself to think of," she said, a world of meaning in her words.

"True, but you have servants to obey any orders you might give. You can have them pack up your clothes, or whatever it is you think you need, and ship them to London. That should not amount to much, since you can purchase everything else there new, your wardrobe, household items, even your grandfather's paints."

She blew out a breath of air. "That shows how much you know about artists. Grandpapa has his paints specially compounded for him by a chemist in York. He would never leave without them, or his brushes and canvases and props and costumes. Besides, you forget I am a banker's daughter. Why buy new when we already have what we need?"

Once again, what she did not say was evident in her voice, that West was a spendthrift wastrel just like his father, ready to toss his money around on foolish ventures.

"I stand corrected, but you will find that London fashions have changed."

"I am not speaking of gowns and slippers. I know my country-made gowns are not suitable for a viscount's wife."

"But they are lovely," he told her, trying to sweeten her mood. He might as well have poured more sugar in her tea.

"Aside from the monetary aspect, I do have a sentimental attachment to a few belongings of my mother's, a couple of books, some childhood treasures."

Which meant that, once again, West had trampled on her tender emotions. "Then of course you must take them. I will help you prepare for the move to London. It is the least I can do."

His offer of assistance surprised her. Her acceptance surprised him, until he realized she'd figured out a way to get rid of him, if not kill him outright.

Before he had eaten his fill of breakfast, West found himself out inspecting the Littleton traveling coach and her grandfather's cattle. The lumbering old coach was nearly as ancient as the driver, but both looked sturdy and reliable. Jem Coachman also looked after the horses, the pony cart, a gig, and Penny's mare. His nephew, Harry, was groom, stableboy, and sometime footman. They might be adequate to convey Mr. Littleton and his niece to Bath once a year, but they were not up to the task of moving the entire household to London.

So West rode to all three nearby villages in the pouring rain. Little Falls did not boast a coaching inn—it barely boasted a church and a general store—so he had to ride farther to find enough carriages and wagons and horses for hire, along with drivers, grooms, outriders, and guards. The additional conveyances were for the servants, the luggage, and the kitchen supplies Cook demanded be transported.

Only she knew exactly how Mr. Littleton liked his eggs, Mrs. Bigglesworth declared, so she was going along. Besides, her sister lived in London, and so it would be like a holiday for the cook. Since Westmoreland House in Town had no resident chef, West was happy to agree. Mrs. Bigglesworth did not trust West to have the proper pots and pans, so she was taking everything.

When he returned, Penny informed him that her grandfather did not trust him to have an adequate wine cellar, so another well-sprung coach was needed to carry Littleton's best bottles. West rode back to Upper Falls, again in the pouring rain.

Penny next assigned him the job of sending messengers ahead to reserve rooms at decent inns along the way south. Separate rooms, she insisted, not trusting him, either.

"You might have mentioned that before I rode out the first time," he said, donning his damp greatcoat once more. "Or the second time. I'll have to ride back to the inn where your father stayed to consult the innkeeper about the best accommodations, and to hire someone knowledgeable about the roads." Her own footmen were too busy to go, she told him, and too seldom out of Little Falls to select routes and rooms for overnight.

In the late afternoon, when he had changed into dry clothes, West considered his equerry duties ended. Littleton's brandies had not been packed in straw yet, so he thought he'd sit by the fire with a glass or two, warming his toes.

Penny thought otherwise.

"You did offer to help, didn't you? The sooner we get packed, the sooner we can leave."

So she had him boxing up the *few* cherished belongings she could not part with, the *couple* of books Grandpapa liked her to read to him, *some* things it would be wasteful to leave behind. Hah! She might as well have put the whole house on a barge and towed it to London!

They started in the library. Most of the Littleton servants, West learned, were too old for the backbreaking work of crating up her grandfather's favorites. She swore she was not going to bring every single book, although it felt like it to West, after an hour of climbing up and down the ladder, filling boxes. He kept reminding her that although his collection was small, London was full of booksellers and lending libraries.

"Of course it is, and I am quite looking forward to establishing an account or a subscription at each of them. I already have an extensive list of the books I wish to purchase, after I see your library, of course. But I do like to have my favorites with me, too."

He looked over at the section of novels whose shelves were nearly bare by now. "I thought you were bringing the ones your grandfather particularly enjoyed."

She waved her hand, the one not holding her endless lists. "But these are my old friends."

She had a lot of old friends. She pointed; he packed.

After an all-too-brief rest for tea, they moved to the attics, room after connected room that traversed the entire upper story of the house. The ceilings were low, the windows few, the air stale, and the dust thick. Boxes lay atop trunks; sacks sat on sofas; paper-wrapped parcels hung from the rafters. Penny had to inspect it all.

Her mother's collection of porcelains and her monogrammed linens and china had to be taken to London, of course. They were part of Penny's heritage, the same as West's entailed heirlooms, so he could not argue. Some had been handed down from her mother's mother, or her mother. He could not expect her simply to leave them here, could he?

"I am not certain we'll find room for everything in London. And the monograms are wrong, naturally."

"Then we can take them to Westfield in the country. Surely there are attics and cupboards there."

What, carry them again? The silver tea set alone weighed a ton, and would take up half a carriage. So would her mother's harp that Penny did not play, but intended to have lessons on in Town. Or should she try her great-aunt's spinet?

"I have a pianoforte. It is out of tune, but I can have a man in as soon as we return," he offered, in vain.

She decided to take both instruments. They were not much more difficult to wrestle through the mounds of boxes and down the stairs than the five trunks of fabrics.

"I purchased the dress lengths in London, and some more in Bath, or whenever there is a fair in the neighborhood. And my stepmother sends me a few every year for my birthday and Christmas, but I do not need many clothes for the country."

No one needed that many gowns, not even the queen. West simply grunted as he hefted another trunk to his shoulder.

"You see?" she asked when he went past her. "I can have these made up in the latest styles, by the most fashionable modistes, without wasting all of the funds Father allotted for my trousseau. Just think of the money you can spend on your horses. You should be pleased you have such a thrifty wife."

He would be if he did not keep bumping his head on the low rafters. He'd be pleased if he did not see stars for the rest of his life.

Penny even had to take—and he had to carry down—a beloved wooden dollhouse from her childhood. Her father's new stepdaughters had been hellions who would have wrecked the miniature architectural marvel if it were left in the nursery at her father's house. The tiny furnishings would have been splinters in a day. Instead they were packed in yet another crate.

"I suppose that was uncharitable of me," she mused, checking the dollhouse off her list. "But the little girls got my father and my London home. The dollhouse was something of my own I could claim."

Now his head ached from the attic and his heart ached for the girl she had been, waiting for the rescue that never came. "Well, you could not have taken any of this following the drum."

"No, but I might have moved it to Westfield, or Westmoreland House."

"Then my little brother would have destroyed it."

Life would have been far different for both of them if they had wed eight years ago, and they both knew it. They might have had a little girl or two to play in the dollhouse.

West carried it down the stairs as quickly as he could.

When he returned, Penny was in another area of the vast attic, locating the furnishings rescued from her stepmother's redecorating efforts. Selected by her own mother as a bride, they had to come with them, too, all the elegant chairs and carved end tables, mirrors and rugs. Penny seemed to consider each piece essential, as if his own house were a tent in the wilderness. Well, it might have been, West conceded. Most of the public rooms were stripped of furniture, and what remained was under Holland covers in who knew what condition. If Penny would rather be surrounded by familiar pieces instead of the new fashion for Chinese lacquerware, he would not complain. Until he bumped his head again. And again.

Next she pointed toward an entire room filled with Littleton's valuable early paintings, the masterpieces Littleton had promised to Penny before losing his eyesight. They could not be left behind, nor be handled roughly by draymen when they arrived. Oh no, West had to carry them down himself, in their heavy frames.

As he trudged up and down the narrow attic stairs, he passed servants who were too busy or too clumsy for his wife's precious horde. They got to carry sheets, by Jupiter! Clean sheets, at that.

West was filthy, covered in dust and cobwebs that were stuck to his face and neck and clothing by perspiration.

Lady Westfield, the dainty darling, was covered in a shapeless apron that stayed spotless, while she sat with her lists atop a trunk, one he'd moved three times. She was humming; he was panting, every muscle protesting. And he'd thought he kept fit, sparring, fencing, riding. Hah!

"Oh, and when you are done here," his bride cheerfully chirped, "you can help Marcel box up Grandpapa's paints and canvases. He won't let any of the servants handle them, but you are family now."

He was family, oh joy. He felt more like a coal heaver than any kissing cousin.

She let him stop hauling near dinnertime. Most likely she did not want to starve the beast of burden, he decided. Then she added, "I told Cook to serve it later, to suit your usual Town hours. And so that we could get more done in daylight."

He was too tired to be hungry, and too dirty to think of food. He needed a bath first—if Her Highness could spare a servant to carry cans of water for him—and a second shave of the day, to be ready for the night. He planned to claim a reward for his hard work; lud knew he deserved it. He'd been Penny's serf all day. He fully intended to be her seducer after dinner—a smooth-shaven one.

His bath arrived mercifully quickly, and he soaked away both dirt and sore muscles. West found it so relaxing, in fact, that he thought he'd just lie down for a few minutes to dry off, before dressing. He lay on his back, a smile on his face, thinking of the night ahead. He still had that bottle of champagne, and still had not had a wedding night. Now he had a grateful bride. Surely the gods were smiling, too.

Chapter Eleven

Miss S. dutifully wed the man her parents chose. She dutifully bore him three children. Then she dutifully died, so her husband could marry a woman who did not bore him.

—By Arrangement, *a chronicle of arranged marriages, by G. E. Felber*

The gods were not smiling. They were laughing out loud. A maid woke West up at dawn, bringing fresh hot water. She fled, screaming, spilling the water. Thinking he'd be blamed for the puddle, George the pug tried to burrow under the covers, at the same time West grabbed for them to hide his nakedness. A growling, grumbling tug-of-war ensued, all of which brought Marcel, West's robe, and Penny from across the hall, but not in that order, unfortunately.

When West came down to breakfast, Penny was still blushing. She stammered out that Marcel had gone to help the viscount dress before dinner last evening and found him too deeply asleep to awaken.

"Too bad it wasn't you. You could have tried to revive me with the kiss of life, like you'd do for George."

Now she sputtered: "M-Marcel swore he covered

you, but you must have thrown the blanket off." The problem was not what Marcel did when he went into the viscount's room, but what he said when he came out. Monsieur would miss dinner, he announced, but, la, what Madame was missing! What a magnificent body, what luck that my lord had finally come up to scratch, and what an imbecile my lady was.

Worse than advice from the flamboyant Frenchman was the urge to go look for herself, with West so sound asleep. Penny could check if he was warm enough. Or if he snored. She could bring a plate of food, in case he woke up in the night. She could bring George. Whom was she lying to? She could finally see what a naked man looked like.

She resisted the temptation, more for fear of being caught than respect for West's modesty. He obviously had none, and he was her husband, after all. Gracious, though, he'd think she was ready to join him if she was in his bedchamber, staring like a child at a pastry shop. Buns, biscuits, and baguettes, oh my.

She had not gone peeking, but she had stayed awake all night wondering. No innocent maiden would have such questions in her mind. Every married matron would have the answers. Penny was neither. Caught betwixt and between, she was confused about her own desires, duties, and debts of honor. So she had made more lists, through a very long night.

The glimpse she'd had this morning did nothing except confirm Marcel's opinion: Westfield was perfect; Penny was a perfect ninny. But, she told herself, handsome is as handsome does, as her mother used to say. Unfortunately, her husband was looking incredibly handsome this morning after his good night's rest. He was dressed for riding, with fawn-colored breeches that hugged his thighs, a bottle green coat, and high-top boots. And he was eating enough breakfast for three men, having missed dinner. He was a real man, as Marcel might have said, but in French, with innuendo. Penny nibbled on a slice of toast with jam.

When West's appetite was partly satisfied, he smiled and asked, "What Herculean tasks do you have for me today, my dear? As you see, I am ready to ride to the ends of the earth for you, lift the moon, or fetch a star."

"Nothing so demanding as that, I am afraid. In fact, I shan't need you at all." In actuality, she would be better off without his disturbing company.

That was what he was afraid of. "Nevertheless, I am at your service."

"I am merely going to drive the pony cart to deliver baskets around the neighborhood, foodstuffs Cook deems too perishable to transport to London, other things too good to throw out when there are those in need. I make these rounds often, alone. There is no need for you to come along."

West could not like the idea of his wife, no matter what strength in her right arm or that she was no dewy young girl, traipsing around the countryside by herself. She was dressed in a shapeless brown wool gown whose only virtue could be that it was serviceable and warm, not the least fashionable or revealing, but there were always highwaymen, beggars, returned renegade soldiers, who would not care if she sparred with Gentleman Jackson himself or wore flour sacks.

"In Little Falls?" she asked with a laugh. "They could not find their way here, and they would have poor pickings if they did. No, the most danger is if a rabbit runs in front of old Molly."

"Nevertheless, I shall accompany you," he said. He decided that Penny looked tired, as if she had not slept again. The new pages of lists in front of her confirmed his guess, as did the dark shadows under her blue eyes. She was still lovely, with those blond curls falling out of her neat bun to frame her face, but now she looked like a wounded angel. Once again he had let her down. He'd slept the night away thinking delicious, decadent thoughts, while she had been poring over her notes, thinking of her grandfather and her neighbors. Then he had awakened her early, wrestling a dog for a decent cover.

Lud, he had to stop making things more difficult for his wife if he had any hope of getting into her good graces, or getting into her bed. Dragging baskets to the poor was not his idea of a romantic interlude, but he was willing to try anything.

"It will be the perfect opportunity for us to become better acquainted," he told her before she could reject his offer. "And your neighbors will ask embarrassing questions otherwise. I would hate them all to think that I am lazing by the fireside, brandy in hand"—which sounded delightful to West, on this second gloomy day in a row—"rather than at my new wife's side, helping her do good deeds."

He was right. There would be curious stares and awkward conversations when yesterday's bride appeared by herself today. Penny reluctantly agreed to his company, then was glad she did when she saw how many hampers Cook had filled, how many bags and boxes she herself had decided to discard.

They took the filled pony cart to the orphanage, the poorhouse, and the vicarage, then came back and refilled it for deliveries to invalids and oldsters and indigent widows. They argued briefly over who should drive.

"I am the man."

"But I know Molly and the roads and where we are going."

Somehow being stronger, older, and supposedly wiser was not enough. Nor was membership in the Four Horse Club. "But I am the man," West repeated. If he gave up the reins now, he'd never regain the upper hand. "The gentleman always drives."

Penny scowled at him but took the other side of the driving bench. He pushed a basket out of the way, sat, and gathered the reins. Then he clucked at Molly.

Molly turned her head to look at him. He flicked the whip over her ear, said, "Walk on" in an authoritative voice, and jiggled the reins. Molly stayed glued to the stable yard.

"You need to kiss her."

First she wanted him to breathe into the dog's mouth. Now he should kiss her horse? Like hell he would. But the blasted mare would not move.

Penny reached over for the reins. "You can drive home. Molly is always in a hurry to get back to her oats." Then she made a kissing sound and the mare stepped out.

West balanced a bundle on his lap and waited for Penny to overturn the loaded cart. She did not, of course, and they reached their first destination without incident. Without speaking, either. West's only consolation was that he did not know any of the field workers or sheepherders they passed. He'd wager none of them let their wives drive the family wagon.

After a few stops, West decided that Penny was trying to kill him a different way from landing them in a ditch or destroying his dignity. Yesterday it was hard work; today it was with arrows to the heart. Every sad farewell, every hug good-bye from this old crone, that little moppet at the orphanage, was another shaft of pain. Everyone knew her; everyone was going to miss her. Worse, she was going to miss them.

When they left the orphanage, Penny wiped a bit of moisture from her eyes before taking up the reins. The tears kept falling, though, as they watched the children wave. Good grief, West thought, she was crying. The intrepid Miss Goldwaite, who struck first and asked questions later, was weeping. He knew she was not crying to get sympathy, because she was trying her best to hide the sniffs and gulps. Nor did she look pretty, with her eyes turning red and her cheeks getting splotchy. That made it all worse. Proud Penny was crying because she could not help it, because she was miserable, because of him. He was plucking her away from the life she'd made, all her friends, the worthwhile and rewarding work she had found. The arrows hit their mark.

A single tear West might have managed; this flood unmanned him. "Pull over, dash it, and let me drive. I can throw kisses to your wretched horse."

"I am fine. I am simply tired, that is all."

"No one turns into a watering pot when they are weary. Now pull over."

She listened to him, mainly because she could not see through the tears, and because she could not reach her handkerchief. When Molly was at a standstill, he took the reins and handed over his own soft linen square.

He did not kiss Molly, but he reached for Penny's hand after she blew her nose. "My dear, I am so sorry."

She left her hand in his but sniffled and looked away, embarrassed that he was seeing her so foolish, so unrefined. Ladies never showed their emotions or made scenes. "For what? You did not do anything."

"But I am the one dragging you away. You would not have to endure these wrenching farewells otherwise."

"Heavens, you are taking the blame for that? I always knew it is a woman's duty to follow her husband. You are the man, remember?"

He felt like a maggot now. "That is the way of the world. I have lands to manage, a voice in the government. I cannot stay here, but we can come back to visit your friends. And all that trousseau money you are saving can go to your special causes. The children here are so much better off than the poor waifs in Town. You can help them, and the scores of people at Westfield who must be needing a caring mistress. You'll see. Your grandfather will be with us, so you do not have to fret over him. And you will like London, I know."

Her lower lip started to quiver; a new tear started to form.

"Do not cry, sweetings. Lord, do not cry." West was in a panic, ready to weep himself, or leave her and the horse right where they were.

"I am not crying."

"Of course not. You are simply tired, as you said."

She nodded and brushed at her cheeks while West looked on, feeling as helpless as a flea. Then she said, "I grew up in London and I was happy there, but now things will be different. I know no one; I will not know how to go on." West would leave her for his wanton widows.

It was London that was making her cry? Zeus, West realized, his strong-willed wife had butter for a backbone. She was not just sad to be leaving; she was afraid of what was ahead, of facing the *ton,* of playing the part of a peeress. He relaxed. He might not be able to handle a woman's tears, but he had guided plenty of raw army recruits through their first battles. "Of course it will be different. You are no girl having to follow every ridiculous rule; now you can make your own. Remember, you will take precedence over nearly everyone. If the high sticklers do not like you, so what? I have never cared for any of those stiff-rumped, long-nosed crones anyway.

Besides, you said your friend Lady Bainbridge will help.
She can make introductions."

"What if she is too busy? She always has a young lady
under her wing. That's how she makes her living."

"We'll offer her more money." He paused for a minute. "It is your father's blunt, isn't it?"

That won him a tiny smile, so he rushed on: "And do
not forget the city has so much to offer, the theater, the
opera—you do like music, don't you? Of course you do,
you are going to take harp lessons."

"I prefer the theater."

"Good, so do I." And he hated the harp. "Remember
the museums, the lectures, the circus. And the stores. I
never heard of a female who did not like shopping."

She dabbed at her nose with his handkerchief. "I suppose I will enjoy some new gowns or a fancy bonnet."

West wracked his brain to think of something else
that might appeal. "You'll have my house to make over
as you see fit. You can even let Marcel help you, unless
you have other friends in London."

"I used to, but they are all married with children.
None of them are in Town."

"Well, you'll have your stepsisters."

She clutched the sodden handkerchief to her mouth
to stifle a gasp.

"Well, my brother, then. No, you wouldn't come to
Town at all if you knew him and his rackety friends.
You'll make new ones. You'll see. My friend Endicott's
wife runs a charity school for girls, and another friend's
wife holds a literary salon you would enjoy. You can
meet some of the authors whose books you have been
reading."

She tried to smile but failed, her blue eyes awash in
tears.

West could not help himself from reaching out and

pulling her closer to him, caressing her back, letting her weep on his shoulder. "You'll be happy, I promise. You will. I never meant to ruin your life, Penny, and I will spend forever trying to make it up to you. You will not have to worry about anything. You have a husband now."

She looked up at him. "That's what scares me the most."

So he kissed her. And Molly headed home.

Penny's grandfather retired right after dinner that evening, leaving them alone in the parlor. West offered his arm to Penny for a stroll on the terrace, where the clouds had finally blown away and the stars were out.

Neither spoke for a minute or two; then West put his arm around Penny, drawing her to his side. "So you do not take a chill," he said, liking how she fit so perfectly.

She liked it, too, by how she stayed close and put her arm around his waist.

He feathered kisses on the top of her head. "I do mean to make you happy, with all my heart."

She looked up, moonlight in her eyes. "I believe you mean that today."

"Not just today," he told her. "Marriage is forever." The words would have chilled West to the bone a week ago, but now they were warm on his tongue.

She shook her head. "You cannot promise what you do not have to give."

"I can try. That is all any of us can do."

Penny started crying again.

West stepped away from her so he could find his fresh handkerchief. "Good grief, what now?"

"You have been so kind, helping with the packing without complaining, playing with the children at the orphanage, charming all the poor widows and old men when we delivered packages. I saw you hand that crippled soldier a coin from your own pocket. And you have been patient and understanding."

"That is what you are crying about? I thought I was being a good husband. I am not proficient at it yet, of course."

She threw herself back into his arms and pounded on his chest, sobbing. "But I did not want to like you."

He held her hands before she could think of inflicting serious harm. "Ever?"

"Not yet."

"Ah." He kissed her lightly on the forehead and pushed her in the direction of the stairs. "Go to sleep, my dear. We will speak more tomorrow. You must be more tired than I thought if you cannot even carry your grudge."

Chapter Twelve

*To avoid marrying the woman his parents chose,
Lord F. tried to elope with the girl next door. The
ladder broke. So did his neck.*

—By Arrangement, *a chronicle of
arranged marriages, by G. E. Felber*

Yes, Penny was sad, and yes, she was tired. Mostly,
yes, she was a buffle-headed beanwit. She'd all but
told West that she liked him! She might as well have
handed him a lance, then stood before him without a
shield.

Penny knew she never had a fair chance to start with.
Viscount Westfield was a practiced charmer and she was
nothing but a bookish spinster. Still, she might have with-
stood compliments and kisses, no matter how gratifying,
no matter how glorious. Those were a rake's stock-in-
trade, after all, and she knew better than to trust them.
But kindness? She had no defense against that.

Very well, she told herself as she rebraided her hair
for bed, she liked him. She might as well accept the inevitable. He was her husband; a slight degree of affection was acceptable, especially since she knew him for
what he was. Now she had to draw the line at liking and

save what was left of her poor, bruised heart before he skewered it.

Unless, she thought, setting the brush aside and climbing into bed, West was being nice for his own scurvy, slimy motives. He wanted a woman and he wanted an heir. She was the only available woman—unless he went back to the inn in Upper Falls—and she was the only one who could give him a legitimate heir. Once he had his son, and his mistresses back in Town, he'd have no more use for her.

Fine, Penny told herself as she snuffed out her candle, the sooner he left, the better. She wanted children of her own and an independent life. So she would draw the line *there*. She would permit him to consummate the marriage, but she would not enjoy it. Passion was merely another practiced ploy of his, another chain binding her to a pipe dream. Pleasure would only raise her expectations, and they already had too far to fall.

So she fell asleep thinking about the fences she'd built around her feelings, the lines she had drawn. She dreamed, however, about the line of West's straight nose, the line of his well-muscled leg, the line of his lips as they touched her.

She liked him! West saluted his victory with a glass of brandy raised to the moon. Now he knew he had a chance of a comfortable marriage. This wedding business was more complicated than he'd imagined, not that he ever believed he could understand a woman, but he knew he had to try. He did not want to live with a rebellious, reluctant bride, or like a monk. He touched the garnet ring on his little finger, a gift from his mother. He wanted a better marriage than his parents had, too.

He liked his wife, especially now that he had seen her softer side, so winning her heart would be no hardship.

He had never considered a woman's affections to be more than a convenience at the beginning of an affair, a burden at the end. But a wife was different. Penny was different. He wanted to take her to London and show her the sights and show her off, instead of dragging her there. He wanted to make her happy, to atone for the past. Mostly he wanted her, now.

Lud, the few kisses he'd taken had been heaven, the way she responded, the little murmurs she made, how she pressed herself against him. Straitlaced Persephone Goldwaite had far more heat than she knew, waiting for him to fan the flames. Once he had her burning with desire, he hoped, the rest would follow.

He had a few more days to work his way further into her affections and into her bed. Tomorrow she was going to be busy with meetings of her charity boards and bankers, and the following night the Whitstanleys had asked them to dinner, to celebrate their marriage and bid Penny and Mr. Littleton farewell. After that, they could leave for London, husband and wife by decree, lovers by choice, he hoped, partners by the grace of God.

He raised his glass again before swallowing the last sip, and made a toast. "To a good marriage."

The moon winked back.

"Shall I accompany you, my dear?" he asked over breakfast the following morning. Penny was looking rested and confident again, far more tempting in a bright raspberry-colored gown than the raspberry jam on the table. She had her ubiquitous lists, but no frown, for once.

She even smiled. "What, come with me to the Ladies' Guild meeting? Now, wouldn't that cause a stir, like a new rooster in the chicken yard? No, my lord, you would only be a distraction from the business of the day."

"Laying eggs? I always thought a rooster was necessary for that."

For once she did not blush. Penny was proud that she was getting used to his teasing. "Our business is running the church bazaar. I need to hand over all my notes for the fair so someone else can run it next year. And I have been acting as secretary of the guild, keeping the lists for whose turn it is to arrange flowers, launder the altar cloth, that kind of thing. You would find it all boring."

Not if he could watch his wife.

"Besides, I doubt anyone would expect you to accompany me there, since gentlemen never do, so your absence will not stir up more gossip."

"What about after the meeting?" He hoped they had time for a picnic, a stroll, an afternoon cuddle, a kiss in the carriage, anything.

"After the meeting I have to deliver the vicar's sermon notes. The man would repeat himself forever, I swear, with no one to keep track of his lessons. And then I have instructions for Mr. Edmonds at the bank about transferring my funds. After luncheon I meet with the governing board of the orphanage. That should take the rest of the afternoon, because no one wants to accept the new responsibilities. We need another instructor, now that I am not here to help teach the girls needlework and such."

In other words, no cuddling, no kissing. West rode alongside the pony cart when she went to her first meeting, and made sure the ladies saw him hand her down, kiss her hand before leaving. The vicar saw him, too, and the banker. No one was going to think his Penny was alone, unprotected, uncherished.

After a brief stop for luncheon, Penny asked West to stay behind when she went to the orphanage.

"I have been neglecting Grandpapa these past days.

Would you stay and keep him company? He is used to having me read to him, or playing chess. I have to warn you, he remembers all the moves even if he cannot see all the pieces, so you cannot cheat. Not that you would, of course."

"But you tried?"

She laughed. "Once, just to see. And got my hand slapped."

He handed her into the pony cart, threw kisses to her and Molly, and watched them drive off before he returned to the house. He wondered how she would get on in London, when no woman of standing went anywhere unaccompanied by a footman and a maid, if not a gentleman escort.

Her grandfather thought she would do fine. "She ain't stupid, my girl. She won't do anything to embarrass you."

"I never thought she would. I was merely concerned for her own sake."

"And about time, too."

What, did he have to court the old man, too? West tried to return the book of Penny's poems, but Littleton said they'd be no good to him anymore, since he could not read them and would not share his granddaughter's private thoughts with Marcel or another servant. He asked West to read them aloud, one last time.

The meter was still as ragged, the images just as melodramatic.

Littleton wiped his eyes with the back of his sleeve. "She was all heart, my girl. I'd like to see that back, in the woman."

So would West.

He met her at the orphanage and stole her away for dinner. That is, he convinced her to let him drive, his hired horse tied behind the cart. Instead of going back to her grandfather's house, he drove to the Black Dog Inn in Upper Falls. He ordered a private parlor, a bottle of wine, and, once the meal was served, privacy. There were no lists, no relatives, nothing but newlyweds. They spoke of her errands and her grandfather, the plans he had for Westfield, the friends of his she would meet in London. He was diplomatic; she was demure. No one mentioned the marriage bed or the thirteen years, the pair of demons that shared the meal.

When they were finished, West almost suggested they spend the night in one of the rooms above, but her grandfather would worry, and she had none of the things a woman deemed essential, her nightgown, brush, fresh clothes for the morning. He could do without all of them, especially her clothes, but Penny was already outside, feeding a lump of sugar to Molly while he paid the bill.

Once home, he kissed her good night, fully intending that to be the first kiss of the evening, not the last. She returned his kiss, even weaving her fingers through his hair. She was not going to refuse him, not now.

West undressed, washed, and shaved again, counting how long he imagined it took for Penny to get ready for bed and dismiss her maid. Then he was on his way across the hall to her room, the same unopened bottle of champagne in his hand.

He was about to knock on the door with his free hand when the door opened. She stood there, her hair loose around her shoulders, outlined by the fire's glow in a sheer gown with nothing but ribbons for shoulder straps, like a present. And it was not even Christmas or his birthday.

"I . . . I came to wish you good night," West said when his tongue remembered its purpose. No matter that he'd said the same words not thirty minutes ago.

"I was coming to do the same."

She was? His heart rate, his hopes, and his manhood all rose. Before he could speak, Penny almost pulled him into her bedroom. His eyebrows rose, too.

She looked directly at him, her blue eyes like sapphires in the dimness. "I have decided that we know each other well enough."

"Well enough for . . . ?"

"Must I say it?" She twisted the end of one of the ribbons. "I . . . I thought that we should . . . you know . . . if you like."

He smiled, from the inside out. "Yes, my dear, I do know. There is nothing I would like better. You have made me a happy man."

"Well, this way I do not have to be anxious about it any longer, and we can be comfortable afterward."

He laughed. "You make it sound as if lovemaking is a onetime thing." He had set the bottle down and was touching her bare shoulder, the other hand combing through her hair, watching the play of colors as he lifted the curls. Then he lowered his lips to hers, while his hands pulled her closer, then stroked her back, and lower. "I do not think I will ever have enough of you."

She quickly stepped out of his arms, walking toward the bed.

"So eager, my dear?" he asked, still smiling. "Would you like a sip of champagne first?"

She blew out the candles. "There is no reason to delay."

With an invitation like that, the wine could wait. West couldn't. He did leave on his robe in an effort not to rush the joining altogether.

He followed her to the bed and climbed in next to her, under the covers. She was rigid, trembling, and he did not think it was from passion, not yet.

"Are you frightened, sweetings? There is no need to be."

"Of course not," she lied.

"Then you must be cold. Come, I will warm you." He folded her in his arms and kissed her, meanwhile letting his hand explore the peaks and valleys so thinly covered by her delicate nightgown. He caressed her neck, and then he kissed it, tiny feathery kisses that started at her ear and ended at her collarbone. Between kisses he murmured endearments and encouragement. "Have I told you how I love your hair, your eyes, your firm little chin, your firm . . . ?"

Somehow the ribbons on her gown were loosened and he was stroking her bare breast, his thumb gently rubbing across the nipple, making it harden. His mouth followed, with the same light kisses, until he took her into his mouth.

"What are you doing?" she asked, gasping.

"Making love to my wife, what else?" He paused. "You do know how this works, do you not?"

"I have read books. And the servants gossip. And of course I have seen the animals in the field."

He chose to ignore her inadequate education. "You'll see. This is a lot better than any book."

He went back to fondling and kissing and licking. "Your skin is so soft. And your breasts are so perfect, how they fit in my hand. And your narrow waist—"

His clever hands were there now, making her writhe. Penny thought it was almost like being tickled, only not, especially when he pushed her gown down and kissed her navel. This was definitely not like being tickled. "I think you should stop."

"Stop? I have hardly begun. Have I told you recently how I adore your hair?"

Good grief, his fingers were reaching for *that* hair!

"I would like to see it loose all the time, but I would never want another man to see it."

He returned for another searing kiss on her mouth, his tongue dancing with hers while the weight of his arousal moved along her body. She sighed.

"And now you are perfect, all warm and responsive."

Too warm, too responsive. Penny caught her breath and grasped the remains of her plan before she drowned. "Well, there is no reason for you to pour the butter boat over me. We are already married."

"That is all the more reason. It is part of lovemaking, you know. Loving everything, every inch. We never had a true courtship, so I am wooing your body now." His hands were reaching lower, pulling up the hem of her gown and stroking up her leg, her knee, her thigh.

"What are you doing?"

Was there a name for what he was doing? "Wooing."

She could barely keep herself from flying off the bed. Almost desperate, she said, "Well, I wish you would stop doing that and get on with it."

West rose up on his arms and looked down at her, wishing there were more light so he could see her face. "Get on with it?"

"Yes, you know, just do it. Then we can both go our own ways."

Now he sat up, leaving the covers behind. "You mean, like in some modern marriages?"

"Precisely."

"Over my dead body." He did not have to look down to know that his body was already dead, from the waist down, anyway. "No wife of mine will ever take lovers."

"You did."

"We were not wed yet. Or did you actually expect me to honor a promise I never made for thirteen years?"

Penny retied the ribbons at her shoulders. "I did."

"That is different and you know it. Besides, I told you that I never expected this marriage to occur."

"Well, it has, so go on."

"I cannot."

"Cannot ever?"

"Of course not, I hope. If there are any words guaranteed to destroy a mood, a man's arousal, yours have to be them. 'Just do it' are not what a man wants to hear, let me tell you."

"But I am willing."

"Yes, willing to be the virgin sacrifice, a martyr to the marriage bed." His voice was sharper than he'd intended. His disappointment was greater. "Great gods, woman, I do not want a partner performing her duty. I want one who enjoys sex as much as I do. I want a wife who will touch me, too."

Penny had been clenching her fists to keep from doing that. "Then you are not going to . . ."

"Ravish my reluctant bride?" He let the disgust sound in his voice, along with the dashed hopes. "I could not if I wanted to."

Now she did reach out, and kept reaching. "It's gone?"

He rolled off the bed, rather than face explaining that ignominy to his ignorant wife.

"I am sorry," she said in a barely audible voice, reminding him again how very inexperienced she was.

"No, this entire debacle was my fault. You are so mature and managing—in a good way, of course—that I keep forgetting what an innocent you are. I moved too fast and frightened you, which is inexcusable. I was the proverbial overeager bridegroom, and I apologize. You need more time, that is all. Tomorrow we can try again, moving far more slowly."

Penny thought she would surely die of slowness if tonight's speed almost did her in.

West was going on: "Books are not good tutors. And watching the ram tup his ewes is not a firm foundation for love. Tomorrow we will have a real courtship."

He kissed her gently, without the fervor. "Good night, my dear. Sleep well. Until tomorrow."

Sleep? He expected her to sleep? Just because the cad was no longer interested in his wife did not mean she was ready for bed. What good was having a rake for a husband? She fell asleep reciting the alphabet.

Arrogant, beastly, careless, despicable . . .

Chapter Thirteen

Squire W. and his wife were content with their arranged marriage. They had goose on Sunday, mutton on Monday and Thursday, beef on Wednesday and Saturday, sex on Friday.

—By Arrangement, *a chronicle of arranged marriages, by G. E. Felber*

. . . Useless, vile, wicked, expendable—Penny cheated on *x*; she told herself she deserved the leeway—and why the deuce was he not at the breakfast table for her to rail at? Maybe he'd taken his disappointment or disability or disinclination to Kitty in the next village. Maybe he'd gone back to London on his own. Maybe he'd fallen down the stairs and broken his fool neck.

Penny jumped up and ran around the house, out to the stable. His rented horse was gone; Jem Coachman knew not where.

Penny tried to hide her anxiety in finishing the packing. What if he did not return in time for the baron's party tonight? She could not face her neighbors. She could not face her mirror. How could he do this to her, again? And when was she going to learn not to trust the bounder? He was going to sweep in and out of her life whenever he chose, like a lazy housekeeper. She was dust to him, that was all.

Then Marcel walked by with his lordship's evening tailcoat, the one he had worn for their wedding. "Monsieur asked me to brush it before tonight. George *le chien* may have slept on it."

Now Penny could breathe again, and think about her own ensemble. He was coming back. She was his wife, and he had not forgotten that fact. She knew it was her job to make certain he never did. Tonight she wanted the baroness's guests to think she was worthy of a viscount, and she wanted the viscount to think she was worthy of his name *and* his notice.

She spent the afternoon trying on dresses, then pulling off the lace trim that kept her gowns modest, as befitted a woman on the shelf, no longer looking for a husband. Tonight she was going to make her own husband look at her. He said he liked her breasts. Very well, let him see them. If he'd said he liked syllabub, she would have it on the menu, wouldn't she? So she rejected the trims and the lace fichus and Kashmir shawls, no matter if the Whitstanleys were known to keep their rooms cool. No retiring pastel colors for her tonight, either. Penny chose a cherry silk she'd had made up for a Christmas assembly two years ago. She'd felt self-conscious, as if she were drawing unwarranted attention to herself, so she'd never worn it again. Tonight everyone would be looking at her anyway—those who could take their eyes off West—so she might as well dress the part. The evening already held the excitement, the expectancy, the tingle of Christmas. Too bad there was no mistletoe.

She tried new hairstyles next, practicing wrapping the pearls he had given her around the plaited curls atop her head, like a coronet. She decided to wear her mother's ruby and pearl earbobs, but no necklace to distract from the expanse of skin from her neck to the abbreviated bodice. White gloves completed the ensemble. She'd do. She changed back into her dun-colored round gown, to count the trunks again.

West was shopping. This time he rode farther afield, as far as Doncaster, for more selection. He returned by midafternoon on a disgruntled horse that was not used to having bags and boxes bouncing along its sides. West's arms were full when he reached the library, where Penny was making copies of her lists in case one was lost.

He put his packages down on her desk, and took another armful from a footman before dismissing the man and closing the door.

Penny eyed the mound of tissue-wrapped parcels, a hatbox, a large square covered in paper. "What have you done?"

"I have bought gifts for my bride, of course," he said as he helped himself to a glass of brandy.

"But you gave me the pearls. And I have everything I need."

"Of course you do, but everyone needs presents. Besides, the pearls were for the wedding. These are to show my delight in our marriage. I admit I might not have looked forward to it, but I do not want you to doubt that I am pleased. There are thirteen presents, one for each birthday of yours that I missed. When we reach London, I shall try to find thirteen more, for every Christmas, and another thirteen for the anniversaries we should have shared." He moved the packages around, in some order only he knew. "Perhaps not thirteen anniversaries, for no one intended us to wed when you were so young, but I shall think on that."

"Oh, West, the thought alone is enough."

He quickly reached for a small parcel. "Here, open this one first."

It was a lace handkerchief, with gold leaves embroidered on it. Penny used it to wipe her eyes.

Next he handed her a book of poems. "This Layton chap is all the crack in London. I did not see this volume on your shelves."

"It is on my list to buy. How did you know I like poetry?"

He would not peach on her grandfather. "A lucky guess, that's all."

To change the subject, he uncovered a sheaf of music, some for pianoforte and some for the harp. "For when you learn," he said.

A box of bonbons was next. "Not very original, I'm afraid, but I wanted to get you something sweet." He helped himself to one, and held another up to Penny's lips.

"I am overwhelmed," she said when she was finished.

"But we are not half done. Here, open the largest."

She unwrapped the square box to find a beautiful cherrywood travel desk, all inlaid with flowers and birds. The lid rose to hold pens and ink and paper and pencils. "So you can write your lists while we travel."

As beautiful as the desk was, Penny's eyes kept straying to a hatbox in the distinctive color of the most exclusive milliner in the county.

"Would you like to open that one?"

She held her hands out, instead of answering. Inside the box, in a nest of silver paper, was the most beautiful, frivolous bonnet Penny had ever seen. Of turquoise silk, it had tiny artificial pansies under the lace brim.

"I tried to match the color of your eyes, but could not find anything suitable."

"This is exquisite!"

He handed her a small velvet pouch.

"A lorgnette?" she asked when she opened the drawstrings.

"It is a quizzing glass, so you can look down on all the lesser beings. Ladies use them at the theater, too."

"I am overwhelmed." She was sitting in a sea of papers and wrappings.

"We are still not done."

He gave her a box that held a new fan. "So you can rap the knuckles of anyone who becomes too familiar."

It was beautiful, ruffled lace with purple irises painted on it, with ivory spokes and handle. Unfortunately it did not match her cherry gown.

The next package was a paisley shawl, in pinks and yellows that would make her look like a hot-air balloon in the red silk.

A paper cone contained a nosegay of flowers for her to carry tonight to the party, in a gold filigree holder. The flowers were all blue. "Now, those do match your eyes."

But not her gown. Penny tried to hide her dismay, saying, "Grandpapa will be thrilled. He loves all these bright colors."

"But you do not?"

She picked up the shawl and the fan and the flowers, thinking they were a garden by themselves, a field of vibrant color. "I adore them all, but I was going to wear cherry red tonight."

"Ah," he said, "then this will match." He took a jeweler's velvet box out of his pocket.

"You have been so extravagant," she protested, not taking the gift.

"Remember, I do not have to repay that loan from my father's debt. I am well-to-pass now." He'd pawned his watch, until he could send a bank draft back from London, but West saw no reason to tell Penny that. Just watching her pleasure in the presents was worth every farthing.

She finally opened the box, to find a thick gold chain, with a heart-shaped ruby pendant. "Oh, West, how did you know? This is perfect!" She jumped up, spilling the music and the book and the bonbons, but she did not care as she rushed into his arms. "This truly is Christmas." Then she stepped back, embarrassed. "But I have nothing for you. You should have told me."

"Well, the last gift is more for me, I have to admit. And let me tell you what courage it took for me to enter the shop."

He held up a negligee so sheer she could see him through it. Penny quickly glanced over to make sure the door was shut.

"They call the color maiden's blush, so I knew you had to have it," he said, enjoying the sudden pink in her cheeks. "Will you wear it tonight?"

"To the party?"

"Great gods, this is for me, no one else." Just the thought of anyone else ogling his wife made him say, "Must we go?"

"We have accepted, and we are the guests of honor."

He sighed.

She sighed.

"How long must we stay?"

"Not long, with the excuse of traveling tomorrow."

He smiled.

She smiled.

They did not stay late at the party. West took one look at Penny in her cherry gown, his ruby heart between magnificent creamy orbs, and almost refused to leave the house. She had a shawl around her shoulders, and he hated the thing for covering one inch of her glowing skin.

Then he wished she'd keep it on—or a horse blanket—so no one else could see her. The baroness had invited all the gentry for miles around to come meet a real London lord, so there were plenty of gentlemen to irritate West. Two baronets and a knight were in attendance, but he was the highest-ranking gentleman. From highest to lowest, every man there was drooling over his wife before dinner was served. West wanted to rage that she was not on the dinner menu. She was his.

Except she was hardly his tonight. They had to go into the dining room separately, after Penny was reminded that she led the way, as the highest-ranking female. They were seated at opposite ends of the long table, he next to his hostess, she next to the baron. Then the ladies withdrew and the gentlemen stayed behind, to West's aggravation. Even the dances were country-style, in rows or squares, with no waltzes where he could have held her. Besides, most of her dances were already spoken for by the time he escaped the clutches of a retired general ready to refight the latest battles. He hovered over her anyway, bringing punch, plying her fan lest she become overheated, glaring at her partners so they knew not to go beyond the line.

Suddenly Penny discovered herself the belle of the ball, popular for the first time in her life, with gentlemen tripping over one another for a chance to lead her onto the dance area, or out the open door. She was used to sitting out most dances, joining the matrons and the mothers of younger girls at the sidelines.

"It must be the title," she told West, after refusing yet another invitation to stroll through the secluded gardens.

He laughed. "My sweet innocent. Your title has nothing to do with it." He pulled her through the open doors himself, and into a dark corner of the terrace.

Who needed mistletoe?

After an interval sure to have tongues wagging, Penny tucked back a curl that had come loose from her intricate arrangement and said, "Grandpapa must be getting weary."

West straightened his neckcloth. "Of course. We must think of the gentleman." West had, which was why he'd hired another coach, so they could return separately.

"And we still have packing to do."

"Hmm." He was nuzzling her ear, dislodging another curl. "And I am tired of sharing your company."

Now he was kissing where the ruby pendant touched her skin.

Penny was suddenly out of breath.

"We are newly married," he added, licking at the crease in her décolletage. "No one expects us to stay."

"They'll all know." Maybe she did not need to breathe anymore.

"They already know. They're all jealous."

They left before the gathering had even more to gossip about.

The carriage ride was torment. With Penny in his lap, every bump in the road jogged West's desire. Unfortunately, he could not rip off her gown and make love in the coach. Not her first time, he told himself, not with the coachman apt to hear, not to face her grandfather at the door when they arrived home. Still, he could not keep his hands off her.

Penny had the same problem. The elaborate knot in his neckcloth was gone, and so were the top buttons of his shirt and waistcoat, landing on the floor of the carriage. Now Penny could put her hand against his warm flesh, the way he was heating hers.

That was not enough for either of them.

"What are you doing to me?" she asked, almost frantic with need.

"Making you want me. The way I want you."

"If I wanted you any more, you'd have to carry me into the house."

He did anyway. West carried her through the entrance, down the hall, up the stairs, and straight to her room. The groom who came for the horses turned his back; the footman at the front door faded into the paneling; her maid disappeared through the dressing room. West was out of breath, but not from the carrying.

He put her down and pointed to the blush-colored negligee on her bed. "Don't bother. I might rip it. With my teeth if I had to."

Penny was snatching the pearls from her disheveled hair, while he unfastened her gown and corset. Soon his clothes were on the floor. Her clothes were on the floor. West and Penny were almost on the floor.

"No, not here, my sweet." West lifted her again and carried her to the bed. "Should I douse the lights?"

"No, let me look at you."

He was splendid. And hers. She held her arms out. "Come, husband. We have waited long enough."

She was naked, panting, her lips swollen from kisses in the coach. More importantly, she wanted him, not a mere cursory bedding to seal the marriage bargain. He sat beside her on the bed and said, "Say it."

"Say what?"

"That you want me."

She smiled. "I have no way to say it. You have stolen my breath and my wits. If you do not come to me now, I shall perish."

"We cannot have that, by heaven." He did not rush, though. He caressed and stroked and suckled, until she was almost screaming with want, which meant he had to stop her with more kisses, lest her household hear. "Sh, sweetings. I need to know you are ready, so I do not hurt you."

She was hot and wet and taut as a bowstring. He played a concerto with his fingers and his tongue.

"Oh, oh, *oh,*" came the crescendo, then, "Oh, my. I never knew."

"Well, the maids in the upper floor know now, too," West said, but he was grinning with pride and power and her pleasure. "And that is only the start." He raised himself up, poised above her. He slowly started to enter— as slowly as he could go, considering he was about to burst into a thousand pieces. "Lud, I do not want to hurt you."

Penny did not think she could feel pain now, in the euphoric afterglow. She pulled him closer, her legs around him. He pressed deeper, his mouth on hers, as if to absorb the discomfort he feared causing. Then he pulled back, ready to thrust fully, ready to find his own release.

But there was a noise.

"What was that?" Penny asked, pulling back, pushing him away.

"Nothing. Just a sound."

"It was not nothing. I heard it."

"It was George," he said, trying to reposition himself.

"George is never in my room."

"Then it was me, by Jupiter," he cried in desperation.

"You did that, in my bed?"

"Lud, Penny, it was nothing. Making love is messy and noisy."

"It was me! Oh my heavens, I know it was!" She shoved him off her altogether and curled into a ball, her head burrowed under the pillow. In muffled moans she lamented what a failure she was, how no true lady made such noises, how she could not do this anymore.

"Not . . . ?" he asked in disbelief.

"I cannot. Go away. Oh, how can I ever look at you again?"

Easily. If she would take the pillow off her head, she would see he was as eager as ever. "Please, sweetings, do not fret about this. Truly. In another two minutes you would not have heard it. You would not have cared." He practically pleaded for those two minutes.

She shook her head, or the pillow. "No, it is too terrible."

Terrible? West thought it was glorious. "Come, now, you saw how beautiful lovemaking could be. Let me show you the rest." He touched her back—all he could reach of the knot she was curled into—but she pulled away, grabbing the bedcovers to pull over her. Next thing he knew, West was looking at a mound in the mattress, his manhood minified, his marriage a muck.

"Are you certain?"

"Yes," came a muffled reply. "I am sorry."

Not as sorry as West, he'd wager. Since he could not force himself upon her, his only option was to leave. So he gathered his clothes and what dignity a man had after such a fiasco, and trudged across the hall to his lonely room. And his roommate, George.

Penny uncurled herself, straightened the covers, and stretched luxuriously.

Revenge was sweet.

Chapter Fourteen

Lord and Lady P. made the best of their arranged
match, until Lady P. fell down the stairs, aided by
his right knee to her arse.

—By Arrangement, *a chronicle of*
arranged marriages, by G. E. Felber

The trouble with denying her husband his conjugal rights, Penny realized, was that she was denying herself the pleasure of her husband. Against all her plans for self-preservation, she had enjoyed his lovemaking far more than she'd supposed possible. Now she understood why no one spoke of carnal matters to young, unmarried females: They would be too eager for their own good. Penny certainly was.

Maybe, she worried, only the lower classes enjoyed sex. Surely no wellborn women could act with such abandon; if they did, they never giggled like the maids after the May Day fair, or glowed like the blacksmith's daughter after her wedding trip. Penny worried that she'd acted like a wanton last night, almost ripping West's clothes off in her haste. He already knew she was no lady, neither mild-mannered nor demure. Now he'd think her a trollop, besides a shrew.

If he did not think her a doxy, he'd consider her some priggish female with feelings too rarefied for the earthiness of sex. Her own thoughts were in chaos. She did not want to like her husband's attentions, but she liked his skin next to hers, the sweet words he whispered, how his hands made her feel cherished and more alive than she had ever felt before. Of course she had never done *that* before. She might never again, from the grim look on West's face in the morning before they left for London. She almost apologized, showing she was ready to try again, but he did not give her the chance.

West ate in a hurry, then busied himself with the carriages and carts, the loading of the luggage, the instructions to the drivers, the comfortable arrangement of the passengers. He chose to ride alongside at first, making sure they stayed together, that the drivers and postilions were competent and careful. Then he rode ahead to check on the roads and the accommodations.

As soon as he was out of sight of the cavalcade, he set his horse to a fast and furious pace. He'd never do anything to hurt a horse, but he was not so sure about his wife if he had to share a carriage with her or watch her staring wistfully out the window.

Now he knew why married men still took mistresses.

Now he knew why they took to wife those doll-like debutantes that mothers were always foisting off on unsuspecting bachelors. The sweet little innocents had no opinions of their own, no will, no spirit. They were used to obeying orders, good soldiers in the fight to win a better place in society, a bigger fortune, a higher title. They were taught from birth that whatever a husband did was right. Their mothers told them to think of England in the marriage bed and endure, without complaint.

Penny a soldier? Hah! Half the time the female acted like a general at least, all confident and courageous—

and wrongheaded, besides having no idea what the ordinary infantryman wanted or needed. Other times she was like a raw recruit, not knowing how to march or whom to salute.

The problem was, if West had to have a wife, he wanted one with a mind of her own. He never enjoyed a clinging female who needed coddling and cajoling. He also wanted a passionate partner, not a biddable bride, in his bed. Penny could have been ideal, but, lud, for a mature, independent woman, she did have an odd kick to her gallop. Or two.

Now he knew why so many married men drank.

The trip took longer than anyone expected. Mr. Littleton got a cough; Penny got her courses; George the pug got carriage sick. West grew restless and took side trips to a horse fair and a breeder he'd heard of, making purchases to be sent on to Westfield. Penny grew resentful that he could meander around, while she was confined to the carriage. Once again he was ignoring her existence. Apologize for being finicky? Never. Invite him to share her bedroom? When hell froze over.

Whenever they stopped, they all had separate rooms, as Penny demanded and West approved, which made her madder still. Her maid slept in hers. George slept in his.

When they reached London, West rode ahead again, to warn his household. He'd sent messages to the Parkers, who acted as butler and housekeeper of the family pile, advising them he was bringing guests. The small staff should do what they could, he advised, before the party reached Town.

He pulled up at Westmoreland House on Prospect Street. At least he thought he was at Westmoreland House. He checked the familiar buildings on either side, to make sure. This was his house, all right, but now the windows sparkled, the brass rails gleamed, and the bricks were free of London's soot and grime. He handed his horse over to a groom who materialized out of nowhere—surely not out of West's payroll—and went inside. If Parker himself was not beside the door, West would have thought he had the wrong address indeed. The entry hall had been painted a sickly yellow color, but the parquet floors were freshly waxed, under a bright and brand-new Aubusson carpet that looked as if it cost more than his last racing curricle. A spindle-legged table he'd never seen held a huge naked statue of some gilded Greek goddess with an unlikely bouquet of silk flowers and stuffed birds in her hand. Over the statue hung several portraits, and heaven knew he'd never seen those people before, either. Even Parker, who had been with the family since before West was born, was a new man in powdered wig and spotless coat. Before West had set out north, the old butler's black coat was as faded gray as his hair.

Before West could ask questions about what other changes had been made, by what magic genie, the first of the baggage carriages from Yorkshire arrived. Bemused, West went back outside to hand Penny out of the coach.

"Why, your house is lovely," she said, surprised after hearing of its disrepair.

"It is, isn't it?" he replied, equally as surprised.

He led her up the stairs and then stopped. "Should I carry you across the threshold of your new residence?"

Penny recalled the last time he had carried her, in a fevered rush. Perhaps he'd keep going now, to the bedchambers, and they could start anew, in a new place. She could feel her cheeks grow warm at the very idea. Then she recalled that he might have spent his recent nights in the arms of some willing serving wench, for all she knew. "That will not be necessary."

West ignored the ice in her voice. "It is supposed to be good luck, I always heard." He turned and slid his hands beneath her knees and across her back. Penny shrieked and threw her arms around his neck for balance, and West laughed as they swept into the front hall.

When he set her down, the skirts of her green traveling costume were all twisted, her turquoise bonnet—the one West had given her—was hanging by its ribbons down her back, her hair was coming undone, and she was laughing, too. Here was her new life, willy-nilly, in a viscount's arms, and it felt good.

West thought he'd never seen a prettier sight, so he kissed her, right there in the doorway of his home. Their home. That sounded good, too.

"I say, bro," came a drawling voice from one side of the double stairs, "you might wait until you are upstairs, you know."

Penny looked up to see a tailor's dream making its way downstairs. A young gentleman of about twenty years was wearing wide yellow Cossack trousers, a spotted Belcher kerchief instead of a proper neckcloth, a waistcoat glittering with gold and silver stripes. He had West's dark coloring, but nowhere the breadth of shoulder or the finely chiseled cheekbones and jaw. He did have red shoes.

"Grandpapa is going to love him," Penny whispered in West's ear.

West gave a long-suffering sigh. "As you have probably guessed, my dear, this pink of the *ton* is my brother, the generally Honorable Nicholas Westmoreland. Nicky, come make your bows."

"I say, with pleasure." The Tulip pulled a quizzing glass on a ribbon from his pocket and held it up, inspecting Penny. "I knew you were too downy a bird to let Gold Pockets foist his old-maid daughter on you. But you've done even better, bringing home a bit of fluff that will be the envy of London. I don't suppose you'd put in a word with Lady Greenlea for me now that you've moved on, would you?" He swung the quizzing glass in the air in circles. "No, I could never afford a dasher like her. Which reminds me, bro, about my allowance—"

Penny had gone rigid again. West cleared his throat. "Nicky, may I present my bride, the former Miss Persephone Goldwaite."

Nicky dropped his quizzing glass, and his jaw. "Never say so! Why, you lucky dog." Then he bowed. "And my apologies, Miss—ah, Lady Westfield." He held out his hand, to take hers to kiss.

Penny could see a garnet ring like the one West wore. She kept her own hand by her side. "That is Lady Gold Pockets to you, sir."

West laughed. "I must warn you, Nicky, the lady does not forget an insult. And she has a punishing right, so mind your manners."

"No insult intended, to be sure."

Penny was not quite as sure. The fop appeared to be a typical London swell, to whom anyone without a title was a nobody.

West was going on: "Besides, if she does not hit you, I will. So go make yourself useful and help unload the coaches."

"What, when we have a score of footmen standing around for just that?"

"We had the Parkers' two nephews and a couple of day maids when I left."

Nicky shrugged. "These chaps just appeared, along with the painters and carpenters and cabinetmakers."

West could see the evidence of the workmen. "And you never asked what they were doing here?"

Nicky shrugged again. "I thought they had the wrong

address. I wasn't about to tell them, was I, and have them take everything back? Besides, you told Parker to get the old place ready for guests. I figured he knew what you were about."

West would look into that later. For now he had to play host. "Well, then help Parker show Penny's grandfather to his room. You did give Mr. Littleton the south suite, didn't you, Parker, the one with the sitting room overlooking the garden?" When the butler nodded, West told Penny, "There is plenty of light, and a bare floor no one needs to worry about staining."

His brother shook his head. "It ain't bare anymore. None of the rooms are."

"Well, no one will be painting today anyway." He turned to Penny. "I will show you around myself." Before he led her into the front parlor, he bent down and picked up George. "Here, Nicky, meet your new roommate. He snores and he swoons. But do not worry. All you have to do is breathe in his mouth to revive him."

Nicky started to argue.

"You mentioned your allowance?"

Nicky held his arms out. "Nice doggy."

West and Penny toured the house, forgetting their differences as they marveled at the new furniture that filled the rooms to overflowing, colors clashing, in higgledy-piggledy styles. "I never thought I would miss the faded old chairs. Even the dustcovers were better than some of this."

Parker announced a caller before they went to inspect the kitchens.

"No need to announce me. I'm family," Sir Gaspar said as he strolled into what used to be West's book room. "Nice, eh?"

"You did all this?" West waved his hand around, encompassing the statues, the chintz-covered chairs, the cabbage roses on the wallpaper, the animal heads mounted on the paneling.

"Me and Lady Goldwaite, of course. Constance does love to decorate. I said I would freshen up the place, didn't I?"

"No, Father," Penny said, "you offered to pay for it."

Sir Gaspar pulled out his pocket watch to check the time. "Same thing. Didn't want you coming home to such a shabby place. Besides, the sooner this house is ready, the sooner you can start entertaining. The Season's started and the gals have hardly been seen by any of the right people."

Penny's head was spinning. "I cannot think about Lady Goldwaite's daughters now."

Her father frowned. "They are your stepsisters."

"Yes, but we have just arrived."

"Of course you have. I got the message, didn't I? That's why I am here instead of at the bank. You are expected for dinner tonight. We figured that the cook you brought with you won't have time to make up a meal. The gals want to see you again." He eyed her rumpled traveling gown with disdain. "They have all the latest fashion journals. And Constance is anxious to discuss plans. Lady Spincroft's ball is next week. And you'll want to seek vouchers for Almack's before too much time is past. You'll need to pick a date for your own first ball before the social calendar is full, to let the gals make their bows here."

"But we are not even unpacked," she insisted.

"You have servants for that, my girl. You are a lady."

Penny started to tap her foot, but West accepted the dinner invitation, for the following day.

Sir Gaspar had to be content with that. Then he had to leave, to inform his own household. Before he left,

West had a few questions about the new staff. "Would you mind waiting a moment, sir?"

West told Parker to gather all the servants, all the new ones. He told Penny she should go rest, or unpack, but she stayed, her lips pursed and her brows knotted.

When the servants were lined up, three-deep, in the hall, West asked who paid their salaries.

Sir Gaspar grinned. "I do, of course." The men in their immaculate livery all nodded.

"And which one of you sent Sir Gaspar the message that we had arrived?"

"That would be Freese," one of the older men answered, and a fit-looking footman stepped forward, smiling, envisioning a handsome reward.

"Then you are the first to leave, Freese. You see, this is my house, not Sir Gaspar's. I will not employ anyone who is not loyal to me alone, putting my and my lady's comfort and welfare ahead of anyone else's. I am afraid I cannot afford so many in staff, either, nor pay as much as Sir Gaspar obviously has. I suggest you all seek employment with him, since he hired you." He spoke to Sir Gaspar: "You may use the carriages and wagons outside, sir, to carry your new servants."

Sir Gaspar looked to Penny. "Come, now, my girl, tell your husband you need these fellows to add to your consequence. Can't let a man's foolish pride keep you from your rightful due."

"No, Father, I will tell Lord Westfield no such thing. You have meddled for the last time."

The servants shuffled their feet, waiting to see whether they would stay or go.

"I only meant well, poppet."

"No, you mean to continue to manage my life and Lord Westfield's. We will not tolerate it. Not to decorate our home or put spies in our midst or organize our social calendars or criticize our wardrobes. Is that plain?"

West clapped, which drew Penny's attention to him. He stepped back a pace when he saw that her fists were clenched.

"And as for you, my lord, you are almost as bad."

If the fists and the frown didn't give him pause, the use of his title made Penny's displeasure obvious. West said he was sorry. "But I simply do not have the kind of money your father does to keep an army on my payroll."

"Money has nothing to do with this, nor the number of servants. No, you said I was to have the running of our household. We have not been here an hour and you are riding roughshod over my wishes, accepting dinner engagements without consulting me, dismissing servants without asking if I require them."

"I honestly thought you would have the refurbishing of Westmoreland House, and you cannot blame me if someone else did the work. I suppose I should have asked before accepting your father's invitation, but he is your father. I thought you would be pleased. As for the servants, do you truly wish to keep on retainers with divided loyalties?"

Penny raised her chin. "No, but I wished to be the one to dismiss them."

Sir Gaspar slapped his thigh. "Damn if you ain't acting the lady already. I knew you'd make a proper viscountess."

They both glared at him.

The footmen left.

Chapter Fifteen

Miss T.'s parents wed her to a drunk. He stayed drunk and they stayed married until she found something else for him to swallow. That is why they call arsenic the widow maker.

—By Arrangement, *a chronicle of arranged marriages, by G. E. Felber*

Nicky was upset to be carrying luggage after all, alongside the Parker nephews and his brother. His puce coat was becoming wrinkled. "I do not see why we cannot keep on some of the new servants. Certes, it was a nicer style of life for the last few days. And what is the point of wedding an heiress if you cannot enjoy the benefits?"

West was not seeing much benefit right now, nor much enjoyment. He simply grunted under his end of a large trunk.

"I don't think your wife likes me."

West didn't think she liked either of them, which was nothing he was willing to discuss with his little brother. "She is just sensitive about being wed to a rake for her father's money. And for not being a member of the *ton*." And for being neglected all those years, while he enjoyed other women, he thought, but did not say aloud. "You must give her time," which was something else he'd been saying to himself for a sennight now.

"I do not mind giving her time, but sweat?" Nicky set his end of the trunk down, then dabbed at his face with a lace-edged handkerchief. "At least her relations like me. Mr. Littleton has offered to paint my portrait."

"Have you seen his recent work?" That was what the trunk contained, too valuable, Penny said, to be entrusted to mere servants.

"No, but he is famous, ain't he? And Marcel promises to invent a neckcloth just for me."

Anything would be better than the spotted rag Nicky now wore.

"Marcel is going to call it the Westmoreland Fall. I prefer the Nicholas Knot, don't you know. But capital fellow, Marcel. Knows everything there is to know about bootblacking. And Mrs. Bigglesworth patted my cheek, just like an old auntie."

"Mrs. Bigglesworth, the cook?"

"That's right. She promised to make me raspberry tarts. What a treasure, and she is already thick as thieves with Mrs. Parker, who is thrilled to be getting out of the kitchens, what little time she spent there. I am looking forward to a decent meal at home, let me tell you, after sharing the tray Mrs. B. sent up for Mr. Littleton."

West hadn't received any food at all. That must be why, he realized, his temper was so foul.

He also realized that Nicky would rather talk than carry, so he pointed him to his end of the trunk.

His brother was not finished. "When a chap dines in company, he is expected to pay, you know, either with coin or reciprocal invitations or with doing the pretty for the host's ugly daughters. Now that we are above hatches, we will be able to hold dinner parties for our chums. So this marriage thing is going to work out fine. I had my doubts at first, but now I see the advantages. You did well, bro."

West thought so, too, except for the spying servants, the three wagons still to be unloaded, his interfering father-in-law, and the fact that his wife was as prickly as a hedgehog.

Some backbreaking hours later, West passed his bride in the hall. She was as disheveled as he was, still in her creased green traveling gown, her hair fallen entirely out of its knot. She looked as irritated as he felt, but he doubted her pique was from too much physical labor without enough physical loving. Most likely he'd done something else to rile her. Heaven knew it did not take much.

Before she could rail at him, West said, "I hired back two of the menservants after they swore allegiance to me. They are willing to work for a fair wage rather than have no position at all, because your father had no use for so many footmen. I did not have time to consult you."

Penny was mortified at her father's actions and she'd spent hours trying to right his meddling. After the long journey all she wanted to do was settle into her new surroundings at leisure, and she thought West must feel the same, but neither had a moment's rest, thanks to Sir Gaspar's grandiose schemes. Now her husband was rubbing at the sore spot, reminding her that her father was manipulative and managing. He was still her father.

She stood toe-to-toe with West, ready to do battle. "I know. I sent one of them to Lady Bainbridge with a note. And I told Mrs. Parker to hire whatever maids she thought we required." She added, in curt tones, "I did not have time to consult you, either."

West heard no thank-you for trying to lighten the

work for all of them, no joint discussion of household expenses. He supposed she must feel entitled to spend whatever of his money she could. Like her sire, she obviously thought money gave her the power to act with impunity. Well, he still had some authority in his own home.

"I instructed the men to remove the dead animals from my book room."

She countered with, "I told Mr. Parker to dispose of that naked statue in the hall."

"I ordered the maroon velvet bed hangings removed from my room."

"I had the rickety escritoire taken away from mine."

"That was my mother's writing desk."

Penny was mortified all over again, but she could not back down. If she let this man call the tunes, she would be dancing to his music for the rest of her life. She was done letting any man dictate to her, not her father, not her husband. "Very well, I will tell the Parker boys to put it in your room."

A dainty lady's desk, with its matching small-scale chair? He'd rather have the maroon draperies around his bed. West took a deep breath, trying to control his temper. "I told Parker we would dine out."

"I told Mrs. Parker that we would take potluck here. Cook and she are already bosom bows, so they will manage." She raised her chin. "And I invited Lady Bainbridge to share our meal."

"Without asking me?"

"You accepted my father's invitation, without asking me."

"What happened to a man's home being his castle?"

"What happened to friends, partners, companions? It seems to me your promises are as poor as your memory."

He frowned. She frowned right back.

West knew he was being childish, but, hell, it was his house. If he did not stand tall now, he'd be stepped on, a laughingstock among the other henpecked husbands. "I shall take supper at my club. I have a great deal to catch up on with business associates and political allies."

"Good. Lady Bainbridge and I have a great deal to discuss also."

"Good." He started to leave, then said, "I'll take Nicky. He does not feel welcome."

"Your brother is a fool."

Now, there was something West and Penny could agree on, if he was in the mood to be agreeable. He was not, being forced out of his house on his first night home, after laboring like a coal hauler half the day. "Nicky might have more hair than wit, but he is still my brother. I will thank you to treat him accordingly. I tolerate Mr. Littleton and Marcel for your sake."

She tilted her head and narrowed her eyes. "What is wrong with them?"

"Ah, nothing, nothing at all. But nothing is wrong with Nicky, either, or nothing a few more years won't cure. He has been coddled his whole life, being so young and coming so late in my parents' marriage."

"He dresses like a clown."

"Yes, but that is better than when he wanted to file his teeth down to look like a coachman, or when he decided to be a tragic poet, and dressed in black from head to toe, spouting lamentations."

"You put up with that?"

"I am not Nicky's keeper, only his brother. I do not rule his life."

No, he ruled only Penny's. She left to cancel the lovely dinner she, the cook, and the housekeeper had planned with what supplies were on hand.

West took Nicky to his club. Grandpapa took a tray in his room. Penny and Lady Bainbridge dined in Penny's sitting room, which was comfortable, if one liked pink, fluffy furnishings. They would be gone before the end of the week ... into West's sitting room if Penny had her way. The dastard had left her alone on her very first night in a new house, not even staying to meet the only friend she had in London.

Penny apologized for her husband's absence, but Lady Bainbridge brushed that away. Now they could have a more comfortable coze and catch up on the past eight years, the way letters never could. Mostly the older woman wanted to hear about Penny's marriage.

Penny wished to discuss marriage in general, not hers in particular. She waited until Matthew Parker—or was that Michael?—finished serving Cook's excellent meat pie, along with crusty rolls and claret. When he left, Penny blurted out, "Do ladies usually enjoy their husband's attentions?"

"Of course. What woman would not want to be complimented and cosseted?"

Penny shredded her roll. "I do not mean those kinds of attentions. I mean in the bedroom. Do ladies like it?"

Lady Bainbridge almost choked on a sip of wine. "Heavens, child, what a question. Don't you?" She held up a hand. "No, do not tell me. I can see from your blushes that you do."

"But real ladies?"

Lady Bainbridge clucked her tongue. "You are a real lady, my dear, and a woman is a woman, no matter her social standing. Oh, I know some ladies protest that their husbands' appetites are burdensome." She held up a forkful of meat pie. "I do not mean for food, of course. But I think most women enjoy the intimacy of the bedroom.

It is one of the joys of marriage, part of the cement that holds a couple together." She took another sip of wine, as if needing it before continuing. "And I do believe that if a lady does not find pleasure with her husband, then he is no true gentleman. I cannot believe your viscount would fail in that regard, not with his reputation."

Penny did not want to hear about West's renown as a lover. His past was already as constant as a bad toothache. "So passion is not reserved for fast women?"

"Foolish girl, you still blush as easily as when you were eighteen. No, nothing is wrong with enjoying your spouse's ardor. In fact, it is a consummation to be devoutly desired."

It was by Penny, despite her own wishes. Having once tasted West's lovemaking, she wanted another serving, the full meal this time.

Lady Bainbridge was not finished. "And an eager husband is far preferable to a disinterested one who saves his best efforts for his mistress."

Could West be visiting a mistress, even tonight? He had been without a woman since their wedding, for all practical purposes. Who knew how strong a gentleman's appetites were? Penny lost hers altogether.

After discussing such personal matters, Penny felt she could ask her friend and mentor, "But what of you? If you found wedded life so enjoyable, why have you never remarried?"

"Oh, I was never interested in finding another husband. There could never be a man as fine as my Julius."

"Then you could take a lover, if intimacy is such a pleasure."

Lady Bainbridge fanned herself with her napkin. "Goodness, Penny, I hope you do not mean to ask such things in public or we will never get you accepted into the beau monde. I know other widows have their discreet liaisons. Some even have protectors to support them. But I do have my principles, you know. Not every woman can be comfortable with an affair. And lovemaking without love is not half as rewarding."

Penny paused to think about that, and Lady Greenlea.

"I did think of remarrying for financial reasons," Lady Bainbridge confessed. "Julius did not leave me well-off, as you know, and the cousin who inherited his estate has seven children of his own to support."

"Which was a blessing for me, that my father could hire you to assist me at my presentation. And now I can have you to help again, thank goodness."

The older woman smiled. "Well, I did not have much choice but to seek employment, especially since I chose to preserve my scruples and my self-respect. Few enough gentlemen wish to wed a widow of little fortune, even if I were willing. My Julius and I were not blessed with children, either, so a gentleman in need of an heir would not glance my way. Now it is too late, of course, considering my age. Gentlemen want younger wives, to warm their beds and look pretty on their arms."

"Why, you are not that old. You are barely forty, I'd wager, and a handsome woman. You are elegant and intelligent, and know how to go on."

"Thank you, my dear. Who knows? Perhaps this Season, helping you, I shall find a man as good as my husband was." Lady Bainbridge laughed. "One who still has all his teeth, and still knows how to sport between the sheets."

Nicky had wandered off to watch a game of hazard, but West stayed behind in the dining room of his club, sharing a bottle of port with his friend Michael Cottsworth. Some ten years older, Mr. Cottsworth had been

West's commanding officer in the cavalry on the Peninsula before being invalided home. When West came into his title, sold his commission, and decided to try breeding and training horses, Cottsworth had been a big help in getting contracts with the army. He also helped West find his feet in London's social quicksand, where a green lad could sink without a guide. The two were good friends now, good enough that West could discuss his marriage. After all, Cottsworth was a widower. He ought to understand.

West studied his glass of port, then said, "Damn, this business is more complicated than I thought."

"Your stud farm? I thought you were making a tidy profit now."

"Not the horses. Being a husband."

Cottsworth smiled and raised his own glass. "It's the best thing that can happen to a man. Simply begin as you mean to go on."

"That's right, take the reins, just like breaking in a new horse. I intend to do that very thing. Tomorrow."

The former officer laughed. "No, you'll get thrown for certain that way. I meant surrender now. Concede. Admit defeat and stop fighting the inevitable, for you can never understand a woman, so you can never win whatever war you think you are fighting. Hell, half the time you won't even know where the battle lines are. It is far easier to make peace in the beginning. You'll see how much more rich your life can be with a contented wife." He extolled the married state, the comfort, the joys, the sharing and caring and warmth. And the sex.

West could imagine Penny sighing with pleasure, but he could not imagine it happening any time soon. As for the rest? Pigs would fly first. He poured another glass of port. "What about you? If marriage is such a fine institution, why have you not taken another wife?"

"I am no nob who needs an heir to his titles and estates, and I have no taste for courting." Cottsworth tapped his right leg, which resounded with a hollow, wooden sound. "And I don't cut the same figure I did when I was young. I can't dance or stroll with a pretty female down some secluded path. Hell, if I got down on one knee to propose, I'd never get up. And it's not like I have a fortune to compensate. Besides, I had a good marriage, but I doubt I could find its equal."

"So you don't miss all those advantages you kept nattering on about?"

Cottsworth emptied his glass. "Every day."

Chapter Sixteen

To save his boot-making shop, a man promised his daughter to his landlord. Every day the daughter wrote her husband's name on the bottom of one shoe and her father's name on the bottom of the other, and walked on them.

—By Arrangement, *a chronicle of arranged marriages, by G. E. Felber*

Eleven o'clock and he was not coming home. This was to be the story of her life from now on, Penny knew, waiting for her husband, wondering whose bed he was in if not his own or hers. That widow's? A paid courtesan's or a chance-met tavern wench? Why had she thought things might be different, that she could change him, that marriage would change him? West was a rake. He'd always be a rake. If he could not find pleasure with his wife, he'd find other arms to welcome him. She knew it; she just thought he'd wait a few weeks. He'd said he would wait for her to be ready. He'd said he would be faithful. He'd lied. And she'd lied to herself.

Twelve o'clock and she was not sleepy, not with her hopes in shambles. So Penny decided to continue with the work of making her new home more comfortable.

She might not know anything of intimacy, but she sure as Hades knew how to run a household.

Most of her efforts had to wait for daylight, for footmen to move furniture and maids to dust behind it. She needed help removing her father's ugly choices, and she needed the stores to be open in the morning, the linendrapers and showrooms and warehouses Lady Bainbridge had recommended. Westmoreland House would not be up to her standards in one day, but the fine old house would not embarrass its residents one hour more than necessary.

Penny did not want to chance waking her grandfather, either, opening his crates to hang his paintings instead of the horrid pieces on the walls downstairs. So she went into West's empty rooms.

She was not trespassing, not precisely. A good wife knew her entire domain, Penny told herself. How else was she to know what to replace or rearrange for her husband's comfort? Men did not care about fabric swatches and furniture styles, she knew, but she might get a hint of what he preferred without bothering him with such petty matters. That's how she justified her snooping, anyway.

In case West's valet was there, or if his lordship returned—twelve thirty, where was the dratted man?—she brought her lists and a pencil to take notes.

The small dressing room that adjoined hers smelled of his soap and his cologne. That was the first thing she noticed. Then she saw his shaving supplies on the washstand, his comb and brush, all lined up in military precision. Penny often forgot that her husband had been a soldier, since he was so much the polished gentleman, yet here was evidence of his former training, or his valet's.

She opened the doors of his wardrobe—she had to

know if the standing piece of carved wood was adequate,
didn't she?—and again smelled West's distinct spicy cologne. His clothes were all neatly arranged, with room to
spare. Penny supposed Nicky needed extra shelves for
his apparel, but West had plenty of room.

His drawers, too, were in order, not that Penny exactly
fondled his stockings and handkerchiefs and inexpress-
ibles. Feeling like a Peeping Tom, she hurried into the
adjoining bedroom. She could not tell which furniture
was his, which was her father's doing, but the massive
bed that almost filled the room made her think either it
was a new addition, or else her husband threw orgies.

She could understand why West disliked the heavy
hangings that surrounded the huge canopied bed on
three sides. The maroon velvet was so dark and thick
it made the bed more of an imprisoning cave than a
welcoming nest, even with one corner pulled back by a
gold-tasseled tie. She recognized her father's taste here,
for Sir Gaspar did not believe in fires in the bedchambers until the depth of winter, making an enclosed bed
necessary for comfort, holding body heat in and the chill
night air out. In fact, Penny thought, these same maroon
velvet draperies might have come from Sir Gaspar's
own house, since they did not appear brand-new to her
experienced eye. West hated them, so they were a recent addition. She had thought she recognized some of
the paintings and chairs earlier, but now she was certain.
Her father's wife had taken the opportunity of Penny's
marriage to redecorate her own house, and her frugal
father had sent the discards and disasters to Penny. Well,
they could have them back.

The bed might be an heirloom, however, like the lady's desk in her own sitting room. For all Penny knew,
her husband had been born in that enormous bed. Heavens, he might expect the next viscount to be conceived

there! She thought about that for a moment while she
ran her fingers down the sleeve of a paisley robe that
lay across the pillows. Then she thought about how no
nightshirt was laid out with the robe. Oh, my. No, she
would not consider naked men making babies on this
monstrous mattress.

She had to wait to find out if he wished to keep the
bed or use it for kindling, but she could get rid of the offending fabric right now, this very minute.

Penny kicked off her slippers, climbed up onto the
thick bedding, and started pulling. The velvet was sturdy,
the seams well sewn. She pulled harder. She piled the
pillows to stand on, higher, and grabbed more of the fabric in her hands. Then she got down and went to fetch
West's shaving razor. Ah, that made the job much easier, starting the cuts so she could tear the velvet in her
hands.

So her wandering, womanizing husband was out on
the town—rip. So he hadn't wanted to be married—rip.
So she was still a blasted virgin—*rriiip*. And no infant
was going to be conceived, born, or dreamed of, not in
this bed, not any time soon. She pulled so hard she fell
off the bed.

Luckily a wad of velvet cushioned her fall. She climbed
back up and kept cutting and tugging and cursing. Soon
she had shredded fabric thrown all across the bed, the
floor, the entire room, enough to make curtains for the
Drury Lane Theatre, it appeared. Now the bed was open
and airy and of better proportion for the room. If West
was cold under the naked canopy, so what? He had her
money. He could afford more coal for the fireplace. He
would not have her to warm his sheets, not if he came
home from some other woman's bed. Oh, no. Penny was
not going to be just another of his conquests.

On the other hand, the one still holding the razor,

Penny was as torn as the velvet. She wanted to be West's lover. She wanted to lie next to him, to fall asleep in his arms, warmed by his body after a night of pleasure. She wanted what Lady Bainbridge said every woman deserved. She wanted the impossible: West's love. She knew he'd never love a cold woman, not her hot-blooded husband. But how could she live with him—or herself—as the poor, betrayed wife?

Her thoughts were in chaos, but she would not leave West's room looking as if a band of berserk barbers had run through it. She neatly gathered all the fabric and folded it into a pile for the servants to carry away tomorrow. There were enough large pieces for capes or quilts, if any of them wanted to sew for their own use. Her father would approve of that, not wasting good material.

She looked at the soft mound, under the window. No, it should not go to waste. So she went down the hall to Nicky's empty room and fetched George.

"Here is a nicer bed," she told the pug. "And you already like West. He'll need the company, the cur."

Three o'clock, and Penny was finally asleep when she heard the commotion below. She pulled on her robe and rushed to the head of the stairs to look down, grabbing up an ugly vase from the hall table in case she needed a weapon. Instead of housebreakers, however, there was her husband, staggering under the weight of his half-conscious brother as Parker, a coat thrown over his nightshirt, and one of the new footmen rushed to help. Both brothers were disheveled and dirty and smelled of smoke.

He'd said he did not smoke. He'd said he did not drink to excess. He'd said he wanted to make their marriage work. By staying out all night, getting drunk and in brawls—on their first night in their new home together?

Penny was so angry she almost tossed the ugly vase down on his head.

The inconsiderate bounder had even woken her grandfather, who was feeling his way down the hall, his nightcap askew and his feet bare. Marcel was coming behind him, yelling about riots and revolutionaries, waving Mr. Littleton's slippers in one hand, a fireplace poker in the other. Penny was ashamed that her beloved relative and his servant should see her new husband in this state. She was more embarrassed that Grandpapa and Marcel would realize that West had not come home after dinner, had not spent the night with his new wife. She supposed all of London would know, with the Westmoreland brothers' hell raking. The gossip columns were bound to be full of Lord Westfield's philandering in the morning. Sick at heart, she started to go to her grandfather, to turn him back to his own room.

West looked up. "I am sorry to disturb your rest, sir," he said, not seeing Penny in the dark hall, and sounding remarkably sober for a man in his condition. "But there was a fire at General Fitzgerald's place, and everyone at the club raced over to help. Well, some of the members went to watch, making bets on whether the house would fall," he added in disgust.

"I once painted the general's portrait," Mr. Littleton said, straightening his cap. "Is he safe? His family?"

"Everyone in the house got out in time, although I do not know the condition of the rooms or your painting."

"That's all right, as long as no lives were lost."

"The insurance-company firemen were already there, with their bells and whistles. They did a fine job. A spark had landed on a tree in the garden, though, spreading the flames, and I worried about the horses in the mews behind the house. I sold some of those horses to the general myself. We could hear them starting to panic over the servants' shouts and the fire."

The vase slipped through Penny's fingers onto the carpeted hallway. There was a fire?

West had handed Nicky over to the servants, who were half carrying him to the kitchen, where Mrs. Parker could tend him.

"We are both fine," West called up the stairs, "and all the horses were saved, so please go back to bed."

Her grandfather leaned on Marcel's arm and returned to his own room, while Penny raced down the stairs. Before West could follow the others to the kitchen, she grabbed his arm and turned him around, so she could inspect her husband for injuries. He seemed more dirty than hurt. Now she could see the soot on his cheeks, and smell manure. She brushed his hair back from his forehead to make sure, while he stood patiently, a smile on his tired face. He was in one piece, it seemed.

"What happened to Nicky?"

"Oh, he thought I should stay behind, now that I have responsibilities. You." He brushed her cheek with a dirty hand, then winced when his sore knuckles touched her face.

Penny took his hand in hers, gingerly bending the fingers to see if any were broken. "You need some ice on this," she said, starting to lead him after the others to the kitchen, but he held her back.

He kept her hand in his, bringing it to his lips for a whisper-soft kiss on her fingers. "My valet will bring it later. I told Parker to roust him, but your touch is far more gentle than his anyway. Truly, I am fine."

Penny did not want to relinquish him into the care of someone else, either, now that she knew he was safe. There was soap and water in his dressing room, enough to start, so she headed for the stairs, then paused. "But you still have not said what happened to your brother. Should we send one of the footmen for a surgeon?"

"No, he will be fine, especially with Mrs. Parker's ministrations. He's mostly suffering from the general's gratitude, in the form of the most potent rum punch I have ever tasted. My punch barely stopped him."

"You hit your brother?"

"I could hear the horses," he said, as if that explained everything. "We had to move them out, where they could not smell the fire. He was holding on to my arm to keep me from going into the stables. Then he said if I went in, he went in."

"So you hit him?"

"I couldn't chance losing my little brother, could I? I swore on my father's grave to look after him. He came after me anyway, the clunch. Thank goodness he did, because the grooms were busy fighting the fire."

"Nicky was a hero?"

He nodded. "Damned good man to have at my side."

"Nicky?"

"He did complain about his new waistcoat being ruined."

"And you were rescuing horses all this time?"

"Not quite all. The general insisted we celebrate with him after we found other stabling for the cattle. I had no time to send a message."

"Then you were not . . . ?"

"Not . . . ?"

She did not answer, just wiped at his face with the sleeve of her robe.

He grinned, through the grime. "What, did you think I was carousing?"

"I did not know what to think when you did not come home," she confessed.

He kissed her, dirt and all, halfway up the stairs. "Ah, Penny, when will you learn to trust me? I said I would not betray our vows."

She turned away, climbing the last steps. "But you left."

"I came home."

"You won't always. I know it. Someday you'll be gone."

"Never."

"What about Lady Gre—?" Penny would not say the name.

"I ended all my connections before traveling to your grandfather's. You have to start believing me."

They had reached his rooms, but instead of washing the soot and the dirt and the blood off West, they were busy spreading it onto Penny. The fire at the general's house couldn't have been half as hot as the air between them. Then there was no air between them, only a few layers of clothing, which were quickly—

"Your ice, my lord." His valet came in, then a footman with more hot water, and Parker with his wife's salve and bandages.

"Damn," West cursed at the interruption. "The only thing missing is the dog."

"*Grrr.*"

Chapter Seventeen

Miss McC. hated the man her parents wanted her to wed. They hated the man she loved. The young lady pretended to kill herself, having read about something similar in a play. Neither gentleman would chance marrying a female of such unstable mind. Her parents locked her in the attic.

—By Arrangement, *a chronicle of arranged marriages, by G. E. Felber*

Lady Bainbridge moved in the next morning, all abuzz with the news. Most of London was talking about the heroic viscount and his brother. General Fitzgerald was singing their praises to every news reporter who came to interview him. The general's house was smoke filled and water damaged, and his wife was having nervous spasms—but his horses were safe. The papers recounted West's army career to fill more columns, his own horse-breeding efforts, and, of course, his rakish past. His hurried marriage also got its fair share of interest, so West and Penny were the topic of the day. The early, arranged match, the connection to the banking industry, the arrival of an eminent artist at the viscount's house, all were printed, read, and digested over breakfast by the Polite World.

"You'll be inundated with invitations now," Lady Bainbridge told Penny. "So you really do not need me at all."

"Oh, yes, I do," Penny said, thinking that now she would be even more on show, like some sort of circus performer whose whole history was written on the playbill. She'd find no quiet entrances, no gradual joining of West's circles, only more glare, more gossip. Parker had already presented her with a silver tray overflowing with cards from the curious, and it was just after breakfast. Had they written them in their sleep? Tittle-tattle must fly through London like sparrows through the trees.

"I have never met half these people and I have no idea which invitations to accept, which to refuse."

"See which ones your husband prefers. I can eliminate a few as unsuitable, climbers wanting to attach themselves to the newest comets through the social sky. And I know which hostesses will be helpful later, which will be offended if you fail to appear. But Westfield will have preferences."

Which meant Penny had an excuse to visit West in his room after seeing Lady Bainbridge settled in a suite that was not too dreadfully decorated. Regrettably, she encountered West's valet just coming out of the bedchamber. According to the man, Lord Westfield was still fast asleep. He never woke when George barked to be let out, or when a footman came to remove the torn velvet.

Master Nicholas, the man reported, had awoken, clutched his sore head, and swore he was dying. Marcel made him a potion consisting of rum and raw eggs, which cured him of complaining, if nothing else.

Penny decided to spend the time waiting in continuing her survey of the house, with Mrs. Parker assisting to identify family pieces. She was too on edge to concentrate on her lists, though, so excused herself to the housekeeper and went out through the glass doors in the rear parlor to the terraced gardens behind the building. There she found a little piece of the country, a welcome, warming spot with the morning sun shining on overgrown flower beds, untrimmed trees, roses needing pruning, a knot garden gone wild. Her father had not touched a single weed, thank goodness. Of course not, when few would see the results.

Penny wished she could find a pair of thick gloves, her old boots, and pruning shears and start working immediately, but knew she would have to hire a gardener instead. She'd be too busy to play in the dirt, too involved in playing her new role of lady. Still, she'd have the gardens brought back to order as soon as possible, so she'd have a refuge from the coming social storm.

She did stay outside, despite the chill in the air, and pulled a few vines away from the roses, not wanting to face her future just yet. Her husband was a notorious figure, more so than ever. Penny always knew he was dashing and daring. He'd been her ideal for a decade, after all. Now everyone else knew his worth, too, which made her even less of a good match for him. They'd all disapprove of her the more.

Penny's first encounter with society's scrutiny came far sooner than she expected. A gentleman was sitting with West in the parlor when she came back in through the glass doors. Botheration, she had wanted him to herself this morning, and besides, here she was with her hands dirty, her hair windblown, grass stains on her skirts from where she could not resist kneeling to pull up a weed. She thought about fleeing back the way she had come, but both men were standing at her entrance, the stranger slowly and with difficulty, leaning on a cane.

He was somewhat older than West, a dignified gentleman with silver at his temples and a military bearing, but a pleasant smile to counteract the lines etched in his face.

She hadn't thought much about West's friends, but supposed them to be libertines, dissipated, debauched, drunken. This man appeared to be none of those. Before Penny could make her excuses, he politely apologized for calling unannounced, at such an early, unfashionable hour.

"I fear I am used to running tame here, my lady, so never thought twice about coming to see for myself that West survived the fire and the general's gratitude. I understand some of the firefighters are still asleep in the ashes. I am sorry to intrude."

Penny liked him immediately, for his graciousness, for his pretending not to notice her ragged appearance, and for his caring enough about West to hurry to his side. Mr. Michael Cottsworth, formerly Major Cottsworth of His Majesty's Cavalry, was a fine figure of a man despite his obvious limp. He was also West's good friend, she learned, confidant, and adviser. Penny realized that just as West had wed her family along with her, taking in Grandpapa and Marcel and George, facing dinner at the Goldwaites', she had to tolerate his circle of acquaintances. She was glad Mr. Cottsworth was one of them.

She offered to ring for refreshments, but the men had just eaten a late breakfast or an early luncheon, and Mr. Cottsworth had duties at the War Office, although he was retired from active duty. Penny invited him to attend dinner at her father's that evening—Sir Gaspar would be delighted to have another wellborn gentleman at his table—but the former soldier refused, citing a previous engagement. He did not give the least hint of any disinclination to sup with a mere knighted banker, which raised his esteem in Penny's eyes even further.

In return, he asked if they were to attend Lady Aldershott's rout. Penny looked to West, who nodded.

"Then I would be honored if you would sit out a dance with me, that we might become better acquainted," West's friend said. "I regret I cannot offer for a waltz, but I fear your every moment will be spoken for as soon as you arrive if I do not get a jump on the other chaps."

Penny agreed, with pleasure. Now she had another friend. West looked pleased, too, which added to her happiness.

After the gentleman left, West and Penny went over the other invitations that had arrived.

"Zeus, it appears we will need a social secretary to handle this mess or you'll spend half your days answering correspondence."

"Lady Bainbridge offered to help."

"Good." He was studying the names on the cards, putting them into piles. "We do not need to attend every function or go out every night, not as newlyweds. I already told Parker to deny us to callers rather than fill the house to the rafters with gawkers, especially until you decorate the place to your liking and select your new wardrobe. Some of these are invitations to teas or ladies' at-homes during the day. You do not have to accept any but the most important until you are ready. Lady Bainbridge will know which. But you'll want to meet enough people to feel comfortable when it is our turn to entertain. And I wish to be seen with the prettiest woman in London on my arm."

Penny blushed, and West laughed. "Lud, you are so easy to fluster. I doubt that will last past your first ball when every gentleman lays his heart at your feet." He looked down, to see her slippers covered in mud.

"Speaking of feet, why don't you show me what kept you out of doors so long?"

He followed her back to the gardens and listened to her plans to restore them. He did not know a rosebush from a rhododendron, but he loved the sparkle in her eyes and the smile on her lips when she pointed to this scraggly shrub, that broken-limbed bush.

So he kissed her. He'd enjoyed many a tryst in abandoned gardens with pretty women, but few in the sunshine where people might see, and never with one who belonged to him. Not that he considered Penny as a possession—she'd likely darken his daylights for thinking such a thing—but she was his wife, his to cherish, his to kiss in the morning . . . and all night if he could convince her.

"Are you sure we have to go to your father's dinner tonight?" he whispered in her ear, which was already tingling from his breath and his fingers feathering through her hair. "I can think of better things to do out among the roses."

Penny could barely think. What roses? What father?

He sighed and stepped away. "I suppose duty calls. Dash it."

Doubly so.

Lady Bainbridge cried off from the dinner at Sir Gaspar's house that evening. She had a few last commitments to the young lady she was recently chaperoning. A duchess's granddaughter, Miss Lovell was already betrothed, thanks to Lady Bainbridge's efforts. The paid companion's services were hardly required so close to the wedding, but one never offended a duchess, especially not until one had been paid in full. Besides, Lady Bainbridge would be seeing more of Penny's stepsisters than she wished, all too soon.

Penny's grandfather also declined the invitation. He still had a cough. He still needed to send messages to his old friends in Town. And he still remembered dining at Goldwaite's table before.

"And came home needing another supper," the old artist swore. "The man is so wealthy because he never spends a shilling more than he has to."

Penny thought about defending her father with the information that he'd been supporting them all these past eight years, buying Grandpapa's paintings anonymously, but she held her tongue. Mr. Littleton was never going to look with favor on the man who carried his daughter off, then let her die, as if Sir Gaspar's money should have protected Penny's mother from an influenza epidemic.

And he had sent over his unwanted furniture.

Nicky flatly refused to go. He knew Penny's stepsisters, for one thing, and their matchmaking mama. For another, he had to go retell his story of the fire rescue to his chums. Everyone wanted to buy him dinner and a drink. How could he refuse such an opportunity? He was a hero, the man of the hour, a goer among goers. He needed a new waistcoat. Marcel managed to convince him that a true hero did not dress like a caper-merchant, so Nicky wore one of West's, his chest puffed up with pride enough to fit his brother's larger size.

Penny and West went by themselves. They had not been alone in a carriage much since their wedding, and Penny was ill at ease, anxious about the coming dinner, nervous about what might come after, unsure about her reaction to her husband's nearness. Why, her fingers were quivering simply from his touch as he handed her into the coach.

West seemed unconcerned. He was glad, he said, to be going to her father's house rather than going out in public to face the ridiculous notoriety his actions at the stables were causing. Any man would have done the same—Penny disagreed—and the furor would die down as soon as another story or scandal took its place. All those who sent cards or callers had nothing better to do with their time, he told Penny, his eyes telling her he could think of many things. And what did those well-wishers think they were going to do with so many bouquets of flowers or baskets of fruit?

"What, do they think an orange will get the smell of smoke from my lungs?"

Penny instantly asked, "Are you ill? Should we send our regrets?"

He pulled her closer to him on the carriage seat, but shook his head. "No, we may as well get this over with. That is, I am eager to meet the rest of your family."

"Liar."

He laughed, and Penny felt warm all over, not just where their bodies were touching. She wished they were not going anywhere that night.

Chapter Eighteen

*Miss H. married the man her parents chose for her.
She never did learn to love him. On her daughter's
birth, however, she started looking for a wealthy,
titled gentleman to betroth the girl to, the same as
her parents had done.*

—By Arrangement, *a chronicle of
arranged marriages, by G. E. Felber*

Constance, Lady Goldwaite, was obviously disappointed not to have her table full. Penny had made
sure she'd received notice in the afternoon, in time
enough to rearrange her table, but her stepmother was
still annoyed. As always, she blamed Penny.

According to Constance, Mr. Nicholas Westmoreland
was a fribble, a useless younger son with no fortune of
his own, but his name was on everyone's lips. Her girls
could have practiced on him. Lady Bainbridge would
have been a coup, for the widow was known to be excellent *ton,* traveling in the highest circles despite her
lowered circumstances. Penny's stepmother did not miss
Mr. Littleton, she said, who was too eccentric and too
outspoken. Her neighbors and closest friends would not
have been impressed to hear his name in the morning

anyway, if they recognized it. Artists were not quite the thing, she told the artist's loving granddaughter.

At least she was pleased with her new son-in-law by marriage. Constance was in alt that Westfield's first appearance after the general's fire was at her home, and she intended to see that the *on-dits* columns knew it, even if she had to send a notice around tomorrow herself. Perhaps she should have invited a few of the neighbors after all, Constance considered, to see the prize in her parlor.

Penny agreed that her husband was indeed superb. He was dressed this evening in quiet elegance—Constance whispered that she would have preferred a bit of color instead of the austere dark blue and stark white—and showed perfect manners to match. He was more handsome than any man had a right to be, and appeared larger in the cluttered drawing room. Best of all, according to Penny's stepmother, he had a small bruise on his cheek from the rescue, giving him an air of danger, excitement, and daring.

Penny saw Constance glance at her own husband, who was shaking West's hand. Sir Gaspar was short, squat, with thinning hair and thickening waist. Constance would have frowned at the comparison, Penny thought, except that made wrinkles.

"Ah, well," Constance said, for Penny's ears alone, "your father has something your attractive Lord Westfield never had, and that is gold, lots of it, whole bank vaults of it. When a woman has her children's futures at stake, she has to look beyond a pretty face to a full pocket."

Penny knew that Constance took the lines of the marriage ceremony to heart, what she chose of it anyway. She'd married for the better the first time, plain Miss Pease wedding a viscount's grandson. She'd married for

richer the second, taking Gaspar Goldwaite before he
was knighted. To the devil with worse or poorer.

"Not that you have not made quite a catch," Constance
acknowledged, showing Penny a shred of approval,
"even if it took blackmail and bribery to bring the thing
about." The approval faded when she took in Penny's
plain gown, a faded blue Constance's maid would not
have worn. Penny had a simple strand of pearls at her
throat, with her hair pulled into a tight spinster's knot at
the back of her neck. "You could have dressed more in
keeping with the occasion, your first outing as a married
woman, at your father's house, no less, and more in tune
with your husband's splendor. But then you have never
done what anyone could wish, have you?"

Penny had married West. That was enough. She was
not about to trick herself out like a Covent Garden convenient . . . like Constance in her red satin.

Constance shrugged her beefy shoulders, exposed by
the low-cut gown along with more of the woman's assets
than Penny wished to see. "Well, at least your dowdy
outfit will not put me or my girls in the shade."

Nothing could. Besides her skimpy scarlet satin, Constance was wearing half the gems in her jewel box, the
better to impress the viscount. Her girls were wearing
the rest. Constance saw how the viscount was admiring
her daughters, and smiled. They'd caught his eye, all right,
so now he would introduce them to his friends. "Not any
rackety racing crowd, either," she warned Penny, "but
titled gentlemen with property and investments."

The sooner the better, it seemed. As soon as greetings
were exchanged and the newlyweds were seated in the
newly renamed Grecian Room with glasses of sherry,
Constance lost no time. "Now that Westmoreland House
is in order, my lord, when will you and Persephone be

ready for your first grand entertainment? The girls are quite looking forward to it."

The girls were looking as if they had dressed for a ball this very night, Penny thought. She'd worn a favorite blue dinner gown, not too fancy for a quiet family meal. Her stepsisters wore frothy lace overskirts bedecked with sequins and flounces, feathers in their hair, which was a riot of bouncy brown ringlets. Speaking of rings, they each wore several, plus bracelets, brooches, and necklaces and earbobs. Mavis, the older at eighteen, wore orange and yellow stripes, which was unfortunate with her spotted complexion. Seventeen-year-old Amelia's gown was white, at least, all the frills and furbelows of the thing. Even Penny, long out of London society, knew that young females of proper breeding wore white or pastels, and no colored gemstones until they were older or engaged. Her stepsisters were dressed like Gypsies, she decided, or pirates' doxies, decked in the latest booty.

Their manners were no more appealing. Mavis gushed all over West, barely acknowledging Penny's presence. Amelia was as shy as ever, not raising her eyes, barely whispering the civilities at the introductions before fleeing to the corner of the parlor. She could easily get lost among the decor with her white gown and pale cheeks.

Constance had chosen Greek this time, or her version of it at any rate, and a lot of it. White marble busts stood on columns, Ionic, Doric, and Corinthian, all mixed together. White plasterwork plinths and carved caryatids held up armless athletes, headless torsos, and urns. Some had been painted; some of the figures had been draped in white to suit Constance's notion of decency. Every surface was filled with small unidentifiable shards of imitation antiquities. The carpet was bordered in a black-

and-white Greek key design, which was repeated across the ceiling and over the mantel and around the walls and on the window hangings. Even the furniture tried to appear classical, with long, low, uncomfortable benches scattered here and there, as if waiting for a group of to-gaed guests.

Instead, they held a banker, his boorish wife, and the girls done up as bachelor fare. Penny was speechless.

"Stunning, ain't it?" her father asked. "All the rage, you know. Egyptian is gone, and Oriental has been over-done. Can't you just imagine some great orator spouting his philosophy here?"

No, but Penny could easily picture Socrates drinking hemlock. "It's lovely. Truly," she added for emphasis, "but to answer Lady Goldwaite's question, I have no idea when Westmoreland House will be ready for company. There is a great deal yet to be done."

"And you'll need to do something about your ward-robe, too," Constance said with a superior tone. "But you must not wait too long, you know. As they say, time nor tide waits for no maiden."

That was not what they said, but Penny understood that Constance was desperate to see her daughters settled.

Sir Gaspar seconded his wife's urging. "Before you know it, you'll be breeding and wanting to make your nest instead of dancing all night."

West cleared his throat and Mavis giggled. Constance rapped Sir Gaspar on the shoulder with her fan. "Not in front of the girls."

"What, they don't know that married gals have ba-bies? Of course they do. Haven't you been warning them they better have a ring on their fingers afore they drop their handkerchief and raise their skirts?"

"Father!"

"Well, I have been waiting a long time to see my grandson."

And he would have a long wait more.

Penny's face felt so hot, she knew she was blushing like a schoolgirl.

West came to her rescue. "It is far too soon to think of filling the nursery. Lady Westfield deserves to simply enjoy herself on the Town. I am looking forward to taking her to the opera, the theater, the other sights of the city."

Sir Gaspar was disappointed. He'd be more so, Penny thought, if he knew the truth, that his grandson was no closer than a few kisses and some heavy breathing.

Her father was never one to be defeated for long. He pointed to the mark on West's face and mentioned the fire. "Knew you'd make my daughter proud."

Penny was nearly speechless again. She should be proud because her husband ran into burning buildings? He'd taken two years off her life with that bit of bravery.

West changed the subject quickly. He thanked Sir Gaspar for his efforts at cleaning the Prospect Street house, and the loan of the furniture and paintings.

"Oh, those are no loan. Consider it all a wedding gift."

"No, we cannot accept, although we appreciate your generosity, and your charming wife's efforts. You did tell Penny she could choose, however, so she has her own tastes in mind."

Now Penny found her voice. "And you did offer to pay for it all," she reminded her father.

"Now, puss, ladies and gents do not discuss financial arrangements in company, you know."

"Neither do they discuss procreation. You are trying to get off cheaply."

"Me? Your own father?" He looked over at West, whose good favor he still needed if he was ever to get his wife's daughters out of his house and into another man's expenses. "You just send the bills to me."

Penny answered, "I will, never fear. And for my trousseau, in case you've forgotten."

"What's this about a trousseau?" Constance demanded. "You never told me you were going to throw more money away on the drab? That is, on your daughter. She's already wed. Let her husband pay her bills."

Luckily for everyone's tempers and manners, Constance's son, Nigel Entwhistle, strolled into the room right then. A year older than Penny at twenty-seven, he was tall and thin, wearing exaggerated shirt points. His linen was not half as pristine white as West's, Penny noted, nor was his neckcloth tied so expertly or intricately. She also saw the cool greeting the two men exchanged. They reminded her of George when he spotted another dog, his fur ruffled, his stance wide. She would not be surprised if Nigel and West started kicking dirt behind them.

After the pleasantries, which were far less pleasant than before, and they were on their way into dinner, Penny asked her husband, "Do you know Nigel, then?"

His reply was brief but informative. "By repute. I seldom frequent the same venues." He did not say it, but the scorn was in his voice: Nigel was not of his class or character.

Neither was Penny.

Nigel sought to remedy the coolness and the distance at dinner. Talking across the table, claiming they were too small a party to stand on ceremony, he hinted about invitations to West's club, a round at Gentleman Jackson's, a fencing match at Antonio's. "We are family now, of course."

"We'll see," was all West offered. He couldn't see how he was related to the dirty dish when his wife barely was. Nigel Entwhistle was a gamester, and not necessarily an honest one at that. He'd been shipped out of the country to avoid one scandal that West knew of, and barely avoided several more when he returned. He was not welcome in polite society, and barely tolerated at all but the lowest gambling parlors and kens. He was somewhat wellborn, his sire being related to a title on the cadet branch, but only Goldwaite's gold kept him from jail or from getting a knife in his back down some alley. West supposed Entwhistle wanted to use the excuse of his sisters' presentations to edge himself into the *ton* and find some gullible heiress to wed or new lambs to fleece. Not if West could help it, no, not even if they were connected through Penny. A loose screw was a loose screw, no matter whom his mother married.

Penny never cared for Nigel, either, less so after she'd heard he wanted to marry her for her dowry. For once, West's assurance and arrogance were welcome; he put Nigel in his place by directing his own attention to the others. He patiently tried to elicit a conversation from Amelia over the soup. He gently discouraged Mavis's flirtations over the fish course. He subtly deflected Constance's constant matchmaking with his bachelor friends over every unpalatable bite he took.

Penny was finding her own patience, gentility, and subtlety wearing thin, with Nigel seated at her side.

"You'll never hold his attention looking like a country dowd, you know," he told her. "The man is used to dashers, diamonds of the first water."

Penny was wearing a favorite gown, one she had not bothered to alter, since she would soon have a new London-made wardrobe. She intended to start in the morning, but not with Constance and the girls at her side, despite their offers to lend their dubious assistance. Meanwhile the blue merino was lower waisted and higher necked than fashionable, but the color was becoming to her, she always felt, and this was supposed to be a small dinner among family.

"My lord admired the gown," she told Nigel now. "He said the blue made my eyes sparkle like gems, and the cut showed off my elegance. So there."

Nigel ordered the footman to refill his wineglass, then said, in the servant's hearing, "He must want more of your fortune. You can't hold a candle to Maeve Greenlea."

Penny was furious. Perhaps West did hope to get his hands on her personal fortune, despite his denials, but he did not have to give false compliments to get it. Besides, the way his breathing was labored when he first saw her, and his smile started at his mouth and rose all the way to his eyes, showed that he did appreciate her looks. She did not think a man could feign the protrusion in his pantaloons. West wanted her, in whatever she chose to wear, or out of it. He might not love her—he might never love her, which was something Penny had to face—but he did desire her, not some wayward widow. He'd broken off with her, hadn't he?

No, Nigel was simply always one for bursting bubbles. He was one of those nasty creatures who thrived on causing dissension, destroying confidence, creating distress, just for the underhanded pleasure of the thing. As a youngster he used to make his sisters cry by stealing their dolls and smashing them. He seemed still to be a toy breaker. As such, he was not worth her attention. Penny turned her back on him and listened to West's conversations instead. If she had seen the expression on Nigel's face, much less known his foul thoughts, she would not have been so sanguine. No, she would have tossed her wine in his lap.

Chapter Nineteen

To unite their two estates, Lord B. wed his only daughter to the Duke of C.'s only son. The couple had no children. Both estates went to distant cousins.

—By Arrangement, *a chronicle of arranged marriages, by G. E. Felber*

Lady Goldwaite was quizzing West about his friends, his unmarried friends, as prospective sons-in-law.

"None of them would make good husbands, I fear."

Mavis giggled. "Mama says a gentleman with a title is always a good match."

Constance bobbed her turbaned head. "Only if he is ready to settle down."

Penny spoke across the table, as the others were doing. "Nonsense. You would not wish to marry a rake or a fortune hunter just because he has a title."

Mavis giggled again. "You did."

Constance laughed, a high-pitched, girlish sound that was more grating than her daughter's titters. Nigel snorted.

Before Penny could reply, or throw something, by the look in her eye, West said, "Neither Penny nor I had any say in the arrangement our parents made. Neither of us can be accused of greed or ambition." He stared even Mavis into looking down at her plate.

Sir Gaspar slapped his thigh. "But the gal's got the right of it. For all your protests lately, Penny, you must admit you never said nay to the match all those years."

She hadn't, more's the pity. When she was young, she thought of Kendall Westmoreland as Sir Lancelot, not a little in love with the idea of him. Then it was too late and she was a spinster.

"Quite right," Constance said. "As is proper. A daughter's duty is to her father, then her husband."

West smiled at Penny across the table. "But a woman, a mature woman of intelligence and education, has opinions of her own."

Sir Gaspar swallowed his green beans and made a face. "Gals shouldn't have that much education. It muddles their thinking. Look where it got Penny, for all the blunt I spent on governesses and tutors and that fancy academy and Lady Bainbridge to polish her manners."

Once more West came to her defense. "Her education got me a wife to be proud of."

Nigel snorted. "And her dowry came in handy."

Now West set down his knife and fork. "I think the topic of our marriage has been discussed ad nauseam." No, that was the food, but he went on: "Enough ill-mannered strangers will be dissecting the circumstances over their own meals"—which were bound to be better prepared and more generous than this one—"without kinfolk adding to my wife's embarrassment."

Penny raised her glass and muttered, "Amen to that."

No one could miss the steel in West's voice this time, so no one else spoke. They all pretended to concentrate on their meals.

Since part of Penny's pricey education consisted of how to go on in social occasions, the silence felt awkward. She was already irked that West should see her family behaving so badly, without having him think they were totally gauche. So she turned to the younger girls and asked what their hopes were for their own futures. "Do you have any gentlemen in mind? I know you have been out and about London, so have you met any young swains who have caught your eye?"

Amelia never did raise her eyes, but Mavis bounced in her chair. Before she could speak, her mother said, "Tsk. What matter is it if a man smiles at a female in the park or fetches a cup of punch at an assembly? A handsome face is not what a woman needs in a husband. My girls know better than to become infatuated with unsuitable *partis*. Sir Gaspar and I are compiling a list of gentlemen worth considering. I shall send it to you when you are ready to issue invitations to your ball."

"Then the girls are to have no choice in their future husbands?"

"If someone more suitable offers, why, of course we would consider accepting."

"What of their feelings? Are Mavis and Amelia not to be consulted?"

"Do not be more foolish than you are tiresome, Persephone. And do not go putting forward notions into the girls' heads. They shall marry where they ought, as Sir Gaspar and I know better than any chit what is best. But do not worry, with your too-tender sensibilities. Everyone on the list will be a gentleman."

"Gentlemen come in all shapes and sizes, all ages and attitudes. For that matter, they have different moral standards as well as different personalities. Should they not suit your daughters' as well as your ideas of an advantageous match?"

"Give over, Penny," her father said. "The chits will do as they are directed. We will try to find handsome young men. Lud knows enough of them gamble away their patrimony soon enough to need a heavy dowry. No need to fear we'll hitch 'em to some old roué who's killed three wives already, or a man with a different mistress for every night of the week, or a widower with seven children."

Lady Goldwaite was mentally erasing gentlemen from her list.

Sir Gaspar reached for another helping of potatoes. "I did fine by you."

"No."

"No?" West asked. So did almost everyone else at the table, everyone looking at Penny now, even Amelia looking up from pushing her peas around on her plate.

"No, we are not going to talk about my marriage. And no, if you wish my assistance in bringing your daughters to the attention of gentlemen who do not swim in your usual circles, no, you shall not do 'fine' by them. I shall go about it my way."

"What, will you line the brats up and take bids, like you sell your grandfather's paintings?"

"That was hateful, Nigel, and far from the point, which is that the br—the young ladies are entitled to make their own choices."

"Absurd." Constance was scowling, and to the devil with wrinkles.

"It is fair. You sought my help, and you can have it, on my terms. I shall be happy to present Mavis and Amelia once I am assured their manners are suitable for polite company. Which means no brazen flirting." She directed that to Mavis, who predictably tee-heed. Then Penny turned toward Amelia. "And no hiding in corners. Lady Bainbridge can help tutor you so you are better prepared. You must also be dressed like other young misses, demure and modest." Mavis started to whine. Penny ignored it, hoping Lady Bainbridge could work miracles, and told her father and his wife, "After that, I shall invite your listed guests, and anyone else you wish ... and anyone else they wish, so they can make their own choices."

"Nonsense," Sir Gaspar insisted. "What do they know?"

"Precisely. If they do not know their own feelings, then I shall not be party to pushing them into the arms of some man they cannot admire or share affection with. I refuse to take part in forcing a woman to wed where she would not."

Constance was fuming, but she could not shout her refusal of Penny's terms. One did not shout in front of a viscount, and she did need Penny's help. Truth be told, no gentlemen had approached Sir Gaspar about courting either of the girls. Not a single man they met had sent a bouquet. And she simply did not have access to the same grand parties Penny would, where titled swells lined the walls, looking for brides. She chewed her beef—twice, it was so tough—and said, "We shall see. I am not giving my girls to any spendthrift who will waste their dowries, then leave them starving in a cottage."

"If your daughters are old enough to marry, they are old enough to weigh all their options. I know my father's investigators will discover every personal detail, giving them the information they need. That is simple precaution. Men lie."

Nigel made a rude sound; her father harrumphed; West raised an eyebrow. Penny ignored all of them. "But I insist. Amelia and Mavis must not be forced to marry against their wills in a match someone else makes. It shall be their decision, no one else's."

Mavis was clapping her hands, rattling the silverware.

Penny had to smile. "I take it you have a gentleman in mind?"

"Oh yes, he is ever so good-looking. Tall and with straight teeth."

"Those are excellent qualities in a husband, I am sure. What else is attractive about him?"

"He smiles whenever I see him at the bank."

"Ah, so he is smitten, too? Then why has he not asked for your hand?"

"Oh, he is Father Goldwaite's clerk. He would not dare, until now."

"Mr. Crenshaw?" Constance shrieked. "Never! Your father's grandfather was a viscount. I shall not have you throwing your life away on some banker."

Mavis gave one last giggle. "You did."

Penny thought Constance might choke on her chicken. Penny herself had given up on the tough old bird—the sere slice, if not her stepmother. "Well, we shall see if another gentleman takes your fancy. I am sure many will smile at you, once we have you looking like a debutante instead of a doxy."

"But I like pretty colors."

"You can carry a bright bouquet of flowers or a painted fan. What about you, Amelia? Do you hold a *tendre* for any young man?"

Amelia never spoke to young men. They terrified her. She looked at her sister with beseeching eyes.

"Oh, she was moonstruck by that poet we met last year in the Lake Country. Mr. Culpepper was ever so romantic looking."

"And did he return your interest?"

Amelia shook her head, but Mavis said, "He seemed to like the sheep better. That's what he wrote about. Amy likes sheep, too."

"Especially the little lambs," Amelia whispered.

At least she could speak. "Then you might prefer a gentleman from the country, away from the crowds of London."

"Oh, yes, please."

Penny turned to the girls' mother. "You see, she does have opinions of her own to be considered. You would marry her to a city man, willy-nilly."

"Bah."

"No, brava. The young ladies will pick their own mates. There will be no arranged matches without their consent."

Which made West feel as small as the portion of beef on his plate. And as unappetizing.

Sir Gaspar pounded on the table. "There will be no marriages without my consent, not if they wish me to provide fancy weddings."

"You saved a great deal of money on mine."

"I had to purchase a special license, didn't I? Besides, I agreed to provide their dowries. Their own father did not leave them a shilling. That gives me say in the matter."

"I offered to repay Penny's portion," West put in.

Penny paid him less attention than she gave her watery mashed turnips. "Wouldn't you rather a man wed them out of love than out of need for your money?" she asked her father.

Now Nigel laughed. "What a fool you are, Penny, and at your age. You should know better. No one weds out of love, only advantage. Especially in your husband's social circles."

His mother was nodding fondly. Her precious son understood the way of life. Her girls did, too.

Then Nigel added, "Love is for affairs, after you are wed."

Which earned him foul looks from his moral mother, his guilty stepfather, his bemused brother-in-law by marriage, and his angry stepsister. Mavis giggled. Amelia, as usual, sat mumchance.

Constance hurriedly ushered the ladies from the room, leaving the three men to who-knew-what conversation. As far as Penny could guess, they had nothing in common except a connection to her. One was a financier, one was an aristocrat, and one was gallows bait. Sir Gaspar knew banking, Viscount Westfield knew horses, and Nigel Entwhistle knew how to cadge a living. Then again, she herself had little enough in common with her father's second family.

When the four women reached the sitting room—a chamber done in white and gold this time—Constance was still in a pet about having to let the girls take part in choosing their own husbands. What did they know? What did high-and-mighty Lady Westfield know about living with a man, making ends meet, worrying about one's future?

Constance picked up her needlework and began to set fast, furious stitches, leaving puckers on the cloth and not bothering to call for tea or conversation.

Mavis opened the nearest fashion journal and started picking the most unsuitable styles she could. If she had to wear white, she claimed, she'd need a new wardrobe. If Father Goldwaite was buying new clothes for Penny, he could buy them for her, too.

Ignored, Penny wandered toward the pianoforte, where her younger stepsister was seated. "Do you play?" she asked Amelia, who looked at her mother, then bobbed her head. "We had to learn. She said all young ladies are supposed to know how to entertain at private gatherings."

"She is quite right. Will you play for us now?"

"But I hate to perform in front of anyone," Amelia cried. "I only make mistakes."

"Well, there is no one here except family, so why don't you practice on us?

Amelia made mistakes anyway. Penny suffered through one unrecognizable piece, then got up, indicating Amelia should follow her to a sofa. "Why don't you tell me more about your likes and your interests? That way I will know more about the kind of gentleman you might admire."

Amelia was just as relieved to leave the pianoforte and sit beside Penny. She twisted her ringlets through her fingers, though, and said nothing.

"Surely you have some activity you enjoy? Painting? Riding? Needlework?"

Get her hands dirty? Fall off one of the dumb brutes? Spend hours at tedious stitching no one needed? "I like to read."

Penny was relieved the girl knew how, much less enjoyed it. "Novels, I suppose," she said with a smile to show she liked the Minerva Press offerings, too.

"Oh, Mother will not permit us to read such low literature. They are a bad influence, she says. Recently I have been reading Greek mythology." Amelia smiled for the first time, and Penny realized she was actually pretty when she did, with a sweet smile. "Mother thinks anything classic is acceptable and impressive. She has no idea what those Greek gods and goddesses were up to."

Penny laughed. "She'd never have half of them in her parlor if she knew."

"She'd throw my books out, too, so I make up other stories to tell her."

"How creative," Penny said, and how devious.

Amelia bobbed her head, sending ringlets flying. "I read the myths about Persephone. Hers is not a happy story."

"No, but it explains winter, I suppose."

"They say that Persephone's mother was the goddess of agriculture, and she made everything stop growing when the god of the underworld stole her daughter. She must have loved her very much."

"So much so that Zeus made her captor give Persephone back for most of the year so we only have one barren season."

"But why would your parents name you after a child who was abducted and forced to live in Hades with a monster?"

Why, indeed? Penny had always been curious herself. The name was surely not her practical father's idea, but her mother had been the daughter of an artist, with a more open mind. Penny missed her still, and still marveled how that unlikely pair had come together. Her mother would never have wed for money, and Grandpapa Littleton would not have allowed her to, or needed her to. Her father had been softer, gentler in his early days, Penny knew, so maybe they truly did love each other, as hard as that was to imagine. "When I asked, my mother always smiled and said she'd chosen the name because she knew I would be her dearest treasure, and like Demeter, she'd never be able to part with me."

Now Penny wondered whether her mother had known all along that Penny was to be bartered away, sent to another world where her mother could not go. Or else she was prepared to fight for Penny's happiness, like Demeter. She never got the chance. Penny would not discuss the sense of loss she felt to this day, not with Amelia. "I suppose she liked everything Greek, like your own mother."

At least she did not collect it in her drawing room.

Chapter Twenty

Miss K. became a devout churchgoer after the death of the husband her parents chose for her. No one knew whether she was offering prayers for his soul, or thanksgiving.

—By Arrangement, *a chronicle of arranged marriages, by G. E. Felber*

The after-dinner port was sour. So was the conversation between Sir Gaspar and his stepson. They ignored West, but he could not ignore them.

Nigel almost spit out his first taste. "Devil take it, man, are you counting every coin twice, that you cannot afford a decent bottle of wine?"

Goldwaite seemed to find the port adequate. He was on his second glass. "If you do not like it, you can set up your own establishment and dine at your own table."

"I would if I had a decent living allowance."

"Then blame your late father, not me. Damned if I see why I should pay more than I have to if he didn't make provisions for his own children. I am already supporting your sisters, which ought to be your job, not mine. You're a man grown, and not of my blood. So I told your mother, and so I still say. The girls can't help themselves, but you can. Go out and earn a fortune, same as I did."

"I'd rather marry one. Same as he did." Nigel jerked his thumb toward West, who pushed his still-full glass aside, ready to take the dastard by the throat. How many times was he going to be accused of being a fortune hunter, by Harry? And by half of London, it seemed.

His host agreed with him. "You're beating a dead horse, Nigel," Sir Gaspar said, lighting his pipe after West turned down a cigarillo. Nigel took snuff, which was a worse habit than smoking, in West's estimation, in addition to being an affectation. He turned away when the man sneezed several times. Even the sour port was more attractive.

Sir Gaspar ignored the snorts and snuffles. "Asides, marriage between you and Penny mightn't be legal. I looked into it."

That meant to West that Sir Gaspar had considered other alternatives than himself as groom, despite his spoutings about honor and contracts and a gentleman's word. If the banker had seen an advantage to having his daughter marry his wife's son, poor Penny would have been saddled with the ne'er-do-well. West would have been free, but that notion no longer appealed, not when it meant this scurvy fellow could put his slimy hands on Penny's soft skin.

Nigel still had a fondness for the idea of marrying Goldwaite's fortune, if not for the woman. "Persephone and I do not share a drop of blood."

"No, but the law don't care about that. They don't care if you get hitched, either, until someone contests the match. Suppose you are twenty males away from the succession to your grandfather's estates and nineteen chaps ahead of you stuck their spoons in the wall."

"Sounds deuced suspicious to me, twenty swells dying at once."

"Maybe there was an avalanche, or an invasion, an epidemic. That's aside the point. You could inherit, but the twenty-first heir could challenge your marriage on some consanguinity rule or other. He could have the marriage declared null and void, making my grandson illegitimate."

Nigel muttered something about any get of Sir Gaspar's being no better than a bastard either way.

"Well, the boy's father might be more mannered than moral"—now West felt even more like throttling the older man, too—"but at least his parentage ain't in question. Traced back to William the Conqueror or such."

"Not quite that old," West said, but no one listened.

"I looked into that, too, you can be sure." Sir Gaspar blew a smoke circle, and put his ring finger through it. "I hear Mittleman's daughter blotted her copybook so badly that no one will have her. He might come down heavy for someone to take the hoyden off his hands."

Nigel snapped the lid on his enameled snuffbox and shoved it across the table so West could see the erotic picture on the cover. Was he supposed to be impressed by such poor taste?

Nigel was not impressed with his stepfather's proposal. "You think I would take used goods?"

"What, you can afford to be fussy now?"

"But Mittleman is a mill owner, not a gentleman."

Sir Gaspar knocked the pipe against the table to knock out the spittle. Tobacco grounds scattered across his waistcoat. "So Mittleman ain't a gentleman. He ain't the one having to cadge off his mother, either."

Nigel started to let his indignation show, then remembered the stack of overdue bills he had. If he had any hope of Sir Gaspar paying them, he had to hold his tongue.

He drank a swallow of the bad port. "Mittleman, eh? The fellow owns at least a dozen wool mills. What'd the girl do? More importantly, with whom? A chap might be willing to claim a gentleman's brat as his own, but what if she'd serviced the gardener, the groom, and half the local militia?"

West had no interest in hearing of some female's fall from grace, certainly not an unfortunate mill owner's daughter. He decided she'd be better off with the butler than with Nigel. He stood up, saying Penny must be wondering what happened to him.

"She didn't look all that eager to me," Nigel said, earning him another black mark in West's book. Someday those tallies would be counted and repaid, but not today, not in Sir Gaspar's dining room. Decent manners demanded restraint, even if one could not get a decent meal, or a decent drink, there.

West had to find his own way to where the women were sitting. No footman appeared to direct him, another indication of Sir Gaspar's cheeseparing, although the man made sure his own comforts were attended to. Penny gave him such a bright smile, a rush to his side, a swift embrace, when he stood in the doorway of the Gold Parlor, that the whole night seemed suddenly worthwhile. West wished nasty Nigel could see her. Not eager? Hah! West's spirits lifted, until Penny whispered in his ear, "Help."

He took advantage of the moment—what red-blooded man would not?—and put his arms around her, drawing her close for a lingering kiss, despite the watchful eyes of her stepmother and the younger girls.

"That is no help!" she yelped, pulling back, but still

close enough to murmur, "Find an excuse, any excuse, to leave."

"I could say you are breeding," he teased in a low voice, "but your father would bring out the champagne."

Luckily she could hide her blushes in his arms. "Heavens, not that. Do you want to stay?"

He saw the tea tray a servant was wheeling in: nothing but toast fingers and digestive biscuits. "I am sorry, Lady Goldwaite, but I fear we must leave."

"What, so soon? I was going to have the girls perform for you. Mavis has a charming singing voice. Don't you, darling? And precious Amelia plays quite prettily on the pianoforte."

Penny groaned.

"Are you not feeling well, my dear?"

"I, ah, have the headache."

"And we have much to do tomorrow, so Penny needs her rest," he said. To placate Lady Goldwaite, he added, "We have to see about opening the ballroom at Westmoreland House, and making that list of guests to invite."

Constance was content with that. "I'll send my list of names around tomorrow morning."

"Excellent, I'll look forward to seeing which gentlemen you think might be suitable."

Then he could warn them about Precious and Darling.

Once they were in the carriage on the way home, West pulled Penny into his lap and kissed her soundly.

"What's that for?"

"For not making me sit through a recital of amateur efforts."

"Worse, they are ill-trained amateurs, nothing but schoolroom misses." But she kissed him back, to West's delight.

"What was that for?"

"For not being rude to my family, although they deserved it."

Now that they were well away, West could be generous. "Oh, they were not so bad. After Mr. Littleton and Marcel—"

She pulled back. "What's wrong with Grandpapa and Marcel?"

"Nothing, nothing at all. I just meant, ah, I meant that after your grandfather refused to go, I was expecting far worse."

She seemed satisfied, and comfortable on his lap. "Oh. Well, I doubt you could ever be too rude for my stepmother, anyway. You are a viscount, after all."

"And you are a viscountess. My viscountess." He pulled her closer, in the dark carriage, and kissed her nearly breathless.

"What was that for?" she asked when he set her aside to straighten his clothing when the carriage slowed.

"Because I might have starved to death without your kisses."

"No, that is my father's miserly meal."

"No, that is lust for my beautiful wife."

"Lust, not liking?"

"Silly goose, both. A lot of both." He kissed her again, nearly senseless this time. Senseless enough that she said, "I like you, too."

Which meant he had to kiss her once more, nearly home. "I don't suppose . . . ?"

"Yes."

". . . that you would consider making your father a happy man, and me also, of course?"

"Yes."

"You know, by starting a family."

"Yes."

"Yes, truly?" He was nearly ready to ravish her in the carriage. "Now? Tonight?"

"Yes."

Not now, not the carriage, not outside his own house, not with the coachman waiting. No man ever had a woman out of a coach so fast and up the steps to his front door.

Parker was holding the door open, smiling. Penny's face was burning, that the butler knew what they'd been doing. Parker coughed and informed West that Mr. Littleton was abed, and neither Lady Bainbridge nor Master Nicholas had yet returned.

"Fine," West said, almost pushing Penny toward the arching stairs. Then he stopped. "Wait. I, uh, have something important to do. I will be back in an hour, sweetings. Less if I can manage."

Penny could not ask what was so important that he'd delay their lovemaking after seeming so ardent, not with Parker standing a few feet away. Her disappointment must have shown, for he asked, "Do you still have that sheer negligee?"

She looked back to see Parker pretending to polish the hall mirror with his sleeve, as if the proper butler would do such a thing. She nodded at West.

"Put it on, for me."

She would, if he came back. And if he swore he was not canceling a previous engagement with another woman.

West sensed her withdrawal. He raised her hand, tugged off her glove, and kissed her fingers, one after the other. "Trust me, wife." Then he kissed the inside of her wrist, and looked as if he'd work his way up her arm if she let him, with Parker still polishing nonexistent smudges.

"Hurry home," was all she said as she ran up the stairs.

"Oh, you can be sure I will," he called over his shoulder, before racing outdoors and giving directions to the coachman. "And spring 'em," he shouted as he jumped back into the carriage. "My bride is waiting."

Chapter Twenty-one

The match between Lord St. C. and his wife bore no children. He wanted an annulment. He wanted a divorce. He wanted her to accept one of his illegitimate sons as heir. Lady St. C. wanted a family, so she consulted a Gypsy fortune-teller. And a Gypsy lover.

—By Arrangement, *a chronicle of arranged marriages, by G. E. Felber*

A woman could change her mind a hundred times in an hour. She could suffer a hundred doubts and make a hundred decisions. Penny bathed. She lit all the candles. She put on the wisp of nothing and lace. She gasped and blew out the candles. Then she relit half of them, took off the sinful silk, and put on her flannel nightgown. She brushed her hair until it stood on end with electricity, like her nerves. Lie on the bed? Lock the door? Welcome him back? Wish him to perdition for leaving? Demand to know where he had gone? An hour was an eternity, waiting on a man.

Then she heard the carriage. She checked the clock. Forty-five minutes. Was that all? He must have rushed, whatever his business was, proving his hurry to get back to her. Penny tore off the virgin's vestment and donned the soiled dove's. She blew out all but one candle.

West's hands were so full, he could only kick at the door for her to open it.

"Who is there?"

She heard a muffled curse that brought a smile to her lips. "Who the devil do you think is at your—"

She had it open before he finished the sentence. He looked at her smile; then he looked at her near nakedness. He shoved a huge bouquet of flowers at her, enough to make a bower of her bedroom. Then he pushed a sack of scented candles and oils into her hand and started to dash for the connecting door to his room. "I need to shave again. Five minutes. Four."

Penny set down the flowers and the sack and grabbed his sleeve as he raced past. "You are fine." She reached one hand out to caress his cheek and jaw.

He took her hand and turned it so he could kiss her palm. "No, I am not fine." He was out of breath, and nearly out of his skin at her tender touch. The sight of her wearing that bit of silk and a smile of welcome stole his soul. He needed those four minutes to get ready, to get control, to make sure he did not embarrass himself or frighten his innocent bride.

"Three minutes."

"Don't go."

Ah, the sweetest words a man could hear. West couldn't leave now, not even if he still wanted to. His entire body was straining toward her, sure to disobey any command his mind might give. What mind? What matter?

He gave up and took her into his arms, took her lips, took his pleasure in feeling her pressed against his chest, his stomach, his thighs. "My God, you are so beautiful," he murmured, his hands on her soft posterior pulling her closer yet against his hard warrior. He whispered of wanting, between kisses that were of searing intensity, of tongues and teeth and throbbing music.

"Music?" Penny pulled out of his arms and stepped toward the window. She pulled back the draperies and looked down. Three Gypsy fiddlers looked up and waved between bars. Penny recalled her state of undress and hastily let the curtains fall.

"What are they doing there?"

West grinned. "Why, they are serenading you, of course. The singer will arrive as soon as he finishes his piece at Lady Bannamere's Gypsy masquerade ball. I managed to spirit these chaps away while they were on a break. I left her the orchestra, so you need not worry about her party."

"They are playing so loudly they are going to wake Grandpapa."

"I told them to." He went to the window and made clapping motions.

They played louder.

"They'll wake the whole neighborhood!"

"Ah, but there will be no bedroom noises to upset you."

She waved her hand at the musicians, the flowers, the candles he had lit. "You did all this for me?"

"Hell, no, woman," he said, both of them ripping at his clothes, then hers. "I did it for me."

But he did a lot for her, first. He showed her that rising rapture again, with his kisses and his hands and his knowing fingers that understood exactly where she was most sensitive. When she thought she could not stand any more, when her cries almost drowned out the musicians, then he gave her that shattering release. Finally, when her body was still pulsing, he rose on his arms over her, poised to take his own pleasure, and add to hers.

Except she was a virgin.

"This might hurt, sweetings. I am sorry."

Penny was sorry, too, to lose that afterglow of passion, that drifting, floating feeling of satiety and splendor. Fear took over, but she would not let him see it, or disappoint him again. "Do not worry. I'll just close my eyes and recite a hymn."

West gripped her chin and turned her face up. "No. Look at me, Penny. Think of me, of the feelings you just had, of how much I need you, of how much I want you to enjoy every minute of our lovemaking. You will, I swear, after this first time."

"Do you promise?"

He'd promise to hire the man in the moon to play the mandolin next time, if he could get through this time, and soon. "I promise."

He groaned when he felt the hot, moist tightness start to surround him. "Oh, Lord, I don't think I can stand this."

"I thought it was supposed to hurt me, not you."

"It is killing me, sweetings, inch by slow inch."

Now Penny did feel uncomfortably stretched. She squirmed, wanting the other feelings back, the soul-stealing, senses-stirring storm of pleasure, not this almost painful intrusion.

He groaned again. "Lud, don't do that, Penny, or I cannot hold back."

"But you were right, it hurts."

He groaned louder, glad of the musicians or he'd howl the household down, or up. "Do you want me to stop? I am sorry to cause you pain, but I will be sorrier if you tell me to stop. I'll shoot myself afterward, but I will stop, if I can." His arms and elbows were quivering, his breaths coming in gasps, his voice pleading.

For answer, Penny raised her hips to meet him, enfolding him, encompassing him, encouraging him—and enjoying him, especially when he reached a hand between them, touching her again, loving her, giving to her, not just taking.

Oh my. Penny sighed in happiness. West immediately rolled off her. She sighed again, this time feeling the loss of separation.

He kissed her and pulled her into his arms and apologized, all at once. "Thank you, my dear. Next time I'll do better."

If there was better than this, Penny thought she would expire from the experience. Dying would be worth it. "When?"

West pulled the sheet over his lower half when she looked down in curiosity at his now pathetic, puny, but deliriously happy privates. "You'll be sore tomorrow."

She shrugged, moving her breasts against him. "If I am already going to be sore, I might as well see what I have been missing." She raised the sheet again. "Or do men get sore, too, from making love?"

"More so from not making love."

Her forehead puckered in thought. "Shall I kiss it and make it better?"

She did, and he was a lot better, a lot faster than he thought possible.

"Where the hell did you learn that?"

Penny grinned. "You see the advantages of having a broad education and an eclectic library?"

"I see the advantage of having you as my wife." He was feathering kisses across her cheeks, her eyebrows, smoothing that line of concentration, then moving to her breasts, her belly, between her legs. "Lord, I might even thank your father."

She gasped, then said, "You must be grateful indeed."

"Let me show you how grateful." And he did. This time he could wait; she could respond; they could meet at the stars and float back to earth together. They never knew where one began, the other ended, or when the exhausted musicians took a break.

Tangled together, sharing breaths and heartbeats, they were about to fall asleep when Penny bit West on the shoulder, hard enough to leave a mark.

"Ow. What was that for?"

"For making me wait so long."

Lord and Lady Westfield were not to be disturbed . . . that night, the entire next day, and the night after. They were selecting furniture for their rooms, if anyone asked. What they were doing was testing out her bed, which was deemed comfortable, and his enormous mattress, which they decided suited the master bedroom quite well after all. They tried out the new bathing room, which was not as comfortable, not with water and bubbles and wet towels all over, so they made a more careful examination of the sheepskin rug in front of the fireplace. They carefully compared the chaise longue in her room with the leather armchair in the sitting room for sturdiness. Pieces of the chaise were shoved outside in the hall.

When the servants took the broken furniture away, they left food, wine, hot water, fresh towels, and coal for the fire in its place. Sometimes the viscount and his wife ate; sometimes they forgot all about food or drink. They certainly forgot about the rest of the world, including Penny's stepmother and her lists.

Lady Bainbridge felt she ought to receive the woman in Penny's stead, since she was supposed to be Penny's companion and chaperone, and since she would have to deal with the banker's wife and her daughters sooner or later. This was the best position she had had in years, a comfortable household and a good friend to guide through the social shoals. She would not let Penny down.

She accepted Lady Goldwaite's list of eligible gentlemen and quickly scanned it. She mentally crossed off the Duke of Cargell's son, for His Grace would never look so low for a bride for his heir. The Marquis of Brodhurst was too old, the Earl of Sedgewick too debauched.

When she pointed out these facts over tea, Lady Goldwaite bristled and demanded to see Penny. "She is the one who insisted the girls choose their own husbands. Well, they can choose from these men."

Lady Bainbridge tried to explain that Lady Westfield was occupied with getting her house in order, but she would be certain to show Penny the list.

"Redecorating, is she?" Lady Goldwaite was all for charging up the stairs to help rearrange the furniture.

"Oh, but his lordship is helping," Lady Bainbridge said, trying not to blush as red as Penny often did.

"Hmph. What does a man know about what is pleasing?"

Plenty, from the sounds of things, but Lady Bainbridge could never say that.

"No, Persephone needs a more experienced opinion."

"Oh, I am certain his lordship is experienced enough."

"Well, they cannot be at it all afternoon. We'll wait."

Since the pair had been at it all night, all morning, and through the luncheon hour, Lady Bainbridge was not certain how long the wait might be. "I am afraid they might have other plans."

"Nonsense. They knew I was coming. Send a servant to tell Persephone that I have arrived."

Lady Bainbridge choked on the watercress sandwich she was eating.

"Give over, Mama," the elder daughter said, "you are embarrassing Lady Bainbridge," which gained her a warmer place in that lady's heart until Mavis added, with a giggle, "They are most likely still in bed."

"What, in the afternoon? Whatever for?"

"Mama!" the younger wailed, twisting her hair into tangles.

Her mother glanced at Amelia, then snorted. "Never. Persephone has better manners. Not even harlots ply their trade in the daytime."

"But they are married."

"What has that to do with anything? One does one's duty in the dark. And this is not a suitable topic for young ladies," she told Lady Bainbridge, as if that superior female needed reminding of proper behavior. "Now send a servant for Persephone so we might discuss her ball. I thought a Viennese theme, with painted gondolas and flowing fountains. What do you think, Lady Bainbridge?"

Lady Bainbridge thought she was lucky to work for Penny, not this outrageous matron. She also thought she'd cut off her eyelashes before she interrupted Lord and Lady Westfield.

Mr. Cottsworth was easier company. He actually apologized for coming when Lady Bainbridge explained about the Westfields taking inventory of the house.

"I should have known better, but West and I did have an appointment at Manton's shooting gallery this morning."

"Then may I offer you tea? Coffee?"

He accepted, with time on his hands and a pleasant female issuing the invitation. She did not wince at his limp or turn away, but directed him to a comfortable chair.

She did not chatter, either, he was happy to see. Relaxed over tea, he smiled when she started to make more excuses for the absent hosts.

"Finally getting on with it, are they?" he asked with a soldier's bluntness.

She did not take offense, smiling back at the former officer, who had been married and widowed, like herself. They had met a time or two at various social functions, but seldom spoke before this. Now they had affection for the newlyweds in common, so she felt at ease enough to say, "With great enthusiasm, from what I hear from the servants."

"Everyone in London heard about the musicians that other night. Lady Bannamere was furious they left her party early. Were they as loud as the grapevine has it?"

"The grapevine would have withered under the noise. I am surprised the neighbors did not complain."

He laughed, a pleasant sound.

She did not mention the splintering furniture, the bathwater dripping through the ceilings, or the uneaten trays of food, but she did smile at the gentleman.

"I am happy for them."

"As am I."

They both seemed to be thinking of their own marriages, so silence fell. Cottsworth took that as a signal to leave. He used his cane to rise from the chair, sorry Lady Bainbridge had to see his clumsy motions, but knowing there was no help for it. "I suppose I shall be encountering you more now."

"Since you are Lord Westfield's good friend, I suppose so."

He bowed. "I would like that."

She curtsied, hoping he would not see the quick color flooding her middle-aged cheeks. Penny's affliction must be catching. "I look forward to it."

Chapter Twenty-two

Miss V. loved the man her parents chose for her. Unfortunately, he died before the wedding. She never recovered, never married, but had a wide circle of friends, a successful career as a portrait artist, the occasional lover. And a dog.

—By Arrangement, *a chronicle of arranged marriages, by G. E. Felber*

Penny was sore, but she was soaring. She hardly felt the stairs beneath her feet when she went down to breakfast. West had risen earlier and left quickly, before he changed his mind and never left at all, again. Penny had lain in bed, feeling absolutely decadent, watching a virile man get dressed while she stayed wrapped in nothing but contentment. He had an appointment with his bankers, he'd said, but promised to come back quickly to spend the day with her. They would spend it on errands outside the house, they agreed, to avoid the temptation of the enormous master bed. Of course, they had never yet made love in a carriage, which sounded eminently tempting to Penny. She thought West's lovemaking was far more important than a fashionable wardrobe or a new carpet, but he laughed at her newfound appetite, and promised her tonight.

She kissed Lady Bainbridge's cheek before filling her plate at the sideboard, then kissed her grandfather's seamed cheek. She even bent and kissed George's wrinkled forehead. She had never been so happy in her life. Why, everyone should know such connubial joy. Maybe not Grandpapa, but definitely Lady Bainbridge. Penny did not even notice the grins on her companions' faces as she sat, moonstruck and marveling at her good fortune.

West had not said he loved her. Not yet. But he'd shown it in so many caring ways, far beyond the music and the flowers. His gentleness betokened affection; his words spoke of adoration. His knowing when gentle and slow were not enough indicated to Penny that two minds were working as one, not simply two bodies finding mutual pleasure. Surely they shared more than mere lust.

Penny regretted the wasted years, yes, but now she could enjoy West and his magic to the fullest as a woman, not as a young girl. She intended to do just that. He'd say the words soon. Then she could say them back and her joy would be complete.

Lady Bainbridge cleared her throat. "I thought you did not care for kippers in the morning, my dear."

Penny looked down at her plate. She hated kippers. "I am trying new things these days."

Mr. Littleton coughed at the understatement.

"Oh, are you still plagued by that nagging cough, Grandpapa? Should you be out and about?"

"I am fine. Do not be a nag, Penny. I have calls to make." He stood and bowed to Lady Bainbridge, then let the butler help him out of the room.

"Yes, well, it is a lovely day for that," Penny called after him. "Enjoy yourself."

Lady Bainbridge looked out the window. The day was cloudy and overcast, threatening rain. Of course, Mr. Littleton might not be able to notice. She trusted his man to see that the elderly painter had a muffler and an umbrella.

When he was gone and Penny was daydreaming over her breakfast again, Lady Bainbridge said, "Your stepmother delivered her list of prospective bridegrooms."

Penny smiled. "You know, the more I think on it, the more I feel Mavis and Amelia will be better off wed than living under their mother's thumb."

"I thought you believed they should wait."

"Now I am not so averse to marriage. To the right man, of course."

"That's as may be, but I fear none of the bachelors your stepmother has in mind are right for the Misses Entwhistle. Nor will the highly placed gentlemen she named glance at her daughters, who I regret to say have neither beauty nor breeding, and only respectable dowries."

"Oh, dear. Perhaps West will have some ideas of other bachelors, gentlemen who are looking for soul mates, not merely showpieces or shillings. Nicky might know of likely prospects, being more of an age with the girls. Where is Nicky, anyway?"

Mr. Parker bowed as he removed the offending, un-eaten kippers from in front of Penny and replaced them with sweet rolls and butter. "Master Nicholas seldom takes breakfast. We usually see him after noon, before he begins his daily rounds."

"He stays out all night, in other words?"

"In those precise words, yes."

Penny could not approve of such dissolute living. "He might need a wife, too."

Lady Bainbridge laughed. "From what I gather, the

young man is far from ready to settle down. Until he is, he would make some poor girl's life a misery."

Parker silently agreed, nodding as he poured Penny a cup of chocolate.

As soon as the butler left, Lady Bainbridge laughed again. "Look at you, Penny, wed less than a month and already matchmaking. Marriage agrees with you."

"It does. I want everyone else to be as happy."

Penny looked at Lady Bainbridge with such a speculative gleam that the older woman quickly redirected Penny's thoughts. "Your stepmother also reminded me that we need to set a date for your ball, and begin to assemble your wardrobe. Lady Aldershott's rout is this Friday, so we have few days to accomplish much. You need to make a grand appearance, according to Lady Goldwaite, so no one refuses your invitations when they are sent."

"Can we not simply hold card parties or quiet dinners? Amelia would be more comfortable, and both of the girls can become better acquainted with any suitors, far more easily than during a contra dance in a crowded ballroom."

"One would think so, but that is not how it is done, my dear. Whom you know is almost as important as how much dowry you bring. Connections are part of the game society plays. If the girls wish to marry well"—she did not say above their station, in deference to Penny, who did that very thing—"then they have to be sponsored by a popular hostess, not a retiring, quiet female who sits with her knitting."

Penny was thinking of sitting with West, of having him to herself.

Lady Bainbridge was not done with her lecture. That was her job, after all. "Further, you shall be invited everywhere once it is seen that you are accepting invitations. You will be expected to reciprocate. If you hold one ball, in a month's time, say, that will be enough for the Season. Of course, you can still hold small gatherings, especially if the Entwhistle girls wish to encourage a particular acquaintance in more private surroundings, but a viscountess in London is not the same as a squire's wife in the country. And your wardrobe must reflect your husband's standing. And your father's wealth, so mothers with eligible sons will know the family is well provided for."

"Which reminds me, I shall have to find out precisely how generous Father is being with the girls."

"The more generous the better, or our work is cut out for us to make them acceptable. I have already spoken to your estimable cook about complexion potions for the older girl, mashed strawberries and the like. I do not yet have a plan for the younger."

"She likes poetry. And sheep."

"Ah, how much easier to find her a beau in that case." Sarcasm dripped like the raindrops that were starting to gather on the window. "And one acceptable to her dear mother, at that. We have our work cut out for us, my dear."

"Not today. Today West is taking me sightseeing about London."

"What about your clothes?"

Penny chuckled. "Oh, I shall wear some."

Poor Lady Bainbridge. The coming Season was going to be even harder than she'd imagined.

On Lady Bainbridge's insistence, West took Penny to a fashionable dressmaker first.

"But no man likes to shop for gowns and such."

"Oh, West has had plenty of experience at modistes'," Nicky volunteered as he shuffled down the stairs, "or paying their bills, at any rate."

His brother suddenly took offense at Nicky's neck-cloth, or the drooping bow that passed for one. He grabbed Nicky by the limp linen and pulled it tighter. "There, now you might be fit for company."

Nicky couldn't speak, which was what West had in mind.

"Do not let his foolishness bother you, sweetings," he told Penny as he led her out to the waiting carriage. "The past is past. The future is now."

Penny could not help thinking of her husband's expertise in other areas. She could not regret his skill between the sheets, so she tried not to mind his mistresses. His former mistresses.

Nicky was right, though, that West was welcome at the most exclusive dressmaking establishments. Madame Journet greeted him with kisses on both cheeks. When she found that she was to dress the viscountess for her first entrance into society in nearly a decade, with less than a week to do it, she started to shake her head. *"Non, c'est impossible."*

Ah, but Lady Westfield was needing an entire wardrobe for the Season? The Entwhistle misses needed new gowns also, at Sir Gaspar Goldwaite's expense? Ah, anything was possible. She kissed Penny on both cheeks; then she set to work.

West was not overbearing in his opinions, as Penny had feared, but he did know what was stylish. On the other hand, he did not want any other man to see his wife at her barest—at her best, he amended. Penny had not unpacked the dress lengths from the attics, so they selected a blue lutestring that matched her eyes, with gold trim that matched her hair. He wanted pink flowers embroidered on it, too, to match Penny's blushes, but Madame insisted there was not enough time. They settled on a cluster of silk rosebuds at the vee of her décolletage, which was lower than Penny was used to, lower than West, the former rake, approved, and higher than Madame thought fitting.

"Lady Westfield has the bosom to flaunt, no?"

"No!" Penny and West both shouted. They went on to pick several styles from the fashion plates the modiste recommended, for the fabrics Penny already owned.

The choosing and fitting done, West took Penny to the Emporium for new gloves, stockings, and shifts, although she made him wait outside when she selected a new corset.

Then they were free to drive around London, with West pointing out other shops she would want to patronize, milliners, booteries, furniture showrooms, and upholsterers. They toured the British Museum, looking for her grandfather, then stopped at a coffeehouse for a late luncheon. They walked through Hyde Park, despite the slight drizzle that still fell, so Penny would not grow homesick for the country. Few others were out and about, so West could pull Penny behind a tree, a hedge, or a carriage for a quick kiss and cuddle.

They cut the sightseeing short.

That night they attended the opera. West had a box, and they filled it with Lady Bainbridge and Michael Cottsworth, Mr. Littleton, and Marcel in footman's garb. Nicky paled at the idea of the opera, and Penny's family was, happily, committed to a dinner party at a banking associate's home.

West was magnificent in formal white satin knee breeches and dark coat, with a black pearl in his cravat and the garnet ring on his finger. Penny would have felt insignificant next to him in her best country gown, despite its hasty repairs, except for the ruby pendant at her throat—and the admiration in his eyes. She sat toward the back of the box anyway, avoiding the opera glasses trained on Westfield and his new bride. In the dark, no one could see that his arm was around her shoulder, that his hand held hers, that his lips brushed the tip of her ear when he pointed out this notable, that member of the cabinet.

At intermission, Lady Bainbridge introduced the new viscountess to her former patron, a few boxes over. The duchess was so pleased at the match her granddaughter had made with Lady Bainbridge's help that she invited Penny to the wedding, and to tea on next Tuesday.

Michael Cottsworth could not go with West to fetch refreshments, but he could stand guard at the entrance of the box, fending off West's more rakish friends who begged an introduction, or a better glimpse of the female who had caught their comrade in parson's mousetrap. Since half of them were foxed, and the other half unfit for polite company, the former officer felt no compunction about denying them access to Lady Westfield, or Lady Bainbridge for that matter. Why subject such a delightful, refined female to those crude chaps?

So Penny was not bothered by the crowds or the curiosity. West came back and said he missed her, and they left before the end of the final act.

In the following days, Penny did select new rugs and wall hangings, and scores more gowns. She unpacked her mother's china, her crates of books, her rolls of dress fabrics. She hired more maids, approved livery for the footmen, and went on morning calls with Lady Bainbridge, while West was busy with his parliamentary responsibilities and his investments. They drove in the park at the promenade hour, and they visited Astley's Amphitheatre, the Royal Menagerie at the Tower, and three cathedrals.

Nights, however, they spent in each other's arms.

All too soon the date of Lady Aldershott's rout arrived. Penny knew that after that, she would have to be on public view, making the social rounds, performing like the perfect peeress she never wanted to be. She was West's wife, so she had no choice, not without embarrassing him and putting paid to her stepmother's hopes of a higher-ranking hunting ground for her daughters.

Penny's gown was ready. Lady Bainbridge made sure her manners were polished. West made sure the Westmoreland tiara was, too.

"You look like a princess," he whispered in her ear as they stood at the head of the stairs, waiting for the majordomo to announce them to the hordes waiting below, every eye fixed on the elusive Lady Westfield. "Not one of the run-of-the-mill princesses, either," he teased, "but a princess of fairyland, who will enchant every person she smiles at, the way she has enthralled this poor mortal."

Penny basked in the magic dust of his love, even if he had still never said the words. She remembered all Lady Bainbridge's lessons, impressing the dowagers. Her style, her smile, her intelligence—and most of all the reformed rake's obvious devotion—impressed everyone else. A woman who could win over Westfield had to be a true Diamond. And the diamonds in her tiara were nothing to scoff at, either. Fund-raising females wanted her on their committees; young ladies wanted to be her friend; gentlemen wanted to be her lover.

West wanted to skewer all of them, but Penny was a success. Invitations would inundate Westmoreland House. Her own invitations would be accepted with pleasure. Her stepsisters could meet more than bankers' sons and mill owners' heirs. And she would make her husband proud.

Until he left.

Chapter Twenty-three

Lord F. wed the woman his family chose for him, to beget the family's heir. Lord F. took a mistress. His wife took the son to Russia. Heir today, gone tomorrow.

—By Arrangement, *a chronicle of arranged marriages, by G. E. Felber*

"What do you mean, you are leaving?"

Penny lay all cozy and rosy in bed, barely awake. She had actually enjoyed herself at Lady Aldershott's rout, after the initial trepidation. She'd enjoyed herself better, afterward, here in West's bed. His morning kiss, she thought, was an invitation to more of the delicious same. She was wrong.

West was already up and dressed. He looked like a maiden's fondest daydream in tight fawn breeches, shiny high-top boots, and a brown coat that stretched across broad shoulders. His cheeks were smooth from an early shave, and his dark hair was neatly combed. No maiden, Penny was disappointed. Then she noticed he held a cup of coffee in one hand, a letter in the other.

He shoved the written page into his inside pocket. "There has been a fire at Westfield."

"Oh, I am sorry." Penny knew how much his ancestral home meant to West as part of his heritage, his to hold for the next generations to come. "Can the house be repaired?"

"The house is fine. The fire was in one of the outbuildings, near the stables."

That was worse. Now Penny understood the grim look on his face. A building was brick and mortar, but horses and grooms were live beings. "How horrible. Was anyone injured?"

"Slightly, I gather."

"And the horses?" Penny knew his breeding stock meant everything to West, and she never wished an animal hurt, herself.

"My steward sent the letter immediately, before the fire's harm was fully assessed. He was right to inform me as soon as he could. I have to go."

"Wouldn't it be better to wait for his word of actual damage? Perhaps he will find that all is well, once the smoke clears. Then you would have made the journey for nothing." She reached out her hand to him, and he sat beside her on the bed and offered her a sip from his coffee cup. She pushed it away, preferring chocolate in the morning. The very fact that he'd forgotten her preferences showed his distraction. "You cannot know yet."

"He writes of loss. And waiting for my decisions." He set the cup down on the bedside table and got up to pace, obviously impatient to be gone.

Penny pulled the bedclothes up, against the chill in the room. West usually kept her warm in the mornings until someone relit the fire. She frowned. "But we accepted scores of invitations for this week."

"I know, but there is no help for it."

"Very well. Give me an hour, and I shall be ready to go. Lady Bainbridge can make our excuses, and the hostesses shall simply have to understand about emergencies. Lady Bainbridge can spend the time schooling my stepsisters anyway. Lud knows they need it. How long do you think we shall be away?"

West shook his head. "I have no idea how long *I* shall be gone. You cannot come, sweetings. I intend to ride straight through, changing horses wherever I can, riding cross-country to save time. The trip usually takes two or three days, but I hope to make it in far less, sleeping in hedgerows or hostelries along the way. I am taking only what I can carry in my saddlebags."

"That is not safe. There are highwaymen and bands of renegade soldiers on the roads."

"My pistols are already packed."

"No, no, that is absurd. You are a viscount, not a soldier on command. You have to take the carriage and your valet. And your wife."

He brushed a hand across her cheek, then went back to pacing, as if the touch of her could interfere with his intentions. "I am sorry, Penny. I cannot wait, or spend the time a coach needs on toll roads with posting houses. Besides, remember all those invites. Some of those old dragons do not care about anything but filling their ballrooms to overflowing. They will think you are unmannerly, crying off at the last minute."

"Who cares what some fusty old crones think? I cannot go without you, anyway."

"You must. They will cross you off their lists if you are in Town and not on your deathbed. I'll ask Nicky to escort you."

"Nicky? He would not know his way around a ballroom unless it was filled with card tables or highfliers."

"Michael Cottsworth, then. He is a good man, as solid as a rock. He cannot dance, but you will not lack for partners, not if you dress as you did last night. The hostesses will be delighted to have you. You will carve your place in the *ton*, which was what you wanted, so your own parties will be filled."

"No, that is my stepmother's dream." Thoughts of Constance reminded her of that woman's ultimate goal. "Good grief, West, we are to hold a ball in less than three weeks."

"Which is another reason why you have to stay in London, to make the preparations and to school the brats—Mavis and Amelia, that is—for their appearances. You'll be so busy with fittings and furniture designers and dance instructors, menus, and musicians that you will hardly notice my absence."

She missed him when he was out of the room. How was she supposed to manage without him for days? "I cannot hold a ball without a host!"

"Which is why I am in such a hurry, so I can return in time. Furthermore, you are the hostess. You can do anything, with your lists in hand and Lady Bainbridge to help. The Parkers can be trusted, and your grandfather's cook will be *aux anges* to cook for such elevated company." He brushed a kiss across her forehead, set to leave. "I have confidence in you."

She held on to his hand. "No, I need you here. You said you would be at my side in entering your social circles. You know I do not belong there, not without you."

He pulled his hand back and through his hair, disordering the careful arrangement. "I know what I said, Penny, and I intended to be here, but I never foresaw a fire. And you do belong among the haut monde, now that you wear my ring and my name. You have seen how the *ton* took you to its bosom. Lady Bainbridge was speaking of vouchers for Almack's. Some women have to wait for years before attaining that lofty pinnacle of acceptance."

"I do not give a rap about Almack's or acceptance or your blasted aristocracy. You know that. I am a banker's daughter and an artist's granddaughter."

"And a viscountess, an heiress, and a beautiful woman. Please understand, Penny, I have to leave."

"But you have competent managers. You said so yourself, when you said we would live in London much of the year."

"I fully intended to make frequent visits to Westfield, once you were comfortable here in Town."

"And leave me alone?"

"Perhaps I thought that at first, but no longer. I want to show you the breeding farm, the old house, introduce you to the neighbors. But not now, not like this."

"Then wait. Let your employees handle whatever needs to be done now and we can go together, after the ball."

He shook his head. "My steward and trainers and head grooms cannot make decisions. They cannot allot moneys or bargain with nearby landowners for feed or grazing if my stores and acres are ruined. And I need to see to the horses myself. They are terrorized by smoke, you know. Some could have been injured in the panic to get them away, injuries that could take days to discover in all the confusion. Others breathed in smoke, with who knows what results."

"The horses? You are going to Westfield on the horses' welfare and abandoning me here?" She was terrified he wouldn't come back. The fear made her furious.

He pounded the mantel with his fist. "Dash it, Penny, be reasonable. I am not abandoning you. I am looking after my business."

"You do not need a business. You are a lord, a lofty member of your idle arrogant class that looks down their collective noses at people who actually work for a living."

"I am not one of them. I have earned my money."

"Yes, by wedding a wealthy wife. I shall write you a check from my personal account. You can send it to Westfield and be done."

He stared at her as if his lovely butterfly had turned back into a creeping caterpillar. He raised his chin, as angry as she was. "Then I would be a fortune hunter, in fact, wouldn't I?"

"No, you would be a good businessman like my father."

"What if I do not wish to be like your father?"

Penny could not let the insult pass, not when he was deserting her. "You would let your plaguesome gentleman's pride keep you from taking the funds you need for rebuilding?"

"This is not about money or pride or position. This is about my life, what I chose to do with it."

"The horses," she said in flat tones, turning her head away from the sight of him.

"Yes. Can you understand?"

"I understand you are going, with no care for my wishes, my needs."

"I have needs, too. Haven't I proved my need for you? Do you really think I want to dash across England when I could be here, in our bed?"

"Yet you are going, because of the horses."

"Now you are sounding like a spoiled child. Like your stepsisters, whining to get some treat or trinket."

He would compare her to Mavis and Amelia? Penny had to stop herself from childishly throwing the pillow at his handsome, haughty head. "Why, because I want my husband with me, as agreed, at this trying time?"

"Should I be flattered?" He sounded anything but. "You do not want me—you want to have your way. You have a house, jewels, friends, a title, the nod of society—yet you cannot give me two weeks?"

"Two weeks? I gave you thirteen years. Thirteen years, sir. Yet you will not change your ways, despite our agreement that marriage is a compromise."

"Aha! I was waiting for those blasted thirteen years to arise. Time and money, that is all you think of. And yourself."

She balled her hands into fists. "I am not self-centered and spoiled. I am not."

"I suppose you are going to tell me you are not a managing female, either."

That gave her pause. She had always been called a managing woman, usually as praise for running the orphanage, keeping her grandfather's house in order, organizing the Ladies' Guild. She sniffed. "Perhaps I am. There is nothing wrong with being efficient."

He held out a metaphoric olive branch. "Nothing at all. That is why I know you can stand up to the beau monde and plan the ball on your own."

Of course she could. That was no reason to shout like a fishwife, or cling like a limpet. No man wanted a nag, or a wife who lived in his pocket. "Very well, I shall stop acting like a harridan, berating you for doing what you think is right."

He grinned, flashing the dimple she adored. "At least you did not punch me."

"Is that why you are keeping your distance?"

"No, I am staying on the other side of the room so I do not crawl into bed with you, and to hell with the rest of the world." But he did sit beside her, gathering her into his arms for a farewell kiss.

"I do not want you to go," she said when he released her.

"I know."

"I do not want to face your friends and all those stiff-rumped strangers without you."

"I know, and I wish I could be here. But what happened to the self-sufficient, confident Amazon from Little Falls? She could conquer the world on her own."

"You invited over two hundred aristocrats to our ball, that's what happened. My father wants the Entwhistle girls out of his house, that's what. I did not pick those battles to fight, on unfamiliar terrain."

"Life is like that. I did not ask for a fire, or for my brother's title for that matter. But now you have total control over the party, to put your own seal on it."

"I'll cancel the ball, that's what I'll do."

"No. We would only have to do it later. The girls will be older, your stepmother more strident. Do it, Penny. Make it special."

"Very well, in exchange for coming in second to your horses, I will turn your house into a sultan's odalisque, with silk tents and hookahs and dancing harem girls. You will be mortified."

"Will you wear jewels in your navel?"

"And veils, nothing but veils. I shall give your polite society something to speak about besides the weather for a change. And . . . and I will dance." She stood up on the bed, letting the sheets fall away, and improvised what she thought an exotic belly dance might look like.

The horses could wait another hour.

Chapter Twenty-four

In an epic misalliance, Lord Q. married his mistress.
His parents cut him off. She cut off his . . .

—By Arrangement, *a chronicle of*
arranged marriages, by G. E. Felber

Ticktock. Ticktock. The house was so quiet, Penny could hear the clock on the sitting room mantel. West must have built up the fire, then told the servants not to disturb her, because not even the sound of scurrying in the hall reached her ears, not once his footsteps receded down the hall, down the stairs, out the door.

He was gone. Worse, he'd left while she was still bemused by his lovemaking, before she could explain.

He did not understand why she'd acted the termagant, why she'd almost begged him not to leave. West thought she feared the *ton,* like some foolish chit fresh out of the schoolroom, making her curtsies for the first time. Hah. She'd seen what a pack of snobbish sheep they were ages ago, when she'd first come to London. Then she'd been the fiancée of a second-son soldier, accepted in the outer circles of society only because of Lady Bainbridge and her father's fortune. Now she was a viscountess, welcomed with open arms as if she had become more interesting, more attractive, more one of the inner echelons. And she could not care less. Anyone who would not accept her for being a banker's daughter then was not worth knowing now.

She'd accomplished much in the short time they were in Town. She'd seen that West was proud of her and that women in London could be friends, both of which pleased her. She had not had a female friend of her own age in a long time, and welcomed invitations to charitable committees so she could continue her rewarding and worthwhile efforts. As for West, she had not wanted to shame him, and she had succeeded beyond her own expectations. No, she did not fear being a pariah in Polite Society. If no one spoke to her, she could go live at Westfield with her husband, raising her family, if he wanted her there. That way, even if he returned to London on occasion, she'd see him, be part of his life. He would never leave his horses for long.

He left, believing her a coward and believing she wanted to control his life with her money, her demands. He was wrong about that, too. She'd offered him her personal fortune, the one she had tied up in trust so tightly he could not have it without her say-so, because she wanted to make his life easier. Not to own him or dictate its use or make him feel like a supplicant. What was hers was his, once she'd given her heart and her body and her very soul, whether he knew that or not.

She thought about his angry accusations. She wasn't afraid. She wasn't wanting her own way in everything. She wasn't a shrew, at least she hoped not. What she was, was jealous, plain and simple, and she could never confess that to him. She was mortified to admit to that basest, most corrosive of emotions, even to herself.

There it was, though, as green as the ugly fern with hairy roots like spider legs that her stepmother used as a centerpiece.

Penny pulled the covers over her chin, staring at the ceiling. How could she be jealous of a husband she never wanted to like, much less love, and not for the usual reasons, either? His previous women rankled, but they were in the past and Penny was in his bed. He seemed more than satisfied to have her there. But his horses . . . ah, she could never hope to compete with his horses. He loved them better than he would ever love her.

Clip-clop. Clip-clop. West held his latest hired horse to the fastest speed he could, pacing the gelding for the next posting house where he could change mounts. With few travelers on this stretch of the road, his mind kept repeating their argument. He tried to reconcile his needs with her needs, while his thoughts beat in tune to the steady rhythm of the hoofbeats. His need, her need, her knees. They had a little dimple and smooth skin, with a tiny scar from a childhood fall. The backs of her knees were particularly sensitive to his tongue. He'd memorized every inch of her, and the memory was driving him crazy. Damn, he needed to be his own man, not ache with needing her.

She did not understand, and he'd left without so much as trying to change her stubborn, thick-skulled sense of righteousness. Quite simply, a man had to be in charge or he was no man. Why, after a mere two nights of love-making, his innocent bride liked to be on top!

He had to smile, despite the road dust getting in his mouth. His wife was a strong-willed woman, and West told himself he admired that, but damn, he could not give up all he had worked for. He'd be nobody, nobody he respected, anyway, if he let her and her money rule his life. He might as well be her kept man, her hired escort, her underling in every sense of the word.

When his father and brother died, leaving him with debts, West had worked and fought and schemed to make something of Westfield, of himself. He'd given up soldiering, where he was respected and rising in command, to be a better viscount than his predecessors, to take better care of his people and the land they all called home. He could not give up the ground he'd gained. Besides, Penny had no respect for the idle aristocracy. So why, knowing he was working, earning his own living, was she upset when he honored his commitments, nurtured his investments, cared for the living creatures who depended on him, the same as her family depended on her?

His horse pounded down the road, while his thoughts pounded in his head. The mount was fresh, good until the next inn. His thoughts were not, his mood growing blacker and bleaker with every mile.

Penny would do fine in London society without him, whatever her fears. Her money and his title could sway all but the highest sticklers, but even those dragons would be won over by Penny's own personality and inner decency. She'd quickly learn that she did not require him at her side night and day. He told himself that was good, that he was glad, but, gads, what if she did not want him back?

She could insist on separate quarters, separate lives. With his title, he could not afford a scandal. With her money, she could afford as many houses as she wanted, without him in them. Damn.

At least he was certain she liked his lovemaking. No polite endurance for his Penny, no pretending, oh, no. Her enthusiasm for the sport was a surprise and a delight, but was that enough to keep her at his side? She never forgot the circumstances of their marriage, that he'd had to be forced into it, after years of avoidance and abandoning her. Jupiter, he half expected her to cry out "thirteen years" instead of "there, touch me there."

Well, he had every right to be equally as angry. He'd been traded away for his connections, hadn't he? His older brother was expected to make the dynastic match, the grand union of two titled, propertied families. West had been the second son, meant to bring money back to the family coffers. If he'd had the choice, he'd have stayed a soldier, stayed a bachelor, stayed in the country with his horses. Now all he wanted to do was stay close to Penny. Damn, again.

Tick. He did not understand. *Tock.* Maybe he would if she told him she loved him, but a woman couldn't be the first to say the words. West had to know she adored him, because she wanted him so badly, every second. But what if he was so irritated by her carping, he never came back? What if sex and the marriage vows he'd never wanted were the only things binding him to her?

Penny knew West could find another woman, a different one for each night of the week if he wished. She'd seen how females from seventeen to seventy looked at him with hunger in their eyes. She could feel it burning in hers every time he entered a room.

Besides, he'd only say that love and lovemaking were two separate things, although Penny could not imagine wanting any other man but West. Men were different, and dense.

Beyond sex, West had enough funds now that he did not have to return her dowry or pay for repairs to his house. He might even have his heir on the way. It was too soon to tell, but not for lack of trying. He did not need her for anything else. To welcome guests? To pick wallpaper? Select menus? His butler and housekeeper could do the jobs, and better than Penny, most likely. He'd never seen the need for a hostess before. What if he decided he did not need one now, especially a clinging, distempered crone? He could decide to stay in the country with his stables.

She was a fool. Penny bit her lip, remembering their argument. He'd have gone no matter what she said, and she knew that. If her love wasn't enough to keep him, nothing was. She wondered now whether her love was enough to bring him back.

She clenched the sheets in her hands, worrying that she'd given him a disgust of her. Then she dropped the sheets, reminded of poor Penelope weaving her cloth for Odysseus. That seemed to be the cursed role fate had dealt Penny, waiting for West, but she did not have half of Penelope's patience, no matter how close their names or their long waits. Weave an endless winding-sheet like a faithful little wife? Penny would wind his innards into India ink, as soon as she held him in her arms for infinity.

Clip. She did not understand. *Clop.* He ought to be shot for not telling her, but a man couldn't be the one to say the words first, and not during sex for the first time. She'd think that was only his prick talking.

So he'd swallowed the ache and promised to return. His last words were a plea that she trust him. Why should she? He'd said he'd be at her elbow during the coming social season, and here he was, in the saddle. He'd sworn to honor his marriage vows, but his betrothal behavior spoke against him. Knowing Penny, she'd worry that he was going to tup every barmaid between London and Land's End. She'd fret he was gone forever, if she cared at all.

Damn, he should have told her he couldn't want another woman, not with her image so indelible in his mind, dimpled knee to pointed chin, funny pink toes to tousled gold curls, and every soft, silky inch between. He hadn't known for himself, hadn't comprehended the contentment, the pleasure, of having one woman, his woman. The idea that she might be carrying his babe was a joy like none in his life. The notion was more exciting than three mares foaling perfectly at once, more thrilling than one of his horses winning the steeplechase. Not that Penny would like the comparisons. She was not fond of horses, it appeared. Still, she seemed to enjoy the bliss of trying to make a baby well enough, well enough that he'd delayed leaving for an hour, which meant he'd be an hour later returning from what he had to do.

He should have told her he'd hurry, because he wanted only to come back to her arms. Promises and sweet words were easy to say, though, especially during sex, but only time would prove them. How long did trust take to build? Lud, he hoped faster than rebuilding a stable and paddocks. The poets said love could come suddenly or grow gradually, but that tender emotion was not enough. Without trust and respect, West believed, love would shrivel and die.

He urged the horse faster. He had no way to prove his honor, not when he was miles away. Penny did not understand that a man's word was his bond. Women seldom did.

Tick. He left talking about trust, the dastard, not of love. What, did he think she would raise her skirts for the next rake she met? One was enough, she swore, for any woman. Furthermore, just because she'd succumbed to his practiced charms did not mean she was vulnerable to any passing fancy. She was a virtuous woman, by all that was holy, and he should have known that. He would have trusted her if he loved her. No one could have one without the other.

The gudgeon did trust her to ready his house, despite her threats to turn it into a seraglio, for all that was worth. She would live in his stupid stable to be with him. He did not understand. Men seldom did.

Clop. He'd be thinking of her every second, building their future, while she was picking linens and lace.

Sigh. He did not understand.
Sigh. She did not understand.
More than miles separated them.

Chapter Twenty-five

Young Lord A.'s parents actually gave him the choice of three women to be his bride. One was more beautiful, one was more wealthy, one was more good-natured. He chose the one with the biggest breasts.

—By Arrangement, *a chronicle of arranged marriages, by G. E. Felber*

West *was* coming back. He had to be. If Penny truly believed he wasn't, she'd pack up all her belongings, her grandfather, and his dog, move back to Little Falls, and send Sir Gaspar and his second family to Satan. No, if she believed West really had left her, Penny decided, she'd ride after him, a pistol in one hand, a butcher knife in the other, and homicide in her heart.

Since he *was* going to return, Penny was going to be a good wife. She might have been a bothersome bride, but she was determined to be a perfect partner in the marriage. To that end, she spent a great deal of time spending a great deal of her father's money.

Her clothes came first. West liked her in pretty colors, in revealing gowns, as fashionable as other peers' wives. She took the unpacked yard goods to Madame

Journet, who agreed the rainbow shot silk was perfect for Penny's first ball as hostess. She also agreed that the Entwhistle misses had to wear white, but she appeased them all with rosebud embroidery on Amelia's gown, and extra flounces on Mavis's. Since the charges were going on Penny's account, and since she could not step a foot inside Madame Journet's exclusive establishment without Persephone, Lady Goldwaite could not argue. In fact, she decided to have a nap instead of going along for the boring fittings where no one listened to her opinion anyway.

While Penny had the girls in tow, without their mother, she took them to the lending library, where Amelia was in heaven, and Mavis flirted with the clerk. She also took them on a few of the morning calls to Lady Bainbridge's friends and other ladies who had extended invitations, especially those with young daughters or sisters or cousins being presented this Season. Let her stepsisters see how proper females behaved, Penny planned, only to watch the other misses their ages act just as foolishly, some with the same giggles, some with the same shyness, some with less intelligence than an insect.

Lady Bainbridge assured Penny that she had never been so silly, thank goodness.

She was silly enough, however, to suffer stunned stupidity and outright jealousy when one of the other guests happened to be a tall, voluptuous beauty dressed all in green from the feathers in her red hair to the tips of her green-dyed slippers. Colorful indeed. Penny knew the woman's identity well before Lady Bainbridge tried to hustle her away, well before the embarrassed hostess had to introduce West's wife to Lady Greenlea, his former mistress. Somehow Penny made the polite responses, while repeating to herself: "Former mistress. Former." Well, she decided, she had every right to be furious. Here she was, enduring the sly smirk of a known seductress, while West, the cad, was playing at gentleman horse breeder.

Next on Penny's list of priorities was the house; she took her anger out there.

She deserved an orderly, tastefully decorated residence, comfortable but with the elegance her new position commanded.

She hired maids and footmen to clean the town house from top to bottom, throwing out all the useless trash, Constance's castoffs, and undesirable accumulations, like her brother-in-law.

Penny and Lady Bainbridge returned from a shopping excursion that afternoon under a mountain of parcels. Lady Bainbridge made her way up the stairs to direct the burdened footmen, while Penny carried the extra invitations from the print shop toward the library, where she kept her lists of acceptances to the ball and the few refusals. Before she reached the library, however, she heard a crash.

The butler was assigning the grooms to unload the carriage, and the footmen were busy, so Penny traced the sound herself, aided by raucous laughter, applause, and shattering glass.

She hadn't touched the billiard room yet, except to see it dusted and the floor polished. Now, still angry over West's past, no matter how irrational she knew such emotion to be, she decided to sweep the dark, gloomy room clean. "Out!" she shouted at Nicky and his friends, who were lolling in chairs, draped over the green baize table, leaning against the walls. They were swaying on their feet, swearing, singing bawdy tunes, and behaving like the naughty little boys they were too old to be.

Worse, they were swilling her grandfather's finest brandy. She recognized the bottles she'd packed so carefully. "How could you?" she demanded, grabbing the bottle from the inebriated lout who was trying to pour from it into crystal glasses most likely older than he was.

"Best I've had in a dog's years," the dolt replied with a foolish grin.

Speaking of dogs, George was lapping brandy off the floor ... which was littered with plates of food, articles of clothing, betting receipts, racing forms—and a silk stocking. Penny picked Nicky out of the cluster of clunches and pointed at him. Lightning should have bolted from her fingertip; she was that angry. "How dare you treat your brother's house like a ... a ..."

"Gentlemen's club?" one of the young men in his shirtsleeves offered helpfully. "Though they ain't as much fun."

Penny glared at him until he reached for his coat and neckcloth.

Nicky stepped forward, over a broken plate. "M'-brother said I was to stick close to home."

"To be the man of the house, not the town drunk."

"Here, now," Nicky told her, "I'm not castaway, just a trifle on the go."

"Then go. And take all your disreputable friends. I will not have such goings-on in my house, no matter what your brother might have put up with in the past."

Nicky laughed. "Put up with? West was the worst of the lot."

Two of his friends chuckled nervously, looking from Penny to Nicky, wondering if they should bolt for the door or defend their mate.

Another nodded and waved a cue stick. "Good old West would be right here, only he'd be winning."

"Well, he is not here now, and this is the establishment of a gentleman and his lady. If you do not respect him, then you shall respect me." She grabbed the cue stick from his limp fingers and snapped it across her knee.

The billiard player gulped and bowed. "Charmed, Lady Westfield."

Penny had already turned to another of the young sots. "And put that bottle down before you break anything else. My grandpapa collected those vintages himself at great expense."

"And never saw an excise label or I miss my guess," Nicky said, removing the decanter from his friend's hand and studying it through eyes that struggled to focus.

Then someone coughed. Penny looked into the dark corner. "Grandpapa?"

"I sent for the bottles myself, Penny. No need to scold the lads."

Grandpapa? With a billiard cue in his hand? Penny had to clutch the corner of the billiard table.

Mr. Littleton shrugged. "West said to make myself at home. You said to enjoy myself in London."

"I thought you would like to spend time with your old friends, not these young jackanapes." Who were stealthily creeping out the door, waistcoats and fob watches dangling from their uncertain grasps.

"I tried," Penny's grandfather said. "Caswell is as hard of hearing as I am of seeing. Janeaway can't remember either of our names. Bolton has no teeth, and Ffolkes is in a wheeled chair, pushed by some witch with a wart on her nose. These lads are a great deal more fun."

"Fun? Letting them drink and wager?"

"Well, they were mostly betting on if I could hit the balls. A few did go in the pockets!" He brandished several pound notes from his pocket. "This'll help pay for the china and the glass. I missed a couple."

"A couple?" A mirror was cracked, and the wood paneling had round indentations here and there. So did the ceiling. "You are as cork-brained as they are, without the excuse of being young."

"But I felt young, for a bit. And what is the point of saving the wine stock? I am not going to live forever, and wouldn't want to if I could. I can't drink it all myself, so why not share with youngsters who can still enjoy life?"

Penny had no answer. If the silly cubs made her grandfather happier, she could not complain. She could, however, have a few words with her brother-in-law, who was edging out the door.

"Don't you have anything better to do with your days?" she demanded.

He smiled, trying to look as assured as his older brother, and failing. "I am a viscount's son, you know. I am supposed to be a fribble."

"By whose law?"

"Why, all the chaps know the way of things." He waved his hand around, then looked surprised that his chums had deserted him.

"You, sir, are a wastrel."

"I've been called worse."

"Then parasite, leech, hanger-on."

"Here, now. I ain't—"

"Your brother is working himself to flinders, flying across the country to protect his income, while you do nothing but spend his money and wreck his house. Well, sir, no more. He left me in charge, and he left you to help. You will help me get the rest of my books onto the library shelves, and this evening you will escort me and my stepsisters to a waltz party for young ladies. Lady Gossage said she needs extra gentlemen. Too bad your cowardly friends have already left."

Nicky turned green, and not from the fine brandy. "Not a dancing party! I'll find a job. I'll polish the silver. I'll catalog the entire book room."

"Be ready at nine."

Nicky wasted a pleading look at Mr. Littleton, then said, "Is the woman always so cruel, sir?"

Grandpapa coughed, then said, "My Penny doesn't suffer fools gladly, boy. And she doesn't forgive easily, either. Just ask your brother." He coughed again, then fumbled for a glass of brandy.

Penny put it into his hand, against her better judgment. "And you ought to know better than to exhaust yourself, especially by encouraging budding libertines."

"Well, you ought to have more fun, my dear."

She would, as soon as West came home.

At Lady Gossage's waltz party that night, Penny took on the unfamiliar role of chaperone. Lady Bainbridge stayed home claiming a sour stomach, most likely the same one affecting Nicky at the thought of a dancing party among the schoolroom set.

Lud, Penny felt ancient, shepherding her two step-siblings. She was not as old as the mothers of the other debutantes about to make their come-outs, the girls not quite ready for grand affairs. Nor was she as young as the dancers, who would not be permitted to waltz in public until approved by patronesses of Almack's, or some such nonsensical rule. They had to know how to perform the steps, though, in case. Their partners were spotty-faced brothers and underage cousins and raw country connections, all as reluctant as Nicky.

Somewhere between generations, Penny found a seat between two pillars, like a cabbage plant in a rose garden. Her lips rose at the analogy, and a woman close to her own age smiled back at her, as if accepting the invitation to sit in a nearby spindly chair. Mrs. Curtis was a widow, bringing out her younger sister. Penny found a

new friend, someone to converse with, and a new com-
mittee to join.

Together they kept an eye on the dancers. Penny also
kept a careful watch on Nicky, making sure he did not
scarper out the back door while she was discussing the
dire situation of war widows left destitute.

He dutifully danced with the hostess's daughter,
then with Mavis, the elder Miss Entwhistle. They were
laughing, wagering on how many times the other pairs
bumped into them. Mavis's honest laughter, not the
high-pitched giggle she usually affected, was a happy
sound among the glum couples who were concentrating
on the steps and the tempo. In addition, Penny was glad
to see, she was not flirting with Nicky. Of course not; he
had no title. He was an excellent dancer, though, just
like his brother.

He returned Mavis to Penny's side and gave her a
pleading look. Penny was pitiless, however. She nodded
toward Amelia, who was standing nearby, staring at her
feet.

Nicky bowed. "Miss Amelia, I would be honored to
partner you in the next set."

Still looking down, Amelia accepted his hand and followed him to the dance floor to wait for the music to
begin again.

Incredibly, Nicky had Amelia flashing her pretty smile
within minutes, and actually engaging in a conversation.
Penny was amazed, although she realized she should not
have been so surprised. Nicky had a charming manner,
also just like his brother.

Seeing Amelia so animated, other young men later
asked her to dance, and she skipped off with Lady Gossage's jug-eared nephew.

"Good grief," Penny told Nicky, "you have worked a

miracle. What did you speak about to bring her out of her shell?"

He shrugged. "Poetry. She knows a great deal about it."

"Do you?"

"Next to nothing. But I went to school with an almost-famous poet, Gareth Culpepper."

"The one who goes to the Lake District in the summer?"

"Don't they all?"

"Is Mr. Culpepper in London, do you think?"

"Of course. Not even Gary can bore people in the shires all year, can he? And he needs to see his publisher here in Town." He stroked his chin, thinking. "I don't suppose you'd want me to invite him to your ball, would you?"

"I could kiss you!"

He stepped back, looking around to make certain no one heard her. "I'd be content if you let me off your leash."

Penny laughed. "Go. You have done enough for the night."

"Ah, but the night is just beginning. Are you sure you do not need my escort?"

Penny looked around at the other guests, boys who barely shaved and girls who were putting their hair up for the first time. "I think we will be safe enough here, and on the carriage ride home with the footman and a guard Mr. Parker insisted upon."

Nicky looked torn. His brother had asked him to look after his wife, but nothing was said about dancing with budding wallflowers. "How about if we had one waltz together before I leave?"

Penny's new friend nodded her agreement. "Go on and dance, Lady Westfield. You should enjoy yourself, too."

She would, when West came home.

Oh, how she would enjoy locking her bedroom door, after calling him every slimy name she could think of, in return for Lady Greenlea's morning call.

Penny was near her front door waiting for Lady Bainbridge when the widow arrived, so she could not deny West's former lover, who was dressed all in green, of course, with a green-painted carriage waiting outside. But the gall of the woman! The nerve! The emeralds at her throat!

Penny would *not* curtsy, despite being the younger woman. A lot younger, Penny thought with satisfaction, noting the other's careful application of cosmetics. A viscountess outranked a mere baronet's widow anyway. "I am on my way out," she announced in cool tones.

"I seek a mere moment of your time, my dear, to avoid further awkwardness and gossip."

Penny could not see how a visit could halt the inevitable talk, but she nodded and showed her unwelcome guest to a bench down the hall set aside for waiting servants or uninvited callers.

"And I wanted to warn you, before it is too late. Woman to woman, you know."

"Warn me?" Penny's chill turned to ice.

"About West. You'll never hold him, you know. I do not wish to see your heart broken."

"We are married. I do not need to worry over 'holding' him."

The other woman laughed. "You cannot be that innocent."

Penny prayed for Lady Bainbridge to hurry, or Parker to return with her cape. "I will not discuss my marriage, madam."

"That is too bad. West and I discussed it at length."

Now Penny could feel the color drain from her cheeks down to her leaden toes. He wouldn't, would he?

"Oh yes," Lady Greenlea went on. "You see, after years of marriage I never conceived. West needed an heir, naturally, so we could not wed. Not that I would have him, of course. Only a foolish heiress places the keeping of her fortune into the hands of a handsome wastrel. Oh, but you did just that, didn't you?"

Penny found her feet, and her way to the front door. "You waste your time. West and I are married, and he will keep his vows." She put as much confidence as she could into the words, perhaps more than she felt. "So there is nothing here for you."

"But of course there is. The game, don't you know."

Penny opened the door. "Marriage is no game. It is my life, mine and West's. He loves me and I love him."

Lady Greenlea turned on her way out. "Then you are doubly a fool."

Chapter Twenty-six

Lord F. and his lady shared their fine house for thirty years of wedded bliss after their arranged marriage ... she in the east wing, he in the west wing, a false wall between them.

—By Arrangement, *a chronicle of arranged marriages, by G. E. Felber*

One horse threw a shoe. Another threw West. That's what he got for not paying attention to the road and the rabbit that crossed his path. Instead he'd been thinking of his wife, and how quickly he could get back to her.

Not quickly enough. The storage barn was almost completely destroyed, damage to the stables was more extensive than he'd thought, and many of the horses were injured or missing. Worse, the stable manager had suffered a seizure after the steward sent his letter to West. McAlbee was the finest trainer, breeder, and veterinarian West knew—and now he was incapacitated, for who knew how long. Possibly worst of all, the local magistrate suspected the fire had been purposely set, likely by a senior groom that McAlbee had fired for drinking on the job. The man was still on the loose, so the grooms were looking for him, the missing horses, and any further threats.

Most of West's money went to hiring extra men as guards and carpenters to rebuild the barn and the stable. He set up a pension for McAlbee, replaced the burned fodder, and offered a reward for the arrest of Fred Nesbitt.

Most of his energy went to working beside the men or with the injured horses, doctoring what he could, grieving when he couldn't. He fell into his bed at night, barely noticing that his ancestral home was damp, dank, and dirty, with no one caring for it. He hadn't been able to keep on an indoor country staff while he lived in London, or fix the leaking roof and smoking chimneys. How the hell was he going to bring Penny here? Damn, he should have held out for Sir Gaspar to make this place fit for a lady, too.

Or he could borrow money from his wife. The idea made him as sick as thinking of a person who could harm defenseless horses. If Fred Nesbitt was nearby, he was as good as dead.

Unfortunately, he did not seem to be nearby. So how could West leave? The bastard might have left the neighborhood, or he might be hiding out in some gamekeeper's hut, waiting to make another move against McAlbee and Westfield itself. West could not take a chance on guessing wrong, leaving his men, his horses, his property, subject to a drunkard's grudge.

West drove himself and his men harder, raising the reward, battering at the magistrate's door to keep the man and his deputies looking. The missing horses were rounded up, repairs were under way, one of the senior stablemen was promoted to replace McAlbee, and some of the new men had wives willing to clean the manor house in exchange for food and lodgings. Some worked in hopes of permanent positions when he brought his bride home. Hah! As if she'd come.

She'd never forgive him for missing the blasted ball, the date for which was looming ever closer. Nor could West blame her. He'd left her in London knowing few people, burdened with his ramshackle residence and her own impossible relations, in addition to the improbable task of finding husbands for some of them. If he had it to do again, he'd still leave for the sake of their future, but he regretted the need.

Poor Penny, he thought, she didn't even know how to dress or act like a lady, or what was expected of her as a viscountess. She definitely did not know how to weed out the fortune hunters and rakes from her stepsisters' suitors. They'd be there aplenty, like hounds scenting a scrap of meat.

Damn, what if she fell susceptible to one of those hounds—one of those heartless hedonists—herself? A beautiful woman with a fortune of her own and more coming when her father died was an irresistible lure. The hunters might already be circling their prey. They all knew he'd left her on her own days after the wedding. There was no way that news would not spread through London like the fog. Penny would look like fair game to every philanderer in London. And she just might be mad enough, distressed enough, lonely enough, to listen to some silver-tongued devil with evil intentions. She had not known enough compliments in her life, enough caring, to tell real affection from Spanish coin. He blamed himself for that, of course.

And for introducing her to the pleasures of sex. Jupiter, she took to it like a duck to water. He might as well have been the arsonist, starting a fire that went out of control. What if she thought he wasn't coming back? Would she take a lover?

Only if she wanted her lover to join Fred Nesbitt in hell.

West rode to every hedge tavern and cutthroat hideaway in miles. Well-armed, and with murder in his eyes, he was safe enough. No one tried to rob him, which he almost regretted. A good fight might have relieved some of his pent-up frustration. His wife was waiting. He wanted her. He wanted to be with her. He wanted to touch her and kiss her and tell her he couldn't live without her. He wanted to make sons with her, and yellow-haired daughters.

He wanted to borrow money from her? He was a worse dastard than the missing stable hand.

He left bribes, drank foul brews, and visited more whores in one week than he had in a lifetime, only now he was looking for answers, not pleasure. A lot of people knew Nesbitt. No one had seen him since the fire. West kept looking, ready to take justice into his own hands.

If he was forced to miss Penny's party, he might as well be dead. West, not Nesbitt.

He sent a message, but couldn't put into words what she meant to him, what being away from her did to him. He was a man, dash it, not a poet. Everything he tried to write sounded silly or insincere, so he decided to wait until he could see her, face-to-face, hopefully before she shot him.

Penny's thoughts were equally as murderous, and not only about Lady Greenlea's words. The widow was a woman scorned, trying to cause trouble, Penny told herself. That was all the viper meant, to have her vengeance. Penny almost convinced herself, except one note, one short, impersonal note, was all West sent. And it arrived on the day she thought he'd be returning. But no, not only had the miserable worm run off, riding neck or nothing on unfamiliar roads and unfamiliar horses, but now her bridegroom was tracking down a drunk or deranged horse groom! How could he be so uncaring, so reckless, so very, very stupid? Didn't West realize he had responsibilities now? He was probably enjoying himself playing at knight-errant detective, when he could be killed, the jackass! He'd gone and left her to worry, the same as she'd done with him in the army, only then she had worshipped him with a schoolgirl's calf-love. Now she was a woman, a wife, a lover. She cursed his black heart for making her all of them.

She crumpled the note into a ball in her fist and went to throw it into the fire. Then she smoothed it out and reread it, especially the signature line. *Yrs., West.* She touched his writing and his name, and the *Yrs.* The chowderhead couldn't even commit to the *ou* in *yours*.

He was hers. And she was his. To the devil with jealous lovers. If he got killed, she'd ... she'd step on his grave. No, she'd take his lifeless body and hang it from a pole, so every man could see the rewards of a reckless, feckless life, and every woman could be warned about the grief in store for her. No, she'd cement him into the family crypt, so he couldn't run away ever again. No, she'd ... go shopping.

The house was almost ready for its debut, and so were the Entwhistle females. Lady Bainbridge had the young ladies in hand, and was chaperoning them this afternoon to still another gathering for fledglings. Lady Goldwaite was content to let someone else do all the tedious traipsing about, as long as the girls were with the proper sort of gentlemen, which meant of titled families. She was wise enough to know that her presence was a handicap to her daughters' chances, reminding the toplofty nobs of their connection to trade.

Michael Cottsworth had offered to drive them all,

which filled his carriage, which gave Penny the excuse to stay behind. Besides, the former officer and the widow seemed to have a great deal to speak of, and Penny would have been in the way.

Nicky had not been home since the waltzing party, as far as Penny knew. He was most likely avoiding her and any more escort duty. So much for his promise to stand by his brother's wife.

Grandpapa was off to his favorite chemist, having more of his paint colors mixed, then to visit another of his old artist friends, this one married to a woman young enough to be his granddaughter. Mr. Littleton was looking forward to seeing old Jamison, before the man suffered a heart attack.

Penny took her maid along to Bond Street. Not that she felt in need of a companion or the escort of another female. She was not the one in danger. But the gossipmongers in London looked for any chance to stir up a scandal, and breaking with the conventions would set tongues wagging. Besides, Penny knew she would need help carrying the thirteen parcels she intended to buy.

Thirteen gifts, that's what would be waiting for West when he got home, not an angry, agitated wife, no shouts or recriminations or reasons to leave again. He'd given her that number of presents, one for each birthday he'd missed, and she was determined to show West that she held him in equal esteem and affection. She might not say the words, and he might not believe her actions were genuine or sincere, but perhaps this would nudge him into understanding her feelings—and his own.

She knew he needed a new robe, not that he wore it for longer than the steps between his room and hers. Still, his dressing gown was frayed at the cuffs, so purchasing a new one was an easy decision. She selected a dark brown velvet that matched his eyes, and took the garment home to embroider with his monogram and family crest.

He never carried a watch, so she bought him a beautiful timepiece from a fashionable jeweler. The outer casing held an engraved compass, and the delighted clerk assured her they could affix a diamond chip at west. The watch also had a tiny chime for the hour, but that could be turned off with its own winding key. She blushed when the clerk explained that some gentlemen did not wish to hear the chime in the middle of the night.

When he saw her still looking in other cases, the eager salesman suggested a snuffbox. "They are all the thing with the gentlemen," he said to this obviously wealthy patron. "Many of them have a different snuffbox for every day of the week, or to match each ensemble."

"My husband does not take snuff. Or smoke," she offered, when he started toward a gold pipe stand.

"A new stickpin for his neckcloth, perhaps?" The man took a tray of pins from one of the glass cases.

West had his favorite, and several others, Penny knew, but she was attracted to an interesting piece, a tiny gargoyle holding a ruby in its hands. She thought West might like that, so had the clerk wrap it for her to take with her.

"Now perhaps I might show you something for milady?" He gestured to trays of rings and brooches.

"Oh no, I am shopping for my husband today."

The clerk smirked, as if that ever stopped a female customer from looking. "Your anniversary, perhaps?"

"Something like that," was all she said. But the man's question reminded her of something West had said. So she went to Madame Journet's down the street and asked for the direction of the finest maker of lingerie in London.

"For a viscountess?" that wise Frenchwoman asked. "Or for a seductress?"

"For my husband," Penny answered, smiling.

"Ah, in that case you want to go to Noelle's. She makes night wear for the most expensive of courtesans. Monsieur will be delighted."

Penny purchased five, one more revealing than the next, and none in green. The one trimmed with feathers, especially, had all sorts of naughty possibilities. The gowns were for West's pleasure, yes, but Penny could not wait to wear them, for herself, to see the look on his face as his expression softened, then became fixed and intent.

She was glad to leave the suddenly warm shop for the cooler air outside, but had no idea where to go next. She had eight gifts and needed five more. Her maid suggested a nearby print shop, but they already had more artwork than they knew what to do with. None of Grandpapa's paintings were of horses, however, so Penny selected two Stubbs equine drawings in handsome gilt frames that West might like for his book room at Westfield.

A bookstore was directly across the street, and Penny had never been able to resist one of those yet. She found a volume of Mr. Culpepper's poetry for herself, and a thick tome on the bloodlines and breeding of horses since before saddles were invented, it seemed, for West. That one was so heavy she asked to have it delivered, with some other books she decided she needed, eight of them in fact, none for West.

Now she had eleven presents, with only a tobacconist and an apothecary in view. The maid had no suggestions, so they went home. Lady Bainbridge proposed handkerchiefs, of which West had a drawerful, or slippers, which he never wore.

Penny's grandfather had the perfect gift idea, though,

and Penny needed only an hour to unearth it from the crates of unopened paintings from Littleton's earlier years, at the height of his talent and popularity. It was a small portrait of Penny as she'd appeared at sixteen or so. He'd painted her in pink, laughing, with her hair blowing in the breeze, and barefoot. She hadn't liked to see it, to be reminded of Grandpapa's failing eyesight and her own naïveté, so the canvas had been in storage for a decade. In the painting she was a carefree young girl, thinking her life was still ahead of her, before the years of disappointment. She'd give it to West, because he was giving her back her joy.

She needed one more gift. She thought about tying a bow around her middle and wearing that and a smile when he came home, but he'd already opened that present. So she decided on the next-best thing, hoping he wouldn't think it the very best thing. She would buy him a horse. With Nicky playing least in sight, she asked Mr. Cottsworth to help her select a suitable addition to West's stables.

"Do you want to purchase a breeding mare? A town hack? A hunter?" Cottsworth asked. "A horse for his business or for his own pleasure?"

"For himself." She was positive about that, but a stallion could be both ridden and used for stud, so that seemed the best choice. Price was no limit. She wanted the best London had to offer.

She could not go to Tattersall's, where the horses often had longer pedigrees and better manners than the men who attended the auctions there. By luck, Cottsworth knew a gentleman under the hatches who had not yet put his stable on the market. He could take her, with Lady Bainbridge for propriety's sake and by his own preference, to the man's private residence first, before the public got to see the horses.

The solitary stallion was a huge brute of a horse, far too dangerous as a gift for someone she loved, Penny decided. She might give him to an enemy, but not to West. Why, she might as well let the arsonist have him, as let him on that beast. No matter if Cottsworth almost drooled at the sight of the creature and assured her West could handle any horse on earth. She would not permit the former officer to try out the stallion's paces, to show her the animal was manageable. Cottsworth could barely walk, and she would not be party to seeing West's good friend killed. Not even the groom who led the stallion out seemed inclined to get on Diablo's back.

One horse in Butterfield's stable did appeal to her, a sweet mare in foal, who was not up to West's weight, but whose eyes spoke to Penny. She'd be on the auction block next week, going to who knew what kind of owner, instead of coming to the stall's door for pats and carrots.

"This one." Penny stroked the mare's velvet nose.

"A good pick, ma'am," Butterfield's head groom told her. "She's been bred to last year's derby winner. The foal might turn out to be worth more than any other horse here. A'course it'll take a few years to tell if you'll get your investment back. But she's a real lady, is Jezebel."

"West can have the baby. I'll keep the mare. And I'll call her Lady, not some tart's name."

But the foal was not due for another month, so Penny still needed one more gift.

She could tell that Mr. Cottsworth was growing weary from walking through mews and riding rings, leaning more heavily on his cane. Lady Bainbridge looked bored and kept wrinkling her nose at the smells. "I'll find another gift for my husband," Penny offered.

There was one more horse Cottsworth wanted her to

see, not too far away. "The poor chap's blind in one eye," he told her, "after a hunting accident."

It seemed the cow-handed owner shot the stallion himself, then put him up for sale, out of guilt or embarrassment. "Or else he simply does not want to be seen on a mount that is less than perfect," Cottsworth added in bitter tones, from his own experience. "The *ton* is like that, you know. They hide away their old and infirm, preferring to look at beauty, no matter how superficial. Sungod goes on the block tomorrow. If no one takes him, he'll be sold to a hackney driver, or the knackers."

"How awful!" Penny said.

"I thought you'd feel that way." He led her to where a handsome palomino, with lighter gold mane and tail, was being led out by a groom. A scar ran down one side of Sungod's face; otherwise he was a well-built, well-conditioned animal.

"But if he is half-blind, can he be ridden safely?"

Cottsworth took the reins from the groom. "There is only one way to find out."

Lady Bainbridge gasped. Penny asked, "Are you sure?"

The former officer's lips were drawn in a thin line. "Madam, I might not walk as well as I used to, but I assure you, I can still ride."

Penny held his cane. Lady Bainbridge held her breath.

Cottsworth put the horse through his paces in the sand-covered ring, until the two of them were like a centaur, a bronze horse, tail and mane flowing, a strong, confident man with no hint of injury in either of them. The stallion responded to the slightest touch of Cottsworth's knee, so perfectly that Penny could hardly tell when the rider gave a command. Cottsworth appeared happier than he'd ever looked.

Lady Bainbridge sighed at the sight. "Isn't he magnificent?"

"Gorgeous. I'll take him!"

"But you're already married," Penny's companion cried.

Penny patted her hand. "I meant the horse."

Chapter Twenty-seven

*After an arranged match, Lord N. spent all of his
wife's dowry. Then he tried to claim the marriage
was illegal on grounds of insanity. He lost the case.
And his house, his carriage, his hunting box . . . and
his mind.*

—By Arrangement, *a chronicle of
arranged marriages, by G. E. Felber*

Nicky stayed away for two more days.

"Just like a Westmoreland," Penny complained
to Lady Bainbridge, "not caring who is waiting, or worrying, or counting on him to act as escort. Not caring
about his given word."

Actually, she did not care tuppence about Nicky.
West had still not returned, either. The ball was a handful of days away, and he had not sent another message,
the wretch. Penny did not know if he'd caught the arsonist or been burned to a crisp, rebuilt the stable or had it
collapse around his ears, started home—or was never
coming back. Curse him, and his bothersome debauched
baby brother, too.

Nicky staggered home the next morning, just as
Penny was leaving the house. Mr. Parker had gone to

send a footman for the carriage for her when Nicky almost fell through the front door at Penny's feet. He was bedraggled, his clothes in disorder, and he smelled like the Thames at low tide, with dead fish and sewage. She stepped back as he used the door to pull himself upright.

"You should come in through the service entrance when you are so foxed. Or sleep it off in the stables," she said in disgust, "where decent people do not have to look at you, or smell you. You are not fit for a dog kennel, much less a drawing room."

" 'M sick," Nicky mumbled, leaning against the wall after almost knocking over a large Oriental vase used to hold umbrellas.

Penny righted the urn, tempted to take out a walking stick and beat the dunce over the head with it. "That's what you get for staying out for days and nights, drinking and carousing."

Nicky shook his head, then groaned. "No, I'm sick."

Penny looked closer, under her brother-in-law's bent head and tangled hair. He had a black eye, a purple bruise on his cheek, a grayish cast to his complexion, and beads of sweat on his forehead. She pushed him onto a cushioned bench near the door, where callers could wait. "Good grief, what happened to you?"

"Don't remember."

Which put an end to any sympathy Penny might have felt for the nodcock, and her patience, too. She pulled on her gloves, ready to leave Nicky to the butler as soon as her coach was out front. "Most likely you were boxing the Watch, like some schoolboy on holiday."

Halfway out the door, she turned back. "You weren't arrested, were you?" West would be dismayed. Penny knew he'd left Nicky to look after her, but she was older and hopefully wiser—no one could be more foolish—

and she supposed she should have been looking after him. Although how a woman could supervise a grown man she had no idea, other than locking him in the attic.

"Were you in prison? I will hit you with one of those canes, I swear, if you've come down with jail fever. I'll hit you twice if you've stirred up the scandal broth just before my ball."

"I don't think so. Don't remember."

"Well, what *does* your addlepated intelligence remember?"

"I 'member drinking with Bertie Beecham at his lodgings, after the waltz party. Bertie was at the nursery party, too, very respectable, don't you know. Bertie's mother holds the purse strings, so he had to escort his sisters, but he left earlier than I did. Bribed some green lad to dance with the Beecham gals. I should have done the same."

"No, you should have stayed with me and my stepsisters. You would not have ended up looking like you've been run over by a hay wagon. But that was days ago. What happened afterward?"

"I know we went to a club, looking for Gary Culpepper for you. Said I would, didn't I?"

"Oh no, my boy. You are not blaming your binge on me. You know I would not want to invite any reprobate who frequents disreputable gaming dens to the ball, not even if he is a poet, and Amelia's idol to boot."

"You're wrong. Culpepper ain't no 'probate, and the Red and the Black is all the kick this Season. Not for young ladies, of course, but run honestly. You can ask Cottsworth. The owner of the club was a former officer, too. A friend of his and m'brother's."

"I take it Culpepper wasn't there?"

"No, so we went to another place. And another and

another. Never did find Culpepper, but someone said there was a new place he might be, so we tried that one. Not as genteel as the Red and the Black, but a few ladies of the *ton* were playing. We played a couple of rounds of cards, drank a bit."

More than a bit, from the stench of sour wine and smoke mixed with worse odors. "Go on."

"I did not feel so well, so stopped drinking, waiting for Bertie to finish his hand. I think I fell asleep, because when I woke up, a fight was going on. We weren't involved, but you know how these things go."

"No, somehow I have missed the experience of a barroom brawl."

Nicky missed the sarcasm and tried to explain: "Two fellows have an argument, but a bystander gets shoved, so he shoves back, and his friends join in. Then everyone is throwing punches and chairs and bottles."

"Is that what happened to your face?"

"S'pose so. I can't remember. I told you, I didn't feel at all the thing, way before the fight. I only recall the chairs being smashed, and getting dragged to a carriage when someone shouted that the Watch was coming. I woke up in a strange house."

"Not Bertie's?"

"I don't know what happened to Bertie. His mother would have had catfits to see him, or me, like this. Bertie wasn't the one who carried me to Ma Johnstone's."

"Ma Johnstone's?" she echoed, fearing the worst.

He confirmed it. "I woke up in a . . . a house of ill repute."

"What were your friends thinking, to bring you to a bordello?"

They were thinking of having a woman, he'd wager, but Nicky could not say that, not in front of West's wife. "I guess they thought I'd be embarrassed for you to see me in such a state. They must have figured I could sleep it off there. And they must have known Ma Johnstone herself to ask the favor. Only it wasn't any favor."

"Oh, it was so awful you just stayed there?"

He shook his head, then grabbed at his skull with trembling hands. "I don't know. The thing is, I woke up, cast up my accounts, and started to leave. Some ugly bullyboy as big as a house, with a flat, crooked nose, tells me I can't go, that I owe the madam fifty pounds."

"For one or two nights' rest?"

"He said I'd been there longer. And that the others who brought me caused damage, never paid for the girls, and ran off with Ma's best moneymaker. Then he said I'd played cards and signed vouchers."

"Did you?"

He moaned again. "One of them looked like it could have been my initials."

Penny felt like groaning, too. Only an idiot let himself land in bad company, in bed with prostitutes and cardsharps. "How much?"

"I think the total is nearly a thousand pounds. He had a bill from that dive, too, for breakage during the fight. I was the only one they named, it seems."

Penny turned as ashen as Nicky. "A thousand pounds? That's a fortune to most people!"

It was to Nicky, too. "I don't have it."

Now, that was no surprise. "Well, I am not going to pay any jackass's gambling, wenching, brawling debts."

He sat up straighter, or tried to. "I never expected you to cover my bets. Gentlemen's debts, don't you know, nothing to do with a woman. I'll get the blunt somewhere."

"Nonsense, no gentleman plays with a drunken boy and takes IOUs for more than his victim possesses. You should go to the magistrate's office. Most likely you were drugged anyway. The card games were certainly rigged if you cannot remember playing."

"That's what I thought, but it won't wash. I still owe the money. But maybe you could talk to him, get me some more time." His expression brightened. "That's the ticket. He'll listen to you."

Not about money, Penny knew. She told Nicky, "West is working so hard to earn a living, to bring his estate back into profitability. He will be appalled that you have gambled any of it away. Besides, his accounts will be empty after the fire and the rebuilding. So no, I won't talk to him on your behalf. You'll have to do it yourself. After all, you got yourself into this mess, and he is your brother."

Nicky looked at her sideways. "No, he's your brother. Didn't I tell you? It was Nigel Entwhistle who took me to the brothel. Said we were family and all that, so we had to look out for each other." He gave a grim, humorless laugh. "He's the one who holds my vouchers."

Penny shoved him off the narrow bench so she could collapse into it. Nigel? Nigel had swindled a fortune from Nicky, with drugged wine, marked cards, confederates in a house of convenience? Yes, she could well believe it all.

"How . . . how did you get away?"

Nicky looked like he was about to shoot the cat again, on her new Turkey runner.

"Don't you dare," she managed to say, despite her own roiled innards.

He swallowed hard and admitted, "I gave your name. Your father's, that is."

Everyone knew Sir Gaspar Goldwaite was wealthy beyond measure. Everyone who knew him personally knew he'd never pay the wages of Nicky's sins. What, pull a puling member of the useless aristocracy out of the River Tick? Finance a losing lordling who gambled above his means? Penny could just hear him saying that no businessman ever wagered more than he could afford to lose, only the empty-headed toffs. He never mentioned all the investors who went bankrupt when ships went down, trading ventures failed, new inventions exploded.

No, her father would never pay Nicky's debt. Sir Gaspar had already sent his wife's son off to India. He would not throw good money after bad. Nor would he force Nigel to rip up the suspect gaming vowels, not when that meant upsetting his wife, Constance, the maggot's doting mother.

Sir Gaspar wouldn't. West couldn't. That left only one choice for Penny. "I will handle this."

"You will?" From his tone of voice, either Nicky did not believe she would try, or else he did not believe she could succeed.

"Yes, I will." She repeated the words to herself for confidence, adding that she'd find decent husbands for the girls, too. Then she intended to wash her hands of all of them, her father and his second family, the same as they had turned their backs on her until she proved useful. Penny was not about to let Nicky take his dilemma to West, not when her husband had all those other problems, and problems using his wife's money. Furthermore, what kind of start to a marriage was this, with Penny's connection—although they shared no blood between them, thank goodness—chousing West's brother out of a fortune? He'd hold her responsible. Heavens, she *felt* responsible.

Parker came back then, surprised to see Nicky, horrified at his condition. Penny put Nicky in the butler's competent hands, which meant Mrs. Parker's coddling. She did issue firm orders not to let Nicky out of his room until the night of the ball, before he got into more trouble.

When they left, she stayed on the bench, wondering just how she was going to handle this mess, now that she had sworn to do so. Then she got up and walked out to the waiting coach, dismissing the footman who would have accompanied her on her errands.

"No, I have changed my mind. I am only going to my father's house. I do not need an escort."

A gun, perhaps, but not a witness.

West checked the pistol tucked into his waistband as he rode into one more livery stable, a far distance from Westfield. How the deuce was he going to handle this, he asked himself, if no one here had leased Fred Nesbitt a horse, or hired him, or knew of his friends? He was almost out of places to make inquiries, and almost out of time, without finding a trace of the malcontent with the matches. Nesbitt might have fled the country. Or he might be waiting nearby for an opportunity to inflict more harm.

West could not leave his horses unprotected. They were his future, the legacy he wanted to leave to his son beyond a title, a mortgaged estate, and a leaking roof. They were proof of his own effort, not something he'd fallen into by a chance of birth and death, and they were a source of his pride, too, he admitted to himself. Without the stud farm and training fields, he was Penny's dependent, nothing else.

He could not hire enough guards to watch his own dependents, spread throughout his acres, to say nothing of McAlbee in the cottage where he was convalescing. On the other hand, he could not miss Penny's ball, either. He had given his solemn word to be there, at her side, to help find husbands for her stepsisters. The future

of his own marriage—and the heir he hoped to beget—
hung on that vow. Pride, trust, and honor were all tied in
a knot, in his head, in his heart. Penny would never forgive him for letting her down, again. He'd never forgive
himself for losing her love, again.

One more day—that was all he could spare before
riding for London. He raced from posting house to public house to private stables, until he finally found out
that Nesbitt had a relative in the vicinity.

Ah, thank goodness for sisters.

Chapter Twenty-eight

Lady A.'s parents began negotiations to betroth her to the son of a wealthy widower duke. She'd be a duchess someday. She was smarter than that. Why wait? She negotiated her own marriage ... to the duke.

> —By Arrangement, *a chronicle of arranged marriages, by G. E. Felber*

"Ah, thank goodness for stepsisters," Nigel said, coming down the stairs. "I was wondering how long before you arrived on my doorstep."

Penny handed her parasol to the waiting butler, then followed Nigel to the Gold Parlor, where they could be private.

Once the door was shut behind the poker-backed butler, Penny turned on Nigel, not taking the seat he indicated, but standing across from him, her arms folded across her chest, her chin raised. "This is not your doorstep, sir. It is my father's, and shabby gratitude you have shown for his generosity."

Nigel sneered, leaning against the mantel. "What, I should grovel at your father's feet for the crumbs he throws my way? Lud knows he can afford more."

"I meant you should not sully his house with your shady dealings, nor drag his name through the murky paths of your underhanded iniquities and underworld associates. You will blight your sisters' chances of finding proper suitors, and send your mother to an early grave. To say nothing of the effects your dastardly actions will have on my new relations."

Nigel did not pretend to misunderstand. "I pulled the boy out of a bar fight before his skull was bashed, and I kept him out of the Watch's hands. I even found a safe place for him to sober up, instead of leaving him on a street corner where he'd be prey to every yegg and yahoo in Seven Dials."

Penny shuddered to think what could have happened to Nicky. Then she trembled with rage, to think how West's brother got to that neighborhood in the first place. "You led him there, and then you cheated him out of a fortune."

Nigel studied his manicured fingers. "Those are harsh words, sister."

"That is Lady Westfield to you, sirrah."

He curled his lip again. "You are mighty hoity-toity for a wench who's come to ask a favor."

"What favor? That you forgive Nicky's debts? I know you better than that. I would not demean myself by asking."

"That cloak of aristocratic disdain does not become you, our new viscountess. But you always were a proud one, weren't you?"

Penny did not answer; she merely raised one eyebrow.

"Very well, let us not waste one another's time now that we have come to an understanding. Did you bring the cash?"

"Oh no, you mistake my presence, Nigel. I will not pay a farthing. I came to remind you that Nicky is not of age, so his debts are invalid. Contracts with a minor will not hold up in a court of law."

He smiled, but the good humor did not reach his watery blue eyes. They reminded Penny of a puddle reflecting a sunny sky. Pretty, but mud for all that, and without the sun's warmth. His words reinforced her opinion: "Ah, but what of the court of public opinion? I doubt Master Nicholas would like to be known as a man who reneged on his gaming obligations. Play and pay, that is the gentleman's credo, you know. They cherish their honor and all that rot."

"You cannot know anything of honor. Or a gentleman's code, no matter from which elevated family tree you fell. Or got pushed."

His smile wavered at the insult. "But I have studied what the swells think makes a gentleman ... one like your husband, for instance. I could always go to Westfield for the brass."

Penny nodded in acknowledgment of this expected ploy. She'd known she would not get off that easily, not once she realized Nicky's ruin was a carefully orchestrated plot. Nigel had indeed studied his victims well, knowing she would do anything to avoid involving West. Nigel had even been waiting for her, the wily cur.

"As you surmised, I would be embarrassed to have my husband discover that I was related to such a bloodsucking leech," she said, "no matter how tenuous the connection. He warned me you were bad *ton,* but I doubt he knew quite how low you could stoop."

"Ah, but we lowly leeches need sustenance, too."

"Let me see the chits."

He had them ready. "I paid off Ma Johnstone, too. Much tidier to have one debtor, don't you know."

"I know the charges have to be fraudulent, and I know that you and the female are in collusion."

"In that case I suppose I should give Ma's bills back to her and let her send the Butcher to collect from your brother-in-law."

"The Butcher?"

"That's what they call her bodyguard, Boyd. He used to be called Two-Fist Finnegal when he made his living prizefighting, before he pulled a knife on a better boxer. Few people argue about Ma's prices when Boyd comes calling."

Penny put that bill on the bottom of the pile.

Nigel was going on, trying to frighten her, Penny knew. "If you do not believe the reckoning from the tavern, I could deliver the complaints and charges stemming from the brawl to the Watch. They might decide to make an example of your tender sprig, to keep the rowdy boys out of the stews. I could give them the names of your precious Nicky's friends, too. Of course, they would think that Westmoreland peached on them, which is yet another breach in that tedious wall of rectitude your gentlemen cherish."

Another bill went to the bottom of the stack in Penny's hands. The next were so-called gaming vowels, IOUs made out to Nigel, with Nicky's initials scrawled across them. His handwriting was as poor as his judgment, but that was an issue for another day. "No doubt you got him to sign while he was too drunk or drugged to know better. Unless you've turned to forgery in addition to your other crimes."

"Why should I? Westmoreland is a gambler, and not a very good one. Everyone knows that."

Nigel was a gambler, too, only now he was gambling she could not prove the signatures on the vouchers were false. For that matter, he was betting that she would not go to West, her father, or the authorities. And he'd win the wager, the blackguard.

He'd won before she left home. Penny took her checkbook from her reticule. "I will pay you five hundred pounds for the lot, merely to be rid of you. In return, you will leave Nicky and his friends alone. You'll find some other gullible lambs to fleece."

"Tsk. I wish I could, out of family feeling if nothing else. Unfortunately I have debts of my own, you know. The chaps I owe are a lot less easy to deal with than I am. They make the Butcher look like a nursemaid."

"Very well. It is worth a thousand pounds to be rid of you once and for all. I expect you to stay away from me or my family in the future. In fact, I insist upon it, or else I shall go to the authorities. No, if I hear of you playing off your tricks with Nicky, I shall hire a bigger, meaner brute than any you know. Three of them. You won't be able to walk near an alley without looking over your shoulder." She wished she'd thought of that before.

Nigel clucked his tongue and shook his head. "So bloodthirsty, my dear. You see me quaking in my boots. Imagine the scandal if your ruffians lost and named you as their employer. You see, I am very good with a knife myself." He might not take her threats seriously, but he did take her check.

Penny tucked the gaming chits and the bills into her reticule, along with the checkbook. "Then our business is complete."

"I wish I could say it is, my dear. I do wish I could."

Penny looked up from the drawstrings she was tying. "What do you mean? If you find other markers with Nicky's name, I shall not pay them."

"What I mean is that I can afford the style of life I wish, thanks to you and your buffle-headed brother-in-law, but only for a short while, a very short while after I pay my most immediate and dangerous creditors. I would have been set for life if you'd married me, the way I wished."

"I never would have agreed to that."

He shrugged. "Which is why you will have to make me an allowance."

Penny laughed, striding toward the door. "My father won't. Why should I do such a preposterous thing?"

"Because you have the blunt I need, and I will ruin you, else."

"Do not be stupid. I am no maiden to be threatened with the loss of my virtue or my good name. I am already wed, so there is nothing you can do."

"Really? And you thought your brother-in-law was gullible. You would be surprised. After all, you did come to my home."

"My father's home," she insisted.

"Your father is at his bank, counting his coins, as everyone knows. And my dear mother and the brats are out with your own Lady Bainbridge, as you had to have planned. You came here, alone, to visit with a gentleman not quite related, as you are so quick to point out. You did not even bother with a maid, lest anyone carry tales of our . . . shall we call it a tryst? No? A liaison?"

"A business meeting, you swine."

"My, my. Most ladies conduct their business in their own homes, or at their solicitors' offices. But I am sure the *ton* will be agog to hear your denials. As will your husband, when he gets back. Or perhaps Westfield won't care at all. You must have been a big disappointment to him, that he flew off so quickly after the wedding. Perhaps I am well out of it, not that your lack of expertise in bed could affect your bank balance. Warm women are easy to come by, a fortune less so."

Her reticule's strings were in knots. "How . . . how dare you?"

"Oh, quite easily. You see, if you are disgraced, left without that social entry your sire and my mother desire so dearly, then Goldwaite will be ready to leave his fortune elsewhere. Where better than to his beloved wife and her devoted children?"

"Never. My father will never believe your lies, and he will never leave you tuppence. You are despicable." She was out of the parlor and through the front door. Nigel was right behind her.

Her carriage driver had been walking the horses, circling the street. When he saw Lady Westfield at the door, he started to turn the coach around, to fetch her. Nigel waited until the driver's back was turned, but two other coaches were approaching, one from either direction.

"You forgot your parasol, my dear," he called out, taking the frilly thing from his butler's hands.

When Penny turned to take it, Nigel pulled her into his arms and ground his lips into hers, in full view of the butler, two women walking a poodle between them, and the red-haired occupant of a green-painted carriage across the street.

Penny pushed him away, but the carriage had passed and the butler had gone inside and the two women scurried back the way they had come, dragging the reluctant dog. Her own coach was still some distance away.

Nigel sneered. "We'll see what your husband thinks of that. And your new friends. And your father."

Penny wiped her mouth with the back of her hand, then kept drawing that hand back, formed a fist, and punched Nigel in the face with the same force that had stunned West, the day he proposed marriage. Nigel was shorter and weaker than West, so her fist hit him in the eye, not on the chin. He fell back to the paving stones. Unfortunately, no carriages were going by to see that. On the other hand, or foot, no carriages were going by, so Penny kicked him, right where it would do the most damage. Then she broke her parasol over his head.

No one heard his moans or his curses.

"You'll pay for that, you bitch."

She wiped her mouth again. "I already have, you bastard."

But she did not, in the end. As soon as her nerves calmed and her knuckles stopped throbbing, Penny directed her driver to her father's bank. There she closed her accounts, every last one of them, and transferred her considerable funds to the delighted bank where West kept his money.

Nigel would not be getting anything from her—nothing but a black eye.

Chapter Twenty-nine

Miss F.-J. married the elderly man her parents betrothed her to. He politely died shortly thereafter. A wealthy widow, she politely refused every subsequent offer. She raised cats.

—By Arrangement, *a chronicle of arranged marriages, by G. E. Felber*

The widow Beck believed that blood was thicker than water. "I heard you was looking for him," she told West when he finally found the rough cottage where she lived. "Well, Fred's my brother, for good or for ill. You can keep looking." She shut the door in West's face.

On the other side of the thin door, West let a trickle of coins sift through his fingers. "Did you hear there was a reward?"

Silver being thicker than blood, it seemed, Mrs. Beck opened the door and stood aside for him to enter.

The thatch-roofed dwelling was small, a square front room and one tiny bedroom in the back that West could see. The floors were dirt, the furnishings crudely hewed out of logs. The widow herself was gaunt and bent, in a faded gown and a soiled apron. A scrawny cat slept in a patch of sun from a single tiny window, hung with dingy curtains.

Mrs. Beck eyed the flashing coins in West's hands. "My brother is a good man, he is. He works hard and sends me what he can spare so's I can stay out of the workhouse."

West did not see how the workhouse could be much worse than this. He laid one of the coins on the uneven tabletop. "Yours for speaking to me."

The widow bobbed her head, strands of gray hair falling across her cheeks as she tucked the coin down the front of her gown. "It's the drink, you know, riding him hard. The devil owns him."

"No, I own him now. He could have killed someone, and the horses."

"Fred felt real bad about the horses. But none died, we heard. And the headman having a dicey heart, that's not Fred's fault. It was the devil what made him do it, I tell you. Demon rum."

West disagreed. "Men drink. Decent men stop when they have had enough."

"Not all men. My late husband was one what drank till he fell over. Got trampled by a herd of cattle. Never woke up, they told me."

West did not comment.

"Will he hang?"

"I will see that he doesn't if I find him before the sheriff or the magistrate's men. They are all hungry for the reward," he reminded her, trying to hurry her decision.

"He'll be transported, then?"

"That's better than living out his life in jail or on the prison hulks. I cannot leave him loose."

"S'pose not. And that way he has a chance, don't he?"

West did not mention how many convicts died on the journey to Botany Bay, but men frequently died in jail, too, and always at the hangman's noose. "Yes, he has a chance to make a new life."

"And no spirits on the ships out, I'd guess."

"I wouldn't know." He put another coin on the table. "I am in something of a hurry."

"How much did you say that reward was?"

"You do not get it until Nesbitt is apprehended."

"You don't trust me, but I am s'posed to trust you with Fred's life?"

"No, you are supposed to do the right thing, like a good citizen."

She spit on the floor.

West handed over another coin and got what he wanted, the direction to a burned-out herdsman's shack in the woods. Before heading there, he sent a messenger to the local constable, wanting everything to be legal and aboveboard. He decided not to wait, lest the widow have second thoughts and find a way to warn her brother. Besides, the daylight was fading, and he could be on the road for London. He checked the pistol in his waistband. Bad enough that he might be late for Penny's ball; she'd be madder if he was killed . . . before she had that pleasure.

"You ain't going to shoot him, are you?"

"Not unless he resists."

"He won't. He ain't had nothing but my dandelion wine."

Nesbitt hadn't had a bath, either. The smell alone almost knocked West out when he crept up to the charred shack through the brush, not knowing if the man was armed.

"Come on out, Nesbitt. I know you are in there. You aren't going to hang."

Nesbitt called back, "The dandelion wine almost did me in anyway. And m'sister's cooking. No wonder her husband cocked up his toes."

"That is not the issue here. Come on out. You cannot hide forever. And I have places to go. The sooner we get this over with, the easier for everyone. If I miss my appointment in London, all deals are off."

"Come in and get me."

"I am not a fool. I can wait here. With no food or water or heat, you'll surrender soon enough."

"I thought you was in a hurry."

"The constable and his men should have the place surrounded in a few minutes. No telling what they'll do, rousted from their suppers."

They'd likely string him up from the nearest tree. "Damn."

"You should have thought of that before you set my barn on fire."

"I didn't mean it to go so far. I swear."

"I believe you. But it's over now."

Nesbitt came out, hands up. West tucked the gun back in his waistband and stepped forward. The man was a foot shorter, a stone lighter, a decade older, and unarmed. And still he took a swing at West, hitting him squarely in the eye.

Which was all the encouragement West needed to tackle the man and pummel him into the ground. His horses, his money, his wife—he threw all his frustration into his punches, then dragged the half-conscious man to his feet and shook him. "You fool, you should have come easier."

"I got my pride. Couldn't go without a fight, now, could I? M'sister's neighbors'd think I was a coward. And who's to look after her now? I want to know."

"She'll be better off without a bobbing-block like you. I'll see to it."

West saw Nesbitt into the hands of the local authorities, who took their own damned time arguing that West had to sign papers, give a deposition, follow them to the lockup. West gave them another handful of coins and his Town address. Then he left. He did not send a note ahead. The only way a message could reach London before him was to be carried by a pigeon.

No matter the throbbing in his eye—lud, he dreaded to think what he must look like—nor the pain in his knuckles—the last hostler had kept his distance—nor the exhausting, expensive pace he was setting—damn, his own horses were faster and steadier and had more stamina—West was exulting.

Home, he was going home. He might look like the devil in disguise, but he'd be in time for Penny's ball, barring any more misfortunes. No, he would not permit any delays. If a horse threw a shoe, he vowed, he'd run to the next livery stable on foot. Rain, sleet, snow, tornado, cyclone, or earthquake, nothing was going to stop him this time.

He was going home, and Penny would be waiting there, his wife, his lover. He rolled the words around on his tongue, almost tasting her skin, her breath, the scent of her arousal. He urged the horse faster, promising extra oats.

He couldn't wait to see her at the party, all done up in silk and jewels like the elegant lady he'd known she would be, her bright hair piled high, her manners as gracious as any grande dame's. Nesbitt knew nothing of pride compared with the soaring in West's chest at the picture in his mind, Penny at the head of his stairs, welcoming their guests, his friends, the cream of London society. She'd be taking the place where his mother had stood all those years ago, when West and his brothers hung over the ballroom balcony to watch the guests arrive—and, once, toss peas on their heads. West seldom thought of his mother, but he did now, recalling how furious she had been, and how she forgave them with kisses and hugs. He thought she would approve of his bride.

He did, to his own constant astonishment. The skinny thirteen-year-old urchin with skinned knees that he'd met so long ago was now his wife, Viscountess Westfield. At the time he hadn't expected to become his father's heir. He certainly never expected his betrothed to become a diamond of the first water. He might never get used to the idea, but, oh, how he delighted in it now.

And he delighted in the woman she was. As the miles flew beneath a string of horses' hooves, his mind sped to the hours after the blasted ball, and the warm, willing wife he was going to reclaim.

He'd never thought to miss a woman so much. That is, he'd missed having a woman, but never one particular woman, not the way he missed Penny. He felt as if he'd left part of himself in London, something vital and necessary for his existence, for his happiness. That was a difference he'd never understood before. He'd always thought those married friends of his who hurried home from a mill or a horse race were simply henpecked, weaklings suffering under petticoat tyranny. Now he knew better. It was his own feelings that were drawing him back to her like the pull of a magnet, of gravity, of fate itself, not her demands. He'd never had a wife before, of course, but he'd never thought a man could be so close to a female before, either, so very bound by silken threads of want and need and—hell, he was no poet. He did not have the words to express what he felt.

Yes, he did, words he should have spoken before he left her to worry and wonder about his loyalty. He was going to tell her as soon as he walked through the door, even if the whole household heard him. He shouted it out now, for practice.

"I love you!"

The horse stumbled. A goosegirl left her flock and ran after him. A cow behind a nearby fence mooed.

"No, I love Penny. Persephone Goldwaite Westmoreland, Lady Westfield. I love her, I say, and I do not care who hears me!"

This time a swarm of sparrows took wing and a boy pulled his wagon to the side of the road, to avoid the castaway rum cove on the lathered horse. West tipped his hat and smiled. "Someday you'll understand, if you are lucky."

He was the luckiest man on earth, despite the cold rain that started to fall and the wind that carried away his hat. The bad roads did not matter, nor the hurried meals, or the mean gelding that tried to take a bite out of West's leg at every chance. "I don't blame you for taking out your frustrations, old chap," he told the horse. "I'd bite, too, if I never got the chance to make love to my wife again."

He wanted his wife, and no other woman would do. West was amazed at that change, too. He found himself not the least interested in the barmaids, the pretty females at the various inns, the dimpled salesgirls at the bakeshops where he stopped for food. For the first time since he could remember, he barely looked at the women, and not just because he was in a hurry. None of them mattered; only Penny did, and getting back to her bed.

Soon. By tomorrow night, he swore, the night of the party, he'd celebrate his return. Gad, he hoped her new ball gown was easy to unfasten, or he'd have to rip it to shreds, so that he could see her skin, the blond curls between her legs, the blush of passion that covered every inch of her luscious body. Of course, he'd have to wait until the guests left, unless he could entice her out to the garden, or the butler's pantry, or—no, Penny was bound to take her hostessing duties too seriously for that.

Maybe no one would come. He could hope for that, or that the guests all left early to go on to another party. Damn, that would not work, either. He and Penny had to find matches for the misbegotten Entwhistle misses before they could have a life of their own. Very well, he'd look over the bachelor ranks, find some likely fellows, and twist some arms if need be.

He and Penny had to come to some kind of terms about the money, too, her fortune and his lack thereof. Between repairs and improvements to Westfield, the extra men, and the reward money, his coffers were coughing up dust. He was going to find it deuced hard to swallow his pride and ask for a loan, after swearing he'd never live off his wife, but he needed funds immediately and Penny's fortune was sitting in a bank. As soon as the property showed a profit again, he'd put her money back, for their children's futures.

Should he ask before or after telling her he loved her? Before or after loving her witless? Damn, either way, she'd think he was using her, the same as her relations used her, the same as half the *ton* supposed he was using her.

He decided to ask her the morning after, when she was all soft and sleepy and sated. Yes, definitely after, when he'd proved how much he loved her in the best way he knew how.

What if she said no? She had every right to, especially since he left so abruptly. Well, he'd just have to make love to her until she changed her mind.

"Giddyup, you jug-headed jade. My wife is waiting. My life is waiting."

Chapter Thirty

Miss D.-H. was very fond of the gentleman to whom her parents wed her. He was very fond of his valet.

> —By Arrangement, *a chronicle of arranged marriages, by G. E. Felber*

Whatever happened to the woman she used to be? Penny wondered. The one who ran a household, managed an orphanage, organized six different committees with confidence and poise. The one who had learned to rely on herself to make her own satisfactory life. The one who did not need a man to fill her days, her thoughts, her bed.

That female was long gone, lost, or lamentably hard to locate. Instead Penny's mind was in a constant muddle of wanting and needing and missing West. She needed him, here and now, and not simply because the ball was tomorrow. She needed his strength, his assurance, his warmth, his promise of loyalty. Dash it, she needed her heart back!

Curse him, he'd done this to her, despite her best intentions. He'd made her love him, the cad, and depend on him for her soul's well-being, instead of being the comfortable, self-sufficient woman she used to be. Even after the wedding, she had made her own decisions for the most part, and could go her own way. She'd made certain of that. Persephone Goldwaite was not going to be anyone's chattel, anyone's handmaiden, to be used and discarded like a frayed handkerchief.

Now? Now she was all muckle-minded, wondering what West would do: how he would deal with Nigel, Nicky, her money in the bank ... and Lady Greenlea.

Meanwhile, she still had to find husbands for her step-sisters. Mavis had already attracted three men with titles, to her mother's delight. To Penny's dismay, they were a rake, a rogue, and a reprobate. Good grief, they would make wretched husbands, worse than West, if possible, if they deigned to marry Mavis after ruining her. Fortune hunters, all of them, according to Lady Bainbridge and Mr. Cottsworth, they were as interested in dalliance as dowries, no matter how large.

As for Amelia, she had been winkled out of her shell by Nicky's charm. Penny paused in her musings, considering the possibilities. No, she decided, that match would never do. Nicky was polite enough to speak of the girl's interests. He would be bored to tears in a week, listening to her enthuse about poetry and romantic novels. For that matter, Nicky was not suitable husband material, although a bit of responsibility might steady him. If not West's brother, however, who would be kind enough, patient enough, dreamy enough for Amelia, while satisfying her mother's ambitions? West would know.

Where was he when she needed him? Botheration, the most important party of her life was a day away, and everything was falling apart. West was supposed to be her support, her helpmeet, not cause her so many sleepless nights. Gracious, she had slept alone for six and twenty years. Surely she could not miss him so badly that she lay awake worrying where he was sleeping, wishing for his touch, his breath, his warmth next to her, his waking smile, his good-night kisses that lasted all night.

He should be in her bed tonight, now that he'd shown her the pleasures and promised her more. She'd discovered sex was not something one did once, to make a baby. She had not conceived, and she had not satisfied her curiosity, either, or the new burning she felt in her innermost parts, just thinking of West and his interesting parts. She could feel her body heating and tightening, just at the thought of his touch. No, she needed only his smile to start breathing faster, leaning toward him, like a flower to the sun. West had become her light, and she felt cold, dreary, and denied without him.

He should be getting ready for the ball, not leaving her to face his circle of friends without him. Instead of having his strength to buttress her, Penny was so anxious she was bound to make a hash of the whole thing, like spilling her wine on the prince. Goodness, was His Excellence actually coming? What if Nigel came, too? West would know how to act. Penny knew how to panic.

A pox upon him for being a blasted viscount in the first place, for making her love him, for being gone. Especially now, when, instead of the man she wanted, she had to deal with a handful she did not.

First was Nicky. He still looked like the loser in a barroom brawl, which he was, but he was back to being a superior man about Town, which he was not. He looked at the vouchers in his hand; then he looked at Penny through his one open eye and accused her of dishonorable deeds. "You cheated Entwhistle to get them back?"

"No, I was ready to pay. He reneged on his word, making demands I could not accept, so I reneged on mine." She told him how her new bank had instructions not to honor any checks from Nigel.

"Then I still owe him."

"Do not be a goose. You cannot owe a thief for stealing back what he took in the first place. He practically admitted to plucking a pigeon—that is you, in case you thought you ever stood a chance against a hardened gamester like Nigel—just to get to my money."

Nicky glanced at the chits again. "So the bills are not due?"

"You have them in your hand, don't you? I believe Nigel negotiated with the madam and the innkeeper, so those debts are now his, if they existed at all. Neither of those upstanding citizens is liable to go to Bow Street in complaint. I suggest burning the markers. Or keep one as a reminder to use your head occasionally, as more than a target for someone's fists."

"And I do not owe you the blunt now?"

The look she gave him could have blackened his other eye. "You owe me, but not in coins."

Penny went on to relieve some of her frustrations by enumerating his defects in character, intelligence, and common sense. Then she switched to the sins of every male on earth. Without giving Nicky the chance to defend the indefensible—West wasn't where he belonged, was he?—she finished by demanding Nicky's instant reform, his attentiveness at her ball, and the appearance there of the poet Culpepper.

Nicky was willing to promise anything, especially keeping out of the rookeries. He had no desire to face the Butcher or any of his brethren. He would be at the ball, sober and at her side, he swore. Culpepper would come, and other chums who owed him, for abandoning him to a scoundrel like Entwhistle. He would not have left any sick friend in the hands of an ivory turner, he told her indignantly, shifting the blame for the debacle to other shoulders.

Which Penny did not accept, not for an instant. "You went. You lost. You could have been killed, you jackass! And West would have blamed me. So learn from this—learn that you alone are responsible for your own actions! No one else is." That was why she was not going to tell him about Nigel's threats or his assault on her. The cawker was liable to go off in a storm of righteousness, challenging the dastard to a duel. Wouldn't West be happy with her then? In fact, she demanded Nicky's silence about the whole affair.

"There is no reason to discuss any of this with your brother, when the oaf bothers to return."

"Lord, no." The last thing Nicky wanted was another lecture. As angry as West would be over the gambling debts, he'd be furious that Penny was involved. A man did not send a frail female into the fray of swindlers and swine, even if she was stepsister to one of them. "My lips are sealed." And swollen, so West would know something had occurred, but they'd come up with some story to tell him. "So should I drag the other fellows to your dance? They'll do the pretty by the Entwhistle gals, I vow. Or I'll darken their daylights, too."

She sighed, giving up. "Yes, bring them. Polite young gentlemen are always welcome."

Her father was next. "What's this I hear?" he demanded, before the footman could shut the library door behind him.

"Whatever you heard was not true. I did not kiss Nigel."

"Feh. You would not marry the feckless fool when you had the chance. Why would you kiss him?" Sir Gaspar lowered himself into a comfortable chair and accepted a glass of Mr. Littleton's finest. Then he sighed in contentment, enjoying the spirits, the silence, the restful atmosphere of his daughter's house. "I do not listen to foolish gossip. Although Nigel's mother is in a taking over his black eye. A carriage door opening as he walked by, my foot."

"No, that was my fist, although I found another place for my foot."

He nodded, savoring another swallow of the excellent brandy. "Good girl. I always knew you could take care of yourself."

Penny was confused. "If not the gossip, then what brings you here? Not that you are not welcome, of course. But with the ball so soon . . ."

"You took your money out of my bank, closed your accounts. Doesn't look good to the investors. Word gets out that my own daughter, a viscountess, won't do business with Goldwaite's Bank, the rest of the nobs are bound to wonder why. I do myself."

So she told him about Nigel's plan to blackmail her, to see her ruined. Glossing over Nicky's role in the contretemps, she explained how her reputation might be already destroyed, and the success of her ball—and his wife's daughters' come-outs—in serious jeopardy. "If you think moving my accounts to my husband's bank reflects poorly, think how Nigel's assaulting me in the street looked to strangers. I would not be surprised if none of the high sticklers attend the fete, or mothers with their innocent daughters who might be contaminated by my soiled name."

"They'll come," her father insisted. "To drink your wine and speculate on the size of the fortune I'll be leaving you. And I'll dance with you, puss, if that ham-fisted husband of yours doesn't come back in time."

"He promised to be here. But can you not do something about Nigel?"

"I've tried. The boy has bad blood, that's all. I'll make

sure he knows he's not getting a shilling when I stick my spoon in the wall, no matter whom he disgraces, but his mother is too fond of the chap for me to have him, ah, disappear. You should have heard the caterwauling over his black eye." He sighed again, thinking of the difference between Westmoreland House and his own chaotic establishment.

"Can a man change?"

"Nigel won't."

"Not him."

Sir Gaspar set his glass down and scowled at Penny. "What, married a month and trying to change Westfield? Damn if that ain't like a woman. On the other hand, maybe he wasn't the right man for you after all, going off and leaving you vulnerable to every lowlife in London."

"Not every scoundrel. Only Nigel."

"But he left you, with rumors about his former interest. That's not what I like in a new husband. How are you going to get with child if you don't get together with him? That's what I want to know."

West's leaving was nothing she could like, either, but she would not admit that to her father. "He had to go north, after the fire. Furthermore, I would not wish a husband who was careless of his dependents or his investments, or content to live off my fortune without an income of his own." Good grief, she thought. She was defending West! Well, he was hers to criticize, no one else's. "And no, I am not thinking of changing him. He is quite superior as is. I was speaking of his brother. Nicholas Westmoreland needs to do something with his life."

"That scamp? He's young, at least. Maybe he can change if he wants to. If he is interested, send him to me. I'll find a position for him, see if he can amount to anything. Is he good with numbers?"

He was terrible at cards, but Penny did not know if that counted. "I'll ask. But what about Nigel? I cannot be comfortable around him."

"I'll make certain he doesn't bother you anymore. Maybe convince him to go traveling again, for his health, no matter that his mother will miss him." He stood to go. "Deuced sorry about that, poppet. I want you to be happy. I know it doesn't always look that way, but I do."

"Thank you, Father."

Mr. Littleton was next. No matter that she was busy with last-minute preparations for the ball, she always had time for her beloved grandfather. His news was not surprising but disturbing, especially for reaching his ears so quickly, and for upsetting him enough that he wished to leave Town. He looked older, more fragile. She hoped that perhaps that was just the unwholesome London air.

"You must not listen to gossip, Grandpapa. I swear, the London rumor mill grinds at an exceedingly high rate."

"But the talk might ruin your party that you've been planning for so long. I know how much its success means to you."

"None of the gossip is true."

"I am afraid it is."

"What, you do not trust me? I never kissed that mongrel."

He looked around, trying to see if his dog was in the room. "George?"

"Nigel."

"I should hope not. You are a respectable married woman, my dear. You cannot go around kissing other men."

"Oh, I thought that was the rumor you'd heard." She

gave him an abbreviated version of the by-now-familiar tale.

"That poltroon! Now I shall have to stay, to protect you. I ought to take my cane to that henwit of a husband of yours, going off and leaving you defenseless."

She told him about Nigel's black eye. "So I am not precisely defenseless, and West will be back. He promised."

"Then I shall stay in London until I see him, and no matter what anyone says."

"That's the ticket, Grandpapa. Um, if not about Nigel and me, just what was the tittle-tattle?"

"Never you mind. If no one else comes to your ball, you and I shall dance."

Fine, now she had three partners for her ball: a battered boy, a banker, and a blind man.

Chapter Thirty-one

*Their parents matched her pedigree to his purse.
After they wed, regrettably, she discovered he was a
miser. He realized she was a snob.*

—By Arrangement, *a chronicle of
arranged marriages, by G. E. Felber*

A strange footman would not let him pass. He eyed
the bundle in West's arms. " 'Ere, now, you gots to
use the service entrance."

"I am not making a delivery."

"Well, you ain't going in through the front door without I sees an invite to the ball, and Viscount Westfield
ain't about to be asking your kind."

Granted, his kind was wet and dirty, windblown and
unshaven, mounted on a horse not worthy of West's saddle. He was the viscount, nevertheless, and he did not
need an engraved invitation to his own party. No one,
certainly not some lobcock in livery, was going to keep
him from his front door, and from his wife. Before he
and the footman came to blows, his own butler came to
the door. "Milord, is that you?"

"Yes, Parker, and wherever this cretin came from,

send him back. I will not have such ill-mannered servants on my staff."

"Sir Gaspar lent us extra help, milord, for the party. We shan't be needing him, it appears."

The man was already leading West's horse off, as fast as either of them could go.

West bounded up the stairs. He was early. Well, he was days late, but the ball had obviously not yet begun. No crested carriages were lined up in the drive; no elegantly dressed guests were milling outside, waiting their turn to be announced. He burst through the door.

All his efforts were worthwhile, the saddle sores and the three-day beard, the bad food, and the beds in hayricks. He'd do it all again, West told himself, only faster, because there she was, his bright and shiny Penny, his lucky Penny, his golden bride. No, he swore, he'd never leave her again.

The breath caught in his throat, just to see her. Zeus, she was more beautiful than he remembered. Her gown was all shimmery, a rainbow of colors that framed her perfect body, and her hair was sunshine, piled atop her head in glorious gold curls. She was exquisite. She was his. Maybe he could breathe enough to get out the words that had been echoing in his mind for the entire race back to London.

"I lo—," he began, until he noticed her delectable mouth hanging open. And heard a gasp from beside her, a giggle from behind her. While he'd had eyes only for Penny at first, now he noticed that most of her family was in the hall along with his brother, Lady Bainbridge, and Cottsworth, ready to receive the guests. Several servants stood waiting to accept hats and capes. They were all staring at him, at the filthy vagabond who'd stormed into the house. "I look dreadful, I know," he said to Penny, giving the others a curt nod of greeting. "I'll hurry and change. And bathe. And shave."

Penny shut her mouth so she could speak. "You came back."

"Of course I did. I promised, didn't I?" He thrust the bundle in his arms at her, a huge bouquet of yellow roses. "I know I should not have taken the time to find a flower seller, but I wanted to bring them to you."

"Beautiful." But she never glanced at the roses, only at him, through blue eyes that glistened with tears.

Of joy, West hoped. "Do not weep, sweetings. You won't want to greet your guests with swollen eyes or blotchy skin."

Her lip trembled. Damn. West wished her family to perdition. He wished the ball were tomorrow. He wished he were not so filthy, afraid to touch her or the rainbow gown.

He cleared his throat. "There are thirteen roses, you see."

"One for each year of our betrothal?"

"One for each day I was away. You must admit I am getting better."

She smiled then, her sweet, soft, hungry expression telling him that he was good enough, as good as she needed. West did not care who saw. He kissed her anyway.

"Go, my lord, company is coming," Penny whispered, then added as he raced for the stairs, "Or not."

"What did my wife mean, 'or not'? Aren't we expecting the hordes tonight?" West asked his valet as the man scurried around the room, trying to get everything ready while West scrubbed himself in the hastily filled tub. The man knew he'd never find another position in the city, not if he let his employer face the *ton* in such a state

of disrepair. He also knew he'd be out of a job if he repeated rumors Lord Westfield was not going to want to
hear.

The valet stropped West's razor. "Ahem."

"Get on with it, man. I am in a hurry."

The valet stropped faster. "There has been a bit of
talk. The fear in the servants' hall is that no one will attend Lady Westfield's affair. That is, her function. Not
that anyone here believes such calumny, my lord. We are
all quite fond of her ladyship, I assure you. Everyone has
been working diligently to prepare for her ladyship's
gathering."

West was out of the tub. "What kind of talk?"

"I would prefer not to say, my lord. Idle gossip, don't
you know."

West took the razor out of the valet's shaking hand
and held it close to the man's chin. "Tell me."

A naked man with a sharp blade could usually win
any argument. The valet did not try. His hurried account
was understandably garbled, secondhand, full of denials
and disbelief, with frequent swearing that most of the
talk was speculation traced to jealous females, and a bit
of praying that the viscount did not blame the bearer of
such ill tidings.

West started to shave himself while the relieved valet
laid out his formal wear.

Penny and Nigel? Impossible.

Nicky and an orgy of excess? Entirely possible.

Mr. Littleton and Marcel? Probable.

Sir Gaspar's bank failing? A faradiddle.

Miss Mavis Entwhistle joining the muslin company?
Now, *that* West could believe. And that Maeve Greenlea tried to stir up a hornet's nest. He scrambled into
his clothes, shouting at his poor valet when the nervous
man ruined the first neckcloth. "Here, I'll do it myself.

You get to whichever pub the upper servants frequent. You tell everyone you know to spread the word to their employers that I am back, that any insult to my wife or my family is an insult to me. Do you understand?"

The man gulped and fled.

He need not have bothered. As soon as news of West's return reached eager ears—thanks to the flower seller, that footman who'd taken his horse, the caterer, and two neighbors who had been keeping watch before deciding to come or not—the *ton* flocked to Westmoreland House like migrating starlings, eager to scratch in the dirt for a morsel of gossip. Everyone wanted to see how his lordship dealt with his errant wife and his outré in-laws. Why, Lord and Lady Westfield were already providing some of the tastiest *on-dits* of the Season, and they'd been married barely a month.

By the time West joined the others at the entrance to the ballroom, a line had formed, the cream of London society waiting to be introduced to what they thought of as the curds. West stood at Penny's side, daring anyone to find fault with his elegant wife. She was gracious, she was charming, she was stunning in her silk and jewels, and she was as twitchy as a cat in a dog kennel.

West maintained his own smile, exchanging quips and ignoring queries. He'd get to the bottom of this mess later. Now he had to be the perfect host, urbane, unruffled, and above the untruths. When the receiving line thinned, he took a better look at his surroundings. The ballroom was transformed into a garden, with half the blooms in London, it seemed, bedecking every surface. No wonder he'd had such a hard time finding yellow roses to buy.

Lady Bainbridge and Michael Cottsworth were standing nearby—and nearer to each other than convention dictated—helping to make introductions, since

between them they knew almost every member of the
beau monde.

Sir Gaspar and his wife hovered just to the left of
the door to the ballroom, greeting their own friends
and associates, while inspecting the gentlemen for prospective sons-in-law. The guests inspected them, in turn.
The health of the bank was no longer in question, only
the weight of the gold and diamonds dripping off both
the financier knight and his overdressed wife. It was a
wonder to West that Sir Gaspar could raise his hand; he
wore so many rings.

The Entwhistle daughters, at least, were finally
dressed as befitted debutantes, not courtesans, West
was relieved to see. They wore pale colors with demure
styles, and simple strands of pearls at their necks. Penny
and Lady Bainbridge must have worked as hard as he
had, rebuilding his barn, to effect such a change, maybe
harder because he'd had to confront only a felon, not
convince Lady Goldwaite.

Nicky and his friends seemed to be circling the older
sister like sheepdogs protecting a lamb, fending off
wolves like Lord Jessup, who preyed on tender maidens.
West noticed Nicky's black eye and whispered to Penny
between introductions, "Did you punch him, or was that
one of Mavis's beaux?"

She smiled. "I wish I had been the one. But your brother
is redeeming himself tonight. Mr. Culpepper has arrived."

"Good Lord, he is not going to recite any of his dreadful poetry, is he?"

"Only for Amelia, I hope. See? They are over in the
corner, conversing."

To hell with meter and rhyme, West thought the
young man must be a magician, for Amelia was talking
and laughing and actually sparkling. "Is that the same
stepsister I met at your father's house?"

"Lovely, isn't it? I have great hopes in that direction." But she was looking anxiously in a different direction, to where her grandfather sat in another corner with a gathering of his cronies, all waving canes and ear trumpets.

Then Nigel entered the room. The nearby guests hushed their conversations, and Penny went stiff. Without knowing the full story, West wished he still had a pistol tucked into his waistband. He stepped closer to her side.

Nigel bowed. Penny did not offer her hand, but he took it anyway and brought it to his lips.

"What are you doing here?" she whispered harshly, her face gone white.

"Why, I have come to apologize," he said in a tone loud enough to satisfy the gossips—and his stepfather.

Penny tried to get her hand back without being obvious, but Nigel held it tightly. And squeezed it tighter, painfully.

"I did not appreciate your little trick, my dear."

West did not hear his words, but he saw Penny's distress. He would have stepped in, but Nigel dropped Penny's hand, bowed again, and went to join his mother.

"I see he has a bruised eye, too," was all West said.

Penny had already pasted her smile back on for a dowager duchess who was next on line. Before sinking into a deep curtsy that would have made Lady Bainbridge proud, Penny whispered for West's ears, "Now, *that* I did do, and would do again."

Before West could congratulate her, or ask questions, Her Grace harrumphed, looked at West, who had not given his valet enough time to powder his own vividly colored eye, looked over at Nicky, and at Nigel's departing back, then harrumphed again. "I suppose all the young bucks will be sporting black eyes in the morning. Odd fashion you are setting, Westfield, quite odd."

Which did not begin to describe the next guest. "Monsieur le comte du Chambertin," the butler announced.

They were both astounded as a large, broad-shouldered Frenchman, his hair in a queue, his clothes a brighter rainbow than Penny's gown, his fingers sporting more rings than Sir Gaspar's, strolled into the room. He made an extravagant bow, tapping his diamond-studded high heels together and flourishing a lace handkerchief. He kissed Penny on both cheeks, and would have done the same to West if the English viscount had not stepped back a pace. Then Marcel winked at them and minced his way into the ballroom.

"Marcel, a count?" Penny murmured.

"Marcel, a guest?" West muttered. "Good grief."

Instead of going toward Mr. Littleton, however, Marcel headed directly toward Nigel Entwhistle and kissed him on both cheeks before Nigel could move. Nigel turned bright red; then he turned as white as his neckcloth when Marcel patted his arm and whispered something in his ear.

Whatever Marcel said to the dastard, it worked. Nigel left, without bidding his hosts farewell, without so much as taking leave of his mother.

"Good man," West said, watching half the guests watching Nigel depart.

"Nigel?"

"Marcel."

They dissolved the receiving line shortly afterward and opened the dancing with a waltz, just the two of them. For a minute they both forgot all the eyes, all the slander, all the scandal. Only the two of them existed, flowing together, her skirts swirling around his legs, his thighs brushing against hers, their eyes fastened on each other's face, as if memorizing their features all over again.

"Welcome home, my lord."

"I am glad to be here, my lady."

To West's sorrow, that was the last dance they could have, as every man in the room wanted a set with the most beautiful woman in London. Every female wanted to speak with Penny, find out her modiste, her florist, her feelings for Nigel Entwhistle.

West raised an eyebrow at anyone impertinent enough to ask him any awkward questions, and then he tried to corner Nicky, to get some answers. His brother dashed off instead.

"My dance with Mavis, don't you know. Wouldn't want her taking the floor with one of the old roués her mother keeps pushing her way. Foolish chit is liable to let some rakehell lead her out to the gardens."

And Nicky was going to provide propriety? That was Lady Bainbridge's job, wherever she was.

West strolled out the open doors to gather his wits after a night of surprises, and cool his temper after watching Penny and her current partner. The handsome devil was one of West's best friends, which made him a womanizer and a rogue. Darkened daylights might be a new fashion, but if Hazlitt did not loosen his hold on Penny's waist, he would be holding his own privates in his hand next. Ensuring that gentlemen kept their proper distance was Lady Bainbridge's job, too. Where the devil was the companion?

A few steps onto the terrace and West found out. The chaperone, the expert in polite behavior, the respectable widow, was out in the shadowed garden with Cottsworth, who could not dance but could obviously canoodle.

Good grief, West thought again. Good grief.

Chapter Thirty-two

Baron D. and his lady made the best of the bargain their guardians had arranged. He wore waistcoats to match her gowns; he grew stout when she became pregnant. She grew whiskers on her chin. And in their dotage they had matching wheeled chairs.

—By Arrangement, *a chronicle of arranged marriages, by G. E. Felber*

West peeled Lady Bainbridge out of Cottsworth's arms. If he could not hold the woman of his choice, why should his friend have the pleasure?

In turn, Lady Bainbridge tried to drag Miss Amelia away from her poet, insisting they had to dance with other partners. Only spouses—and those seldom did so—or betrothed couples could sit in each other's pockets all night without causing talk.

"Very well," Mr. Culpepper said, falling to his knees right there on the ballroom floor. "Will you marry me, my dearest Amelia, my muse, my inspiration, my beloved, so we never have to be parted?"

Amelia said yes, of course, through her tears and stammers.

Her outraged mother started to say no, of course. Lady

Bainbridge hastily whispered that the young gentleman was second in line for a marquisate, and wealthy in his own right. How else could he get his poetry published?

So the dancing was interrupted for a happy announcement and a champagne toast, with more people congratulating Penny than the newly engaged pair. She gave the credit for her coup to Nicky, of all people. Sir Gaspar shook Nicky's hand, clasped him in an embrace, and walked off with West's brother in serious conversation. Mavis trailed behind, listening to every word.

West started toward his wife and his own celebration, but she was busy with the servants, ordering more wine, more waltzes, more food put out on the refreshments tables because no one appeared to be leaving. When he looked for her again, she was whirling around the room in that cad Hazlitt's arms. And laughing.

This was not the homecoming West had planned. He'd dreamed of Penny rushing into his arms, of carrying her to his bed, of making love all night for the rest of their lives. He'd dreamed of her hair loose, her skin warm, her lovely breasts in his hands, in his mouth. Now he had a glass of flat champagne in his hand, and a bitter taste in his mouth. And an awkward arousal. So he went back out to the terrace, where Cottsworth was smoking a cheroot.

"Have one?" his friend offered, so moonstruck he'd forgotten that West did not smoke.

West was so rattled that he forgot that fact, too, and accepted, then coughed when the smoke filled his throat and lungs, so he drank the warm champagne. "Horrid night," he said.

"Oh?" Cottsworth leaned back against the railing. "The stars are out, the music is delightful, the smell of flowers is in the air, and the company was lovely, until now. What more could a man ask?"

"Straight answers to my questions."

"Oh." If Cottsworth had two good legs, he would have jumped off the terrace and fled through the gardens. Instead, he had to tell West what he knew, from Lady Bainbridge and the servants. "I am not certain what is fact and what is fiction," he concluded. "But the scandal seems to have been averted. Your wife is a success."

His wife was in yet another man's arms when West stormed back into the ballroom. Damn.

He had heard so many accounts of events, been subject to so many innuendos, raised eyebrows, and outright smirks, that even he began to wonder if the gossip grist contained a grain of truth. Some of the men—his former friends—must believe the stories, because they were buzzing around Penny like bees on a flower, or libertines on a loose woman. Damn.

And then he realized his own wife was avoiding him. Damn.

When the current dance ended, Penny found herself near the ballroom entry, facing Lady Greenlea, who was not invited, on the arm of a raddled marquis, who was. Penny had to nod graciously and allow the marquis to kiss her—thankfully—gloved hand. Lady Greenlea waved her fan, making certain Penny saw the flash of a ring on her own gloved finger, a thick gold band, set with a garnet. West's ring.

He wouldn't have. He couldn't have. And where was the toad when she needed him?

Before Penny could demand an answer, or start crying, Nicky pushed past her. "That's my ring," he shouted, "and you were the last person I spoke to before getting sick."

"Dear boy, you were dreadfully drunk that night." The widow kept wafting her fan, and the ring.

Nicky tried to grab her hand to pull the ring off. "You put something in my wine. I know you did!"

The marquis started to make huffing sounds, and Lady Greenlea stepped back. "What, are you foxed again? Tsk. You really must learn to hold your liquor, you know, especially at your new sister's ball."

A crowd had gathered around them, eager to taste scandal broth more potent than the punch being served. Penny's chances of restoring her reputation, of taking her place in proper society, in West's world, were slipping away. She did not care, not if West cared so little for her.

Then he was beside her. "A problem, my love?"

"Take your glove off," Penny demanded, no matter who heard.

West paused. Here he'd been ready to cause a scene in the ballroom, but his lady wife was before him.

"Take it off," she repeated, pulling at his glove, de rigueur for a formal affair. She freed his hand, revealing the garnet ring. Then she threw herself into his arms, right in front of the entire beau monde.

Her stepmother shrieked; Lady Bainbridge staggered into Cottsworth's arms. "I thought I taught her better than that."

"I knew you wouldn't give her your ring."

"Of course not. It was a last gift from my mother." West kept his arm around Penny's shoulder, and raised the eyebrow of his undamaged eye at Maeve Greenlea.

"No woman likes being cast off," was all she said, turning her back on him and taking the marquis's arm.

"Not so fast," West said, but before he created even more of a scandal for the avid listeners, Nicky dived past him, almost knocking Maeve to the ground. He wrestled the ring off her finger. "My mother gave me one, too. I'd never part with it. I bet you were working with Nigel Entwhistle to cheat me."

The marquis sidled away.

West was about to usher Maeve, Nicky, and Penny into a private room when Penny's grandfather shouted from his nearby corner of the ballroom: "I say, ain't that Maeve O'Brien?"

"Eh?" another old gent shouted back, holding up an ear trumpet.

"You know, Maeve who used to pose nude for Froggy Fogerty. I recognize the voice."

Another of his cronies held up a pair of opera glasses. "Sure as the devil. I never forget a bosom like that."

The second aged artist slapped his thigh. "Too bad you can't remember what to do with one. I wonder if Froggy still has that portrait over his mantel. You know, Maeve and the wolfhounds and the fruit."

"Shut up, you old fools," Maeve screamed as she ran past them, but Grandpapa Littleton put out his cane to stop her, not so accidentally setting it on the hem of her clinging green satin gown. Which ripped, right up the back, revealing her lack of petticoat or much else under it.

"That's Maeve, all right," the fellow with the spyglass yelled for the benefit of his deaf friend. "I never forget a—"

"Not in my granddaughter's ballroom," Mr. Littleton warned, grabbing for the magnifying glass. Lady Greenlea was already out the door, the efficient Parker draping a cloak around her.

"Good riddance, I say," Nicky called after her, until West's glare stopped him. "I'll just, ah, say adieu to some of my chums, shall I?"

Penny looked around to see the shambles of her ball. All her guests were scurrying to spread the tale. Even the orchestra had stopped playing. Worse, West's un-injured eye was narrowed, almost black instead of his usual warm brown color, and his mouth was set in a harsh line. The question in her mind was the cause of his anger. The rumors about her and Nigel? Nicky? Her failure as a hostess?

Perhaps, she thought in hope, he was mad at Lady Greenlea, or at himself for leaving her alone, the way Grandpapa blamed him? No, the dagger looks he was sending her way told her exactly the object of his fury. She had not trusted him, or acted like a proper viscount-ess. Now he made no pretense of smiling for the company, no efforts to urge the guests to stay. Penny thought about leaving with her father and his family, but Nicky had already noticed West's dark looks and offered to ac-company the Goldwaites home. "Coward," she hissed as he made his farewells.

Nicky tapped his temple. "Older and wiser." Then he became a boy again, pleading, "You won't tell him, will you? I am speaking to Sir Gaspar about my future. If I can prove to West I am turning over a new leaf, perhaps he won't be so mad. I don't want to join the navy."

"Is that what he threatened? Nevertheless, I do not think he is angry at you."

"Only because he does not know the full story yet. Please, Penny?"

She was starting to get mad herself, not at Nicky, but at West. Half this mess could be laid at his door, for not being in London, for not marrying her when he should have. Besides, weren't proper British gentlemen sup-posed to hide their feelings, not show any displays of emotion? He was doing a poor job of it, brusquely hur-rying the last guests off, looking thunderclouds at the servants who were starting to clean up, glaring at Lady Bainbridge and Mr. Cottsworth as they said their good-nights. Then, without a word to Penny, he disappeared into the library. She took herself to bed. She thought about locking the door in case he was drinking himself into a rage, but West would not do that. At least she did not think so.

She dismissed her maid after being helped out of the rainbow gown, cursing West in her mind. She'd wanted him to be the one to unfasten the shimmering cloth, to see how eager she was to renew their lovemaking. The thought of joining their bodies together made her body grow taut and moist.

A plague upon her husband, he was about as eager as a goose going to market. Penny brushed her hair until it crackled, her temper along with it, while she waited for his huffiness to recall he had a wife.

He came to her door an hour later, still wearing his formal clothes, white satin knee breeches, white marcella waistcoat, dark blue superfine tailcoat, his neckcloth as pristine as when he donned it. He had the same grim lines at his down-turned mouth, the same dour crease between his eyes, one swollen, one skewering her with a steely glint.

Penny did not wait for the attack. She went on the offensive, instead. "I suppose you heard the rumors. You do not trust me."

He was quick to return: "You did not trust me when I said I parted company with Maeve long before our wedding. Nor did you trust me to arrive in time for the ball, if at all. I saw the surprise in your eyes. And you did not tell my valet to lay out my evening wear, which delayed me further."

"Further? You only made the beginning of the ball by minutes."

"While you had nearly two weeks to make a byword of yourself."

Penny started to close the door on him. "I refuse to speak of matters if your mind is already made up."

He put his foot in the door to keep it open. "Blast it, my mind is so muddied I do not know what I think. I needed the last hour to compose myself enough not to tear the house apart. No, not you, so stop looking at me as if I had a horse whip in my hand. Thunderation, are you going to invite me in or are we going to wake up the household again?"

She stood back, reluctantly. He seemed larger and darker without his ready smile and easy charm. She ignored his words and put her dressing-table chair between them.

"None of it is true," was all she said.

"I do not know what *it* is, dash it." West reached out to touch her, then obviously thought better of it. He stroked one of his yellow roses, which were placed on the mantel in a porcelain vase, between two Staffordshire dogs.

Penny wanted to go to him. He should be stroking her skin, not a rose. But she could not give up Nicky's part, and she could not name Nigel. West looked ready to issue a challenge here and now. "You shall have to trust me."

"As I trusted you to handle your moneys yourself? I could have fought to have control of everything you own. A husband has that right, you know. Instead I let you keep your savings for yourself. Now I find out that you have closed your accounts. Without consulting me. I have no idea where you spent the money, and cannot like it."

"You were gone. Furthermore, I did not need your permission to spend it as I saw fit, as we agreed before we wed."

But West needed some of that money, which put him

in a worse mood, if possible. "I gave you that right, not thinking you would abuse it. Or my good name. What, did you pay off your lover? The tittle-tattle has Nigel with a check in your name. Is that why you wanted him gone tonight, before I tore him limb from limb?"

"How dare you! Who knows where you have been for a fortnight? Yet when you finally come home, you accuse me, instead of apologizing for your mistress on my doorstep!"

"For the last time, she is not my mistress." He took a step closer, leaning on the chair in front of her. "Now tell me what has been going on."

"I did tell you, none of it is true."

"You never wrote a check to Entwhistle?"

"Well, that is mostly true. But he never got the money."

"You never called at his house when you knew no one else was home?"

She bit her lip. "Well, I was not thinking about where the family might be. And no, I shall not tell you why I went. I doubt you would believe anything I say. And isn't it odd, don't you think, how you asked first about the money, then about my call on Nigel? I wonder which is more important to you."

He looked at her with sorrow. "If you still think I wed you for your money, then I suppose there is nothing left to say. Good night."

She slammed the door behind him. She'd already said too much.

West could have kicked himself for not saying enough. Instead he kicked the door, and mumbled, "I love you."

The door snapped open. "What did you say?"

"I said I love you, damn it."

Which were the only words Penny wanted to hear. In a heartbeat she was in his arms, weeping. "I love you, too. Oh, West, I would never look at another man. You have to know that."

With her in his embrace, nothing else mattered. He held her like he would never let go. "I do know it, just as I would never want another female."

"And I moved the money into an account with both our names, so Nigel could not get his hands on any of it."

"Both our names?"

"The bank manager said I could. So you can use it whenever you need. I have other investments in the funds, which I left in case I am destitute in my old age, but you will be there with me then, too, won't you?"

"Forever," he said between kisses. "And I don't require a lot of cash, I swear. And I will put it back for our children."

"There is a lot of money."

"Then we better get started on the children."

Her nightgown got in the way. Penny was wearing the new white satin negligee, the one strategically trimmed with fluff and feathers. A feather got in his mouth when he kissed her neck. One went up his nose when he kissed her breast.

"Damn, I am tempted to toss the blasted thing out the window, to see if it flies," he said, coughing and sneezing and pulling the fabric over her head. Penny held her arms up to help, then went back to tearing his clothes apart to get to his skin.

She laughed as she threw his cravat on the floor, atop her nightgown. "I thought you would like it. I bought it as a gift for you."

He pushed her hands aside so he could kiss her naked body, without choking on a feather. When he reached her navel, he whispered, "You are the only present I need, past, present, and future."

She was trembling now, her legs going watery in anticipation as his kisses went lower. "But . . . but there are twelve others."

"One for every year of our betrothal?" he asked, his lips poised above the tight gold curls between her legs.

"No, one for every year I have loved you."

"I will have to think of thirteen ways to show my gratitude." He lowered his mouth. But he could not get past the first way. "I can't wait, sweetings." He did not even finish removing all his clothes. He kicked his shoes aside, ripping at his buttons, then carried Penny to the bed, and filled her with two weeks' worth of wanting. "Sorry, so sorry," he apologized for hurrying ahead and leaving her behind. "I'll . . . make it up to you . . . next time."

That was a bit more eagerness than Penny had bargained for. "How soon until next time?"

"Soon," he answered, rolling off her, pulling her against him, one arm possessively cradling her breast, one of his legs over hers, so she could not move.

She had no place she'd rather be. Penny felt as full as when he was inside her, part of her. This time her heart was full of love. "We'll straighten everything out in the morning—your brother, Nigel, Lady Greenlea, the money, all right?"

"Hmm?" He was almost asleep. "Sorry."

"Don't be," she whispered. "I have everything I need right here in my arms."

Chapter Thirty-three

Affianced at birth to the neighbor's son, Miss R. was pleased that she could keep living so close to her mama. Her husband was pleased with the match, too. Now he could keep living with his mama.

—By Arrangement, *a chronicle of arranged marriages, by G. E. Felber*

West was still asleep after his hard, fast ride. The trip from Westfield must have been exhausting, too, because Penny could not wake him in the morning. She tried with a kiss. Then she whispered "I love you" in his ear. He rolled over. She stroked the hard planes of his back, and he mumbled something into his pillow that may have been "love, too" or may have been "later." A pinch to his derriere did not do it, nor a poke to his ribs.

So much for a lusty start to the day. Reformed rakes might be all well and good, but this one was not good for anything in the morning, it seemed. Penny gave up and got out of bed. She was starving, and not merely for West's lovemaking. Her stomach had been in knots for the last two days, and she had not been able to eat a bite at the ball, either. So she dressed as quietly as she could, although she need not have made the effort, for West did not stir. Then she went down to the morning parlor, where breakfast was served.

Nicky was the only one there. Nicky, at breakfast? She looked to make sure he hadn't just come home, but, no, he was wearing fresh clothes and his hair was still wet from his morning wash. He rubbed at the garnet ring back on his finger.

Penny wanted to eat in a hurry and then get back to her husband, who ought to be awake soon, even if she had to pour water over his head. She wanted to show him his other gifts and talk to him about his black eye, and the black marks on her reputation. Mostly she wanted to hear him say "I love you" again. But Nicky needed her advice.

"Sir Gaspar says he will help me make something of my life. Do you think I have to wait to ask Mavis to share it?"

"Mavis?"

He nodded. "She makes me laugh, and she don't lecture a fellow. We both like London and parties. What do you think?"

Penny spread jam on her toast while she considered her answer. Nicky was looking at her with great expectation of hearing the opinion that matched his enthusiasm, as if pearls of wisdom would drop from her mouth, instead of toast crumbs. Penny supposed she should feel honored that Nicky trusted her with his confidence and accepted her as an older sister, especially after she'd solved his problems with Nigel. What she knew of marriage and courtship, however, could fit on her teaspoon, with room for the tea. So she chewed her toast carefully while Nicky sat on the edge of his chair, waiting.

Well, she thought, she and West had started off with far less in common, and neither Mavis nor Nicky seemed as immature and pampered as they had once had, but gracious, marriage was more complicated than sharing jokes and dances.

"Well? Must I wait until I have made my fortune? That could take years, and might never happen. Mavis could find another suitor. You saw how popular she was with the fellows last night."

Or he might find another young lady he liked better. Heavens, there was more to matchmaking than she supposed, like being responsible for the future happiness of two people she cared about. Penny reached for the dish of eggs.

Nicky pulled the bowl out of her reach. "Tell me what you think."

Penny thought she was still hungry, and West might know better what to tell his brother. But West was sleeping, dash it, and Nicky was hoarding the eggs. "I think . . . yes, I think you should ask Mavis what she wants."

He leaped up, shoved the eggs in Penny's direction, and kissed her cheek. "I knew you would have good advice! West married himself a real winner." He rushed past Lady Bainbridge on his way out.

Lady Bainbridge did not seem to notice Nicky's rudeness, or the platters of food standing on the sideboard. She sat down and waited until Mr. Parker poured her a cup of chocolate and left, then said she needed Penny's blessings.

"That is, if you do not think I am too old to wed?"

Penny set her fork down with a clatter. Had there been something in the punch last night? "I . . . I do not think anyone is ever too old. Do you wish to marry?"

Lady Bainbridge stirred her chocolate without drinking any, studying the swirls and her own daydreams. "I think I do."

"Mr. Cottsworth, I assume?"

"Hmm." The older woman smiled and went back to stirring.

"Does he feel the same?"

"Oh, yes. He says he does not care that I cannot give him children, that he has nieces and nephews aplenty. And then I can hope to spoil your babes when you have them."

Penny looked at the watch pinned to her gown. There were not going to be any infants, not at this rate. "Of course. I expect you to be godmother to my first child."

"Thank you. And Michael says I can help his career, since he wishes to rise in political circles."

"You will make an excellent hostess for a diplomat or a government official. Even better, you will enjoy that kind of life."

Lady Bainbridge leaned closer to Penny, her figured shawl in danger of knocking over the pitcher of cream. "That's what I always wanted, you know," she confided. "And a home of my own. Michael wants to show me his town house this morning, unless you need me?"

Penny shook her head no. She needed time with her husband.

Lady Bainbridge was going on. "I thought we would wait until the end of the Season. You will have those stepsisters fired off nicely. One is already betrothed."

"Two, actually, or nearly so."

"How lovely. Then you will not be needing my services all the sooner, especially with your husband home, and after your grand success last night. Michael's brother has an estate in Ireland where we might honeymoon. If you don't mind."

Penny helped herself to bacon. "I am delighted for you. Just think, no more pesky debutantes to lead through the Season."

Lady Bainbridge took a sip of her chocolate, which

was cold by now, from all her stirring. "No more guarding a young lady's virtue, when she is eager to waltz down the primrose path."

Penny was eager to get back upstairs, but she was honestly happy for her friend, and got into the spirit of the thing. "No more amateur musicales or practice dance sessions."

Lady Bainbridge turned serious. "No more worrying about my future."

"But I told you, you would always have a place with us."

"Thank you, my dear. But that's not the same as having a home of one's own, or financial security. No more counting every farthing." Then Lady Bainbridge giggled like a schoolgirl and added, "No more empty beds."

Which reminded Penny of who was sleeping in hers, but she could not go back there yet. Her grandfather needed her next, to make his farewells. He asked for a cup of tea, which Marcel fortified with a drop of brandy before leaving them alone, before Penny could ask any questions.

"Time for me and Marcel to leave, poppet."

"Not yet, Grandpapa, unless you are worried that Marcel will be found out in a pack of lies?" When her grandfather shook his head no, she said, "You saw how everyone accepted him. Why, he was a celebrity. And you were as much a success. All your old friends welcomed you, and Nicky's friends, too."

He patted her hand. "But I would rather be in Bath, now that Westfield is back to look after you. I don't want to be in Town, waiting for all my old friends to drop off. And I want to get back to my painting, earn my way. The light is dreadful in London, you know, and there are too many interruptions."

Penny looked down at his blue-veined hand with

gnarled knuckles. She could not do anything about the city's perpetual rain and fog, but she could ease her grandfather's worries about money. "You do not need to paint any longer, unless you want to, of course. I have money, enough for all of us. I couldn't touch it until I was wed, but now I can." Well, West technically had the money, but she knew he would not mind. Besides, her father told her last night that he would refill her accounts at his own bank, out of gratitude for Mr. Culpepper and chagrin at Nigel, and to make things look better to his partners.

Her grandfather sipped at his tea and stared out the window, leaving Penny to wonder again how much he could see. He obviously saw that it was time to tell the truth. "If it comes to that," he told her, "I have money, too. Been holding out all these years, I have. It's your grandmother's dowry and an inheritance from my uncle, don't you know. I was making enough of the ready for our needs with my painting, and I liked it that way. So I invested the other sums. Made a fortune, too. Better'n Greedy Goldwaite could have done with the blunt."

"But then why did you keep painting, to sell those—?" She bit her tongue.

Littleton laughed. "How else could I get your father to part with more of his brass?"

"You knew he was buying the paintings?"

"Of course. I had a man investigate the 'gallery' that was buying my work. It was a warehouse, poppet. Where they belonged, I suppose."

Penny served both of them a dish of kippers, from under a silver dome. "But you never let on."

"What, admit that puffguts Gaspar was doing a good deed? We both would have been embarrassed."

"But why? I do not understand. You did not need the money; he did not want the artwork."

Littleton wrinkled his nose at the kippers, or at the thought of his son-in-law. "He did not appreciate you as he ought, sending you away so that woman could take your place, take your mother's place. Not that I wasn't happy to have you, poppet. Brought back the light to the old house, don't you know. You reminded me so much of your grandmother, and your mother, too. I shall miss, you."

Now Penny could not swallow, through the lump in her throat. What if he went away and she never saw him again? "And I shall miss you, too, Grandpapa."

Without seeing, he knew. "Do you know, the one advantage of poor eyesight is that I can hold in my mind the pictures I want? My favorite is you when you posed for that portrait, so sweet and innocent, a rosebud about to unfurl into the magnificent blossom you have become. I will remember that forever."

"And I shall remember all the stories you told me so that I would stand still for you. And, more importantly, how you made me feel loved again, with my mother gone and my father claiming his new family."

"You have a husband now, my dear, to make you feel cherished. You don't need a doddering old man."

Penny tried to hold back a sniffle, but could not. She pushed her plate away. "I will always need my grandfather."

"Maybe you will come to Bath for a holiday."

She blew her nose. "Definitely. That is not so far away."

"Not the way your husband travels. I'll leave you Cook, but I'll take George." On hearing his name, the little dog jumped into Littleton's lap, for pets and kippers.

"Are you sure?"

"Cook has never been happier than when she could fuss over your party, feeding all those toffs. And in Bath we stay at a hotel with its own restaurant, you know. As for George, I could never leave my old friend." He stroked the pug's wrinkled brow. "One day soon old George won't come back from one of his breathing fits. I know that. I should be there with him, don't you think, to say good-bye? He'd be at my side when my time comes, if he could."

Penny was happy her grandfather could not see her tears as he and George left the room on Mr. Parker's arm, to help Marcel with the packing. She needed West's comfort now. What else were husbands for? Surely not to fall asleep during lovemaking. First, her father needed her, too.

A messenger in the ornate Goldwaite livery arrived with a note from Lady Goldwaite. Constance wrote that Sir Gaspar was suffering palpitations of the heart, which his physician deemed dire. Penny should hurry, taking the Goldwaite coach that was ordered to wait outside to save time, since minutes counted. And, Constance suggested in her note, Penny might want to pull the shades, to avoid a repeat of that other nonsense.

Penny's first thought was to fetch West, but he'd take too much time to dress. She did not want him to encounter Nigel this morning, either. For that matter, Penny did not want to see the varlet herself, but she had no choice. Lady Bainbridge had her own affairs to settle this morning, but Nicky would already be there, so she did not bother to ring for her maid, just grabbed up her reticule and followed the groom to the waiting coach, calling back to the footman on duty to tell Mr. Parker and Lord Westfield where she was going.

The messenger helped her into the coach, then jumped up to ride with the driver. The shades were already covering the windows, so Penny fretted in the dark interior all the way to her father's house, until she realized the trip was taking far longer than it should. She pulled at one of the curtains and felt her breakfast sink to the bottom of her stomach. They were not going in the right direction. She banged on the roof, shouting for the driver to stop.

He did, but before Penny could scramble out of the coach, gloved hands shoved her back in. Nigel followed. The driver cracked his whip over the horses' heads and they leaped forward, sending Penny sliding across the seat. Nigel reached out to steady her, but she batted his hands away.

Furious, at herself and at him, she still had to ask, "My father is not ill, is he?"

"I sincerely hope not. 'Twould be a shame if he sticks his spoon in the wall before I get my hands on his gold."

"And your mother did not write the note?"

He raised an eyebrow. "Not even my mama loves me enough for that. She'd think it was laying a curse on Sir Gaspar by claiming him at death's door. Why kill the goose that lays the golden eggs?"

"So you forged her signature the same as you did Nicky's. But why? What do you hope to get? You know I changed my accounts, so I could not make you an allowance without my husband's permission. Which he would never give."

The coach turned a corner, and this time Nigel did not try to hold Penny steady. She clutched the strap near her, wondering if she stood a chance of surviving a jump from a moving vehicle.

"Don't even think about it," Nigel warned. "We are going far too fast. Not that it would make a difference to me as long as your father doesn't find you first. You see, I want what I have always wanted, your father's blunt. He'll pay to see his precious daughter back, in one piece or a few."

"He is dowering your sisters, isn't that enough?"

He sneered, there in the gloom. "Neither brat is wedding as rich a man as I need, thanks to you and your interference. Love matches, bah!"

Penny held on as the coach careened around another bend. "He will kill you for this, you know."

"Your father? He wouldn't dare. My mother would make his life a misery. For all his faults, he seems to care for the old besom."

"No, my husband." Penny knew West would come for her. She had no doubt whatsoever.

"I'll be long gone before anyone finds you. That's if they pay up." He leered at her across the shadows, then licked his lips. "If they don't, soon enough, I might just have to take you with me, which is not a bad idea, now that I think on it. That would serve your high-and-mighty lordship right—him and that fake French count, too. Do you get seasick?"

Chapter Thirty-four

When his uncle told Mr. J. to wed a mill owner's daughter, the young man told him to drop dead. The uncle did, and left Mr. J. out of his will. No one would marry him then.

—By Arrangement, *a chronicle of arranged marriages, by G. E. Felber*

West woke up happy, then went back to sleep when he realized Penny wasn't beside him. He lay abed for a while, dreaming of the ways he could make up for last night, his short temper, and his short performance. Lud, he couldn't wait. That is, he could wait this time, he vowed, until Penny was all soft and sated. As soon as he could entice her back to bed.

Most likely she was at breakfast, he decided, listening to his own stomach's complaints of hunger. He hurried through a hasty meal when he heard Sir Gaspar was ailing and that Penny had rushed to his possible deathbed. He sent for a horse to be brought out front while he grabbed up his hat and gloves and some extra handkerchiefs.

Just as he was about to leave, a carriage pulled up, in Goldwaite's green and gold trim, and Sir Gaspar himself leaped out before the footmen set down the steps.

"Is Penny here?" he shouted, all red-faced by the time he reached West.

The man did not look like he was dying, only out of breath. "You're not sick?"

Goldwaite looked around West, into the empty hall-way. "Do I look sick?"

"Then where is my wife?"

"Devil take it, man, that's what I am trying to find out! If she ain't here, Nigel's got her."

"What does that swine want with my wife, by all that's holy? I won't believe any scandal he tries to cause, and Penny won't believe any former mistresses he drags into my house. Most of all, he can't get his hands on her money."

"No, but he can get his paws on mine. He knows I'd pay anything to get my gal back."

"Ransom?" West heard Lady Bainbridge gasp from behind him, Cottsworth at her side, his arm supporting her.

Sir Gaspar nodded. "That's my guess. I didn't trust the dastard, so I had a man follow him. He got into my other coach—my own traveling carriage, blast him—with the curtains drawn so the man could not see who or what was inside. Then they took off like Satan himself was driving. My man followed as best he could to see the direction, then fell too far behind in his hackney—they were traveling so fast. But he did say they were headed east, for the Dover road."

"Why Dover? Great gods, he can't be thinking of taking Penny to France while we are at war with them."

"No, but he's got a yacht there. He could sail in any direction. But we are wasting time, Westfield. Get in my coach."

Just then Nicky pulled up in West's own curricle, Mavis beside him. "No, come up with me. The curricle is faster and your horses are still fresh. Mavis can ride with her father."

"Nothing but a horse can catch up with them now," West shouted, already running around the house, toward where a groom was leading out his chestnut gelding. "You head out and leave word at the tollbooths if they are still headed for Dover. If not, leave a message where they were last seen. That will save me time."

"Wait," Cottsworth yelled. "You need a better horse."

West glanced at the chestnut before mounting. It was a showy, well-mannered Thoroughbred, not bred for distance or stamina. "Damn, it's the best I've got in Town."

"No, it isn't," Cottsworth called after him, hobbling on his cane as fast as he could. "Penny bought you a hunter, a magnificent stallion that will carry you to hell and back."

West was living in hell right now. He yelled for someone to bring out the new horse, while Cottsworth mounted the chestnut.

"I can't keep up with Sungod on the gelding," Cottsworth said, "but I can send messages back, too. You just have to remember that your mount only has one eye, from an injury."

Bloody hell, he'd sent his gelding off and he was left with a half-blind, unknown animal, picked by a woman! "Which eye?" West shouted before Cottsworth was around the corner.

"The right one, I think."

West touched his own left eye, where the swelling was going down, but not entirely. "That's fine, then. The blind leading the blind."

Speaking of the blind, Penny's grandfather was directing Marcel and two servants in loading Littleton's carriage. He insisted on hying to the rescue also, with Marcel, George, and a case of his best brandy.

West would have started for the stables to save time, but his butler was running toward him, puffing. Parker had West's pistol case in one hand, a heavy purse in the other.

"Good man," West said, shaken that he might have flown after his wife with no way to save her but for the knife he always tucked in his boot. As soon as he stowed the purse and loaded the pistols, his head groom came tearing around the house with the new horse. West blessed him, Penny, and Cottsworth.

Sungod was everything West could have wished: huge, broad-chested, well muscled, his cream coat gleaming with good health, and an intelligent expression in his one eye. West didn't have time to put the stallion through his paces, to let them get used to each other, but he shouted, and the huge horse sensed his urgency and sprang to life. Without the least urging from West, he leaped right over the mounds of luggage left next to the Littleton coach, and they were off, flying past Penny's grandfather, who shouted at him to give the bastard hell.

"No, I intend to send him there!"

They came up on Cottsworth and the chestnut gelding a few streets away.

"Spectacular, what?"

"Incredible," West yelled, feeling as if he had one of the new steam engines between his legs. As long as West kept a firm hand on the reins, Sungod never hesitated, trusting his rider to compensate for the blind eye. West patted his proud neck and waved to Cottsworth as they rushed past, on their way out of the city.

They passed Sir Gaspar, who leaned out his window to yell that Nigel had indeed been seen going in this direction, fast. Nicky said the same a few minutes later, waving him on past the curricle.

"It's just you and me now," West told the horse, leaning over. "You can do it, I know you can. And if we find my wife before that maggot hurts her, or frightens her, or, heaven forbid, gets her on that damned boat, you'll have all the mares you can enjoy, for the rest of your life."

Sungod pricked his ears up and lengthened his stride. West would have relished the speed, the power, except for the purpose of this neck-or-nothing ride. "Penny, I am coming," he shouted into the wind. "I'll find you. Or die trying."

"You seem mighty cool for a woman in your circumstances," Nigel told Penny as she sat silently across from him. Now that they had reached a post road, the carriage was not swaying as much, but she still held on to the strap above the door, weighing her options.

"West will come," was all the answer she deigned to give her abductor.

"Hah. Why should he? He already has your dowry, and now he's got the rest of your fortune, you fool. And you aren't that tempting a morsel, my dear sister. Not compared to Lady Greenlea."

"Parker mentioned she left for her family's home in Ireland. Your evil ally won't be any more help."

Nigel ignored her. "Westfield might be delighted to be rid of you, so he can find another wealthy bride. One with a more pleasing manner and a better figure."

"West loves me, just the way I am."

"Feh, he loves your gold."

Penny sniffled and let go of the strap. She started to untie the strings of her reticule at her side.

"What are you doing?" Nigel demanded.

"I . . . I need a handkerchief," she whimpered.

He looked away, disappointed at her sniveling. A proud woman was one he could threaten and intimidate. A watering pot like his sister Amelia was no fun at all.

Penny sniffled and blew her nose. Then she returned the handkerchief to her purse, at her side, the one farthest from the corner where Nigel was leaning.

When they stopped to change horses, Penny would have made a dash for freedom, but Nigel took a knife out of his boot, a long, thin blade that he used to clean his fingernails, for effect. "I would not try any foolish attempts," he said, "for if I do not kill you, my men will run you down. I do not think your husband will want you back after they have had their little fun with you."

One of the men, the one who had brought the message and opened the carriage door for her—damn his soul—brought a hamper of food back to the coach, along with a bottle of wine. He would not look Penny in the eye, just handed the basket to his employer and rejoined the driver.

Nigel settled back in his corner with the bottle. "You might as well eat, my dear. We have quite a ways more to go."

She would no more share a meal with Nigel than she would with a snake. "I am not hungry," she said, her hand inside the opened reticule.

The horse was starting to flag. Even Sungod's great heart could not keep up the pace all the way to Dover. They had to find Nigel soon.

West brought the stallion to a walk for a time, conserving what was left of his energy. At the next coaching stop the hostler reported that Nigel's coach was a scant ten minutes ahead. West thought of changing horses, but the innkeeper's nags would not match Sungod's strength and ability, even lathered as he was. Who knew what they might face? A guard sat up with the driver, and West assumed Nigel was inside with Penny, but no one could say whether there were others with him.

The smart thing would be to wait for reinforcements, Nicky and Cottsworth, even Sir Gaspar, but Nigel could take a back road, or be heading toward a hedge tavern only he knew about, to wait for a ransom note to be delivered and the payment received. Or he could change carriages at the next town, making him harder to follow. The thought of losing Nigel's trail, of scouring the unfamiliar countryside, of leaving his Penny in the hands of criminals and cutthroats, made West urge his horse onward, after telling the innkeeper to send an officer of the law ahead. He had two loaded pistols, the element of surprise, and a berserker's rage in his heart. That evened the odds, he figured.

They reached a high spot, with the road continuing down, then turning sharply to the right. He could see a carriage past the turn, moving faster than usual. Such speed was unwise on this rutted road, unless the occupants had a tide to catch, a husband to outrun.

"We've got them now, my friend," West told the horse as he nudged him into a jump over the roadside ditch and onto a field of sheep, which scattered when they saw the massive horse thundering down the hill. West guided Sungod on a diagonal, to come back to the road ahead of the carriage.

Gun drawn, he wheeled his horse sideways, blind eye to the oncoming coach, and shouted, "Stop or I'll shoot."

The driver whipped his horses onward. The guard raised his own musket. Nigel tore the shade off the window on his side, so Penny did the same on hers.

She could see West, on the horse she'd bought him, looking like an avenging angel, her angel. "I told you he'd come."

"Shoot him," Nigel yelled.

"No!" Penny yelled.

"Get out of the way," the driver yelled.

The guard took aim.

But West and his horse stayed across the road, so the driver pulled back on the ribbons with all his might. After all, West's pistol was aimed at him, not Nigel. The driver figured he had no cause to die for his employer, who'd likely try to cheat him out of his share of the ransom money anyway, and the nob did not look like he could miss. On the other hand, Joe beside him had his musket out.

In Joe's mind, he was already going to hang for abducting a lady if they were stopped, so he might as well swing for killing a swell. He sighted along the gun's barrel. Meanwhile, the carriage horses bucked and snorted, terrified of running into another animal, but they stopped, bouncing the carriage just as Joe fired. The shot went high and wide, but Joe started to reload in a hurry.

"Dammit," Nigel shouted.

"Criminy," the driver shouted.

"West!" Penny shouted.

West aimed at the guard now, while the driver had his hands full steadying the frightened horses.

There was one problem: Sungod had been shot once by his first owner. He was not about to be shot again. No one had told that detail to West, so he was concentrating more on the two men on the driver's seat than on his own seat.

Sungod reared up in a leap that would have made a circus horse proud. It made West slide right off the stallion's back and onto the road. Joe's second shot was perfectly aimed—at where West would have been. It missed. West's shot did not, hitting the guard in the shoulder, so he dropped the musket. Cursing in the dirt, West tossed aside his spent pistol and reached for the other one, in his waistband. Sungod trotted out of range.

"Drop your weapon," West ordered.

"Drop yours," the driver ordered, his blunderbuss in his hand now, the reins at his feet. "One of us ought to. Not me."

"Shoot him," the guard ordered, clutching his shoulder.

West walked toward the carriage horses, his pistol aimed between the driver's eyes.

Nigel stuck his head out the window. "This is no stand-off, Westfield. You might have one shot left, but there are three of us. My man has his weapon. More important, I have a knife—at my dear Persephone's throat."

"Are you all right, my love?" West called.

Nigel pressed the blade closer, so Penny could feel the edge, and ordered, "Tell him to put down his weapon."

"I am fine, darling. Nigel says you must put down your pistol. Please. He only wants money. That is not worth dying for."

"That's right, Westfield. Drop it."

So West did, knowing he had no choice with Penny in danger. Besides, help would be arriving soon, if he could delay Nigel long enough. "Very well." He bent to put his pistol down carefully. The thing was loaded and liable to go off if he threw it, shooting him or the blasted horse that was watching from a goodly distance.

He rose and walked slowly to the restive carriage horses' heads, to calm them.

"Come on out, Nigel, so we can talk. I have enough of the ready on me to buy you passage out of the country. Leave Penny and go on your way."

"You cannot have enough. Not compared to what her father will pay."

West stroked the horses, holding them steady so Nigel's knife did not slip.

"Shoot him, damn you," Nigel ordered, his head out the window now.

"He ain't armed nor mounted," the driver complained, while Joe complained that he was bleeding to death. The driver took out his filthy kerchief to help stanch the blood, holding the blunderbuss loosely in his other hand.

Nigel was furious. "I don't care. Shoot him!"

Penny was more than a little angry, too. "If you do, your employer is a dead man," she said, from inside the carriage. "I have a pistol on him."

Joe took the opportunity to jump down, bloody shoulder and all. He raced away from the standoff, picking up his empty musket and running for an escape, on the horse that was standing quietly. Sungod turned so his good eye was on the man, and on the rifle. He charged. Now Joe had three broken ribs, besides a wounded shoulder.

Nigel ignored the neighs and the noise, looking at the small ivory-handled pistol Penny had taken from her reticule. Then he curled his lip. "You won't shoot."

"Are you willing to chance it? I already gave you a black eye for kissing me." She ignored West's growl of outrage. "Think what I might do for an abduction. And if you let my husband get hurt . . ." She lowered the pistol toward his lap.

Nigel licked his lip nervously. "That, ah, does change things, doesn't it?" He pulled his stiletto away from her throat.

"Throw it out the window."

He did, but to Penny's surprise, West did not come get it, staying between the carriage horses. Of course. The driver still had him in his sights. "Tell your man to put down his weapon."

"I think not. The odds are not as good, but they are still even. If you shoot me, my driver shoots him."

Penny bit her lip. So did the driver, who'd been listening intently. If Entwhistle died, he wouldn't get anything but a hemp necklace. If the other man died, maybe he'd get a share of the brass the toff said he had. And they still had the gentry mort. He started to raise the heavy blunderbuss. "Sorry, bucko. We've got a boat to catch."

"But no way to get there." West led the lead horses out of their cut traces; then he threw the knife he'd used. The driver clutched his arm, dropping the gun.

"Stalemate over, Nigel. You lose."

Chapter Thirty-five

Viscount W. and Miss G. were married according to contracts and parental decree, after a long betrothal. . . .

—By Arrangement, *a chronicle of arranged marriages, by G. E. Felber*

"May I shoot him anyway?"

"No, my love," West said, pulling open the door and pulling Nigel out by his collar. "He is unarmed, not that the scum deserves any concessions to honor. But did he really kiss you?"

"Yes, and it was dreadful."

So West blackened Nigel's other eye, knocking him unconscious in the process. The last might have been by Nigel's choice, rather than get pummeled into the ground.

West was disappointed. "The craven turned lily-livered, now that he does not have his henchmen or a knife or a woman to terrify."

Penny kept her pistol trained on Nigel, half-hoping he'd awaken and try to escape, while West tied up the injured driver and guard and scooped up all the fallen weapons, placing them in the coach. Then he went to retrieve the horse that had saved his life, and helped save the woman West would have died for. "Do not let the beast see the gun," he warned, leading Sungod back toward the carriage and tying him to one of the wheels.

"He was shot."

"So I gathered." And then he gathered Penny into his arms. "Oh God, I will never let you go again," he said, kissing her forehead, her eyes, her cheeks, her lips.

She lowered the gun. Sungod protested with a loud whinny, so they separated, by an inch, and looked at the stallion, stomping his foreleg. West took the pistol and tucked it behind his waist, under his coat.

"Did you like my gift?"

"He brought me to you when no other horse could. But you are the finest present I have ever held. Oh, Penny, the thought of someone hurting you, carrying you away from me, frightening you—"

He kissed her again, long and hard, trying to express feelings that words alone could never convey.

Penny would have collapsed, but for his arms around her. When she caught her breath enough to speak, she said, "I was not frightened. I knew you would come. And I did have my pistol. But I know precisely what you mean. I felt the same way. My heart almost stopped beating when they shot at you. And I would never have forgiven myself if you were hurt when your horse threw you. I was the one who put you in danger by buying such an unreliable mount."

Cottsworth might be joining the ranks of those with black eyes, West decided, limp or no limp. "Someone might have warned me about the horse."

Penny rubbed his scowl away with her fingers and a kiss. "You fell asleep before I could."

West had to smile. "You are never going to let me forget that, are you?"

"In about thirteen years, I'd wager."

"I'll make it up to you, I swear."

"I know."

He would have started, right there in the roadway, but the sound of horses and vehicles came to them. West reached for the pistol, just in case, but he recognized his own curricle, Mr. Littleton's traveling coach, and Sir Gaspar's town carriage coming down the hill, Cottsworth riding alongside on his gelding. Two other men rode in front—the local authorities, he assumed.

He had time for one last kiss before the cavalry arrived.

Mr. Littleton could see well enough to notice the embrace, when Marcel helped him out of his coach. "I knew he'd make her a deuced fine husband."

Sir Gaspar climbed down from his own carriage and mopped his brow, relieved to see both his daughter and her viscount standing, even if they were behaving scandalously in front of any chance passersby, and the constable. "I picked him, didn't I?"

For once Littleton did not argue with his son-in-law. He did gesture for Marcel to break open a bottle of brandy. "We all need it."

Mavis ran to Penny, crying, half in relief and half because Nicky wanted to shoot Nigel.

"He is my brother!" she wailed.

Nicky came right behind her. "Well, he would have killed mine, and your stepsister, too."

"What will happen to him now?"

"He ought to hang."

The constables gathered up the weapons and checked the accused for injuries, of which there were many and varied. They chose not to ask for details. "No talk of taking the law into your own hands, young sir. There will be a magistrate's hearing, then a trial. They'll likely be transported."